RESORT ISLE

Detective Frank Dugan begins

PAUL SEKULICH

Novel

OTHER BOOKS BY THE AUTHOR

The Omega Formula

A Killer Season

Published by Omnibus Productions
and
Printed in the United States by
CreateSpace,

ISBN-13: 978-0-9915594-7-3
ISBN-10: 0-9915594-7-9
BISAC: Fiction / Thrillers

DEDICATION

To my beautiful wife Joyce whose love and patience
exceed all reasonable expectations.

Acknowledgements

My thanks to Jessica Page Morrell for her professional
guidance, expert editing, and advice on fiction
writing. And for caring about writers.

A special thanks to Detective Jan Ryan and Detective
Mike Pachkoski of the Criminal Investigation
Division of the Harford County Sheriff's Department
for taking their valuable time to show me the technical
inside to real police and forensic work.

A grateful thank you to all the members of The Panera
Writers' Group for their diligence, time and critical
comments that make writing so much less a lonely
business, and novels like this one so much better.

A friend like John C. Rehmert is the best friend a
writer can have; a person who knows, shares and
guides. I'm proud to say he's been one of mine since
we weren't tall enough to go on a lot of Disney rides.

Chapter 1

There are many reasons for screams. Triumph, glee, a warning, fear. But the scream resonating in Frank Dugan's head came from terror, from someone dying. He'd heard it several times that day and once again as he entered his boss's office at the San Diego Police Department. His summons there concerned a peculiar thing a man had said as he lay dying. Frank Dugan took dying declarations seriously, especially when they included his name.

Dom Petrillo, the homicide captain at SDPD, sat at his desk staring at a report. Frank noted the severe expression on his face and anticipated bad news.

"The dying man whispered to the EMS technician, 'Detective Frank Dugan should know,'" Petrillo said. "Then he died."

"So I heard."

Frank pushed his hair off his forehead and waited for his superior get to the point.

"I need you to drive to Huntington Beach to investigate the incident that's left this jewelry store owner dead. I don't know why your name would've come up in a robbery ninety miles away, but I intend to find out."

Petrillo slid a paper across his desk to his detective. "Here's the info you'll need."

"Today?" Frank asked, as he picked up the paper and studied its contents.

"While it's hot. Now saddle up," Petrillo said and pointed to the door.

Frank had requested the day off to celebrate his anniversary with his wife, and wasn't happy about the disruption of his plans, but he knew well that murder is never respectful of special occasions. And he knew something else. The murdered jewelry store owner named on the paper had been the very man who'd sold him the engagement ring he'd placed on the finger of his fiancée, Amy, more than six years ago.

An hour later, Frank's black Bronco roared north through Irvine on the 405 at 10:40 AM. If all went well in Orange County, he could be back home by afternoon, where he and Amy could happily seize the rest of the day.

At least, he could now put the cryptic screams he'd been hearing to rest.

*   *   *

Amy Dugan locked stares with the driver's dead-black eyes and felt a chill, as if she were being examined by a shark. She stood at her curbside mailbox watching the slow passing car and saw something unsettling about the man's sinister smile, like he knew something about her, something private.

The black sedan idling past her home would hardly pique any curiosity, but the four strange men, whose flinty gazes never left Amy as the car crept by, triggered in her a primordial fear. Her eyes followed the car until it turned left at the end of the block. Amy turned from the road and looked over to her neighbor, Barbara Chalmers, working in the yard next door.

"I suppose you thought having two children would stop men from looking," Barbara said as she rose with effort from her flower garden.

"Looks from my husband are all I want," Amy said, retrieving the mail from her box.

Barbara leaned on the fence separating their lawns.

"My nephew's a lucky man," Barbara said. "Got the best looking gal in San Diego County."

"You're pretty hot yourself."

"Used to be. Not so much at fifty-five."

"Youth is overrated. We don't know things like you do."

"I see your five-year-old, but where's the little guy?" Barbara asked, angling her head toward Amy's rancher.

Amy looked at the house and shook an admonishing finger at a blonde girl perched in the bay window snapping a camera button.

"Billy may still be in nap time. Have to get him up or he won't sleep tonight for the sitter."

"Going partying?"

"Anniversary dinner," Amy said. "Six years today."

"My goodness, I had forgotten that. Congratulations, dear. What's six years? Wood? China?"

"I hope Frank thinks it's beef Wellington and cabernet," Amy said, waved goodbye, and strode to her house.

The little girl in the window snapped more pictures as her mother approached the front door. Amy made funny faces at her and gyrated like a rock dancer gone wild. The girl laughed and bared most of her milk teeth, then disappeared from the window.

Amy entered the house, scurried to the giggling five-year-old, and scooped her up in her arms.

"Why, Deborah Ann Dugan, why are you being so rambunctious?" Amy said. "And where's your brother?"

"Billy's watching TV in the den," Deborah said.

Amy let Deborah slide gently to the floor and took her hand.

"Let's just go see what Billy's watching," Amy said and tugged her daughter down a long hallway.

In the den, Billy, age three, sat on the floor cross-legged, four feet from a TV screen blaring cartoons.

"Let's get a shot of you guys and me to show daddy," Amy said, taking the camera from Deborah.

Amy fiddled with the camera for a moment, then sat on the sofa. Billy and Deborah took positions on either side of their mom and tilted their heads into her shoulders.

"All right, everyone, say 'monkey,'" Amy said.

The trio smiled and said the word and Amy clicked the selfie.

"Billy's cartoons are too loud," Deborah said.

Amy rose from the sofa and handed the camera to Deborah.

"You two stay here and watch TV while I get ready to go shopping for a new dress," Amy said. "Mommy and daddy are going out tonight."

Deborah laid the camera on the sofa and picked up the TV remote.

"Why?" Deborah asked.

"Because it's our anniversary."

"Anna...bersury...What's that?"

"It's the birthday of when mommy and daddy got married."

"I like birthdays," Billy said and looked at his mother. "You get cake and toys."

"Is Jill going to come over and watch us?" Deborah asked.

"Yes, she is."

"I like Jill," Deborah said. "She plays hide and seek with us."

"I bet that's fun. Do you hide in good places?"

"I do, but Billy always goes under the kitchen sink. Jill always finds him."

"Yeah, the sink's not as good as in the pantry," Amy said.

"Nope, 'cause Jill takes a long time to find me."

Deborah pointed the remote at the TV and changed the channel to a movie."

"Hey," Billy said. "I want cartoons."

"Play nice, you two," Amy said and slipped out of the den and headed for the master bedroom.

The dresser in the bedroom featured something Amy hadn't noticed before. A small envelope leaned against a framed photograph of a young man in a dress blue, U.S. Marine uniform standing with Amy in a white wedding dress. She picked up the envelope, pulled out a white card, and read its brief words.

Happy Anniversary to my best friend in life.

Six years and still mad about you.

Love always,

Frank

Amy smiled and began removing her yard clothes.

*   *   *

The warm shower felt good on Amy's skin as she luxuriated in the cascading water, more than washing in its flow. As she turned to rinse her back, a dark shadow appeared beyond the translucent plastic curtain, too tall to be a child.

Chapter 2

A masculine voice spoke from inside the bathroom.

"Need a towel, pretty lady?"

Amy gathered the shower curtain around her nakedness and peeked around its edge. A burly young man stared at her and extended a towel in her direction, hanging by a finger.

"What do you want?" she said, trembling.

"Turn off the water and we'll talk. No one's gonna hurt you."

Amy snatched the towel from his hand and spread the curtain to shield herself as much as possible.

"I'll wait outside," the man said and stepped out of the bathroom and closed the door.

Amy's mind raced from thoughts of her children to finding weapons to climbing out the window, but there was no decent weapon available, and the window was too high and too small for escape. And her children were in the house at the mercy of this stranger. She cursed the situation for being the one time she'd neglected to take her phone with her. She had to go find the children. That was first.

Amy tightened the towel wrapped around her, angry that she'd left her clothes and a robe in the bedroom. She eased open the bathroom door and peeked into the hall. No one was in sight.

Did the man leave? Wishful thinking, she was certain.

She sidled along the hall toward the den where she'd left the children. When she reached the opening to the master bedroom, the burly man was standing inside, barely a foot from the doorframe. Behind him were two more young men, high-schoolers at best. Amy noted that they all wore dark green mechanic's cover-alls.

"Step in here," the burly man said and directed her by a firm grip on her bare upper arm with a latex-gloved hand.

"Where are my children?" Amy asked.

"They'll be fine," burly said and pushed Amy into a low boudoir chair. "Do you know why we're here?"

"I can't imagine," Amy said, closing the space between her thighs. "If it's money, you've come to the wrong place. We're just getting by on one income, and with two kids to feed and …"

Amy stopped, realizing her nerves had her rambling.

"How about all that jewelry your husband owns?"

"Jewelry? He has a wedding ring and a Timex watch."

"C'mon, lady. Don't you be bullshittin' ole Ernie. What about the jewelry store chain? Owns about eight of 'em, I figure."

"Sir, you have the wrong people. My husband works for the city and makes enough to keep us off welfare, but that's about it," Amy said, hugging her body to steady the trembling.

"This house is right nice."

"And comes with a 30-year mortgage. We pay by the month to live here. Want to see our bank statements?"

"Naw, I wanna see them jewels," Ernie said and leaned to within an inch of Amy's face.

"Check the jewelry box," Amy said, pressing into the chair back. "You'll see what I have. Costume jewelry, that's what. Now where are my children? I need to see my children. *Now*."

Ernie pulled Amy to her feet and shoved her toward the bed.

"Let's us go see that jewelry box. Then we go see the children."

"Where are they?"

"They're in your nice little family room watchin' the television. They're just fine. Trust me, ole Ernie don't wanna hurt nobody."

Amy pointed to her jewelry box on the dresser. Ernie strode to it and stirred through its scant contents. He glared at Amy and slammed the top down so hard the mirror behind the dresser banged against the wall.

"I'm through foolin' with you, lady," Ernie said and nodded at the two men.

One of the men closed the bedroom door and pressed the lock button in the knob.

"We have good information that you're the owners of Duggan's Fine Jewelry stores that are all over southern California," Ernie said. "You even have a store on Rodeo Drive. Now don't you be tellin' me *that* one sells costume jewelry."

"Our name is Dugan, not Duggan," Amy said. "The Duggans are billionaires. My God, I wish. This is Coronado Estates, not Bel Air."

One of the men grabbed a purse on the vanity bench and pulled out a wallet and handed it to Ernie, who flipped through the credit cards and stared at the driver's license.

"Looks like we got it wrong boys," Ernie said and chucked the wallet across the room. "Dwayne, check to make sure them kids is okay in there with Scottie. Mitch, watch the front of the house for any unwanted arrivals."

The two young men left the bedroom and closed the door. Ernie stared at Amy, then stepped to the door and relocked it. Amy stood, her jaw and fists clenched.

"Now, now, Mrs. Dugan. No need to get all riled up. Ole Ernie don't wanna hurt nobody."

*   *   *

Dwayne entered the den and joined Scottie, who sat on the sofa. Deborah rose from the floor and tugged Billy to his protesting feet, gripping his hand. She

11

held out the remote control to the men in the room, her tiny hand shaking.

"You want to watch TV with us? You can pick."

Chapter 3

Judd Kemp was the second senior officer to arrive. He was the highest-ranking and most seasoned detective in the San Diego Police Department, but when he heard the 9-1-1 request for assistance, the address stopped him cold. The emergency was at 710 Rosita Lane, the home of his young detective partner, Frank Dugan.

"Has the ME arrived, sergeant?" Judd asked one of the army of uniforms spread out over the grounds.

"Inside, detective," the officer said. "With the lieutenant."

"Lieutenant Graham?"

"Yes, sir. He was first on the scene."

"You know who called it in?"

"Neighbor next door. Woman over there next to the fence."

Judd took a good look at the bereaved woman, who stared back at him with sad, red eyes. He turned back to the sergeant.

"Any word from Detective Dugan?"

"He's on his way back from Huntington Beach. He was called twenty minutes ago."

"He know anything?"

"Dispatch told him there was an emergency at his home."

"When he arrives, don't let him inside the house," Judd said. "I don't care if you have to get ten unies to help and subdue him. He does not get into that house. Understood?"

"Yes, sir."

The detective went to the front door, drew a deep breath, and entered the rancher. Nothing in the foyer and living room looked out of place. The adjoining dining room was as neat as a magazine layout in *Better Homes & Gardens*. Candles and the fresh flowers on the dining table betrayed any disturbance; chairs perfectly arranged around the table. He heard voices in the hall and followed the sound.

Lieutenant Mike Graham stepped from the hall bathroom and intercepted Judd.

"You sure you want to see what's in there?" Graham said, indicating a doorway at the far end of the hall.

"I have to," Judd said and pushed past the big man.

Judd peered around the door frame into the bedroom. Everything in that room defied the peaceful setting he'd observed in the front of the home. The medical examiner was directing the photography of the body of Amy Dugan, lying naked on a bed covered in blood. A blood-stained pillow lay next to her head, her long blond hair splayed in every direction. Her mouth was agape as if in a silent scream and her eyes were frozen wide open. Her

14

athletic torso had been slashed so badly Judd had to avert his gaze.

Judd hung his head and tightly closed his eyes. He clutched the door jamb to steady himself. A minute passed before he reopened his eyes and panned the rest of the room where a crime scene investigation team in blue booties scoured the carpet, walls, and furniture for evidence. A man with a dusting machine and brush spread granular aluminum flake dust on all non-porous surfaces and objects. A photographer followed him and snapped photos where he was directed, and a third CSI made notations on a pad as they progressed around the room.

The ME stepped back from the bed and turned his gaze at Detective Kemp.

"I'd like to move her before Frank gets here," the ME said.

"Can you close her eyes?" Judd said.

The ME nodded at a woman near the headboard of the bed who gently drew down Amy's lids.

"The den is next," the ME said, moving toward the door.

"The kids?" Judd asked.

The ME stared at him for a moment and brushed past and into the hall.

Judd Kemp followed the ME toward the den, abruptly stopped and pivoted back toward the front of the house. He had a feeling. It was a feeling that struck detectives often. A premonition. Not always good.

When Judd looked out the large window in the front room he saw the uniforms still out on the lawn and driveway in dark blue clusters, some still searching, but many smoking and sipping. Neighbors shuffled to the crime scene tape and gazed with frozen faces. The lady looked on from the next door fence and dabbed her eyes between waves of sobbing. A moment later, the manifestation of Judd's gut feeling appeared. It was Frank Dugan's Bronco.

Frank leapt from the car and let it drift into the curb as he dashed for the house. Judd bolted for the door and crashed through it to get outside. Two uniformed officers intercepted Frank in the driveway, but found him far too strong and athletic to stop. The young detective barged through the men and spun his way in Judd's direction. Judd extended his hands, to cushion Frank's momentum.

"Frank, listen to me," Judd said as Frank rammed him against the front door. "You can't go in there."

Judd, the much larger man, grasped Frank's jacket at the collar.

"Get out of my way, Judd," Frank said, his blue eyes wide and piercing. "I want to see my family."

"You do not need to see what's in there," Judd said.

"Who are you to tell me what to see in my home? You going to pull rank on me, lieutenant?"

"Please, Frank. I'm begging you as a friend."

"Get out of my way."

Judd released his grip on Frank and reluctantly stepped aside. Frank shot into the house. Moments later everyone outside turned toward the wailing cries from the house.

Every man and woman standing around the house bowed their heads and closed their eyes in helplessness. Judd knew that all in witness there would go home that night and gather their loved ones close.

All save one.

Chapter 4

The funeral for the Dugan family was one of such solemnity that exchanges by the attendees never rose above whispers and facial language.

Frank had difficulty leaving the three closed caskets resting on their biers, and stared at the framed photographs of the children and Amy that sat atop each lid. Pictures from a happier time, frozen in smiling faces.

Judd Kemp hung back. Frank knew he was there to provide comfort, but mainly to keep watch on his friend. He leaned on Amy's casket with extended arms, his head bowed. Judd drifted near and placed his hand on Frank's shoulder.

"Let's leave them to heaven," Judd said.

Frank nodded.

"I want to go to a nice bar," Judd said, "and I don't want to drink alone."

Frank pushed himself off the mahogany lid and faced Judd.

"Tough day. I could use a drink," Frank said, his watery eyes burning red.

"I know you went through some tough ones in Iraq," Judd said. "I'm sure they weren't even close to this."

The two men walked slowly from the burial site. Frank stopped to look back, but Judd steered him toward a line of waiting cars.

*   *   *

Barbara Chalmers stood at the roadside and smiled at Frank and Judd as they approached their black limousine. Judd seated Frank in the limo and stepped over to her.

"Ms. Chalmers, I have your statement on my desk," Judd said. "After the Grand Jury makes its decision to charge those suspects we'll be heading to trial. I'll need you to meet with the prosecutor and me to prepare our case."

"I'll be there, detective. Nothing can keep me from testifying for Amy."

"Thank you. I'll be in touch," Judd said and joined Frank in the limo.

A moment later the limo drove off. Judd grabbed the car phone and pressed a button.

"Take us to the del Coronado," Judd said to the driver.

*   *   *

The Babcock & Story bar at the Hotel del Coronado was one of those five-star lounges that was as good as it gets for ambiance. The elegant rattan seating amid the indoor palms spoke of celebrity, Pacific vacations, and class. The last place Judd wanted to take his grieving partner was to one of their regular saloons slaking the thirst of fifty half-bagged cops from the department. The del Coronado was special, exclusive, and the patrons there were polite and honored individual privacy. One could talk there without shouting, and Judd wanted to assess Frank's mental health in this awful time. Judd was a veteran of reading people. Years of dealing with hard core liars had sharpened his instincts far beyond the subjective accuracy of a polygraph reading. A couple of drinks and a friendly talk with his partner would tell him volumes.

"Your aunt saw those men pass by your house in a car," Judd said. "A little later she saw them behind your house."

"Doesn't prove that they're murderers," Frank said and downed the last swallow of his scotch.

"Puts them at the scene."

"Try to make murder stick on that."

"Barbara puts them in the house," Judd said and signaled the bartender for refills.

"Without hard evidence, it's circumstantial, at best. Besides, they may discredit my aunt's testimony for being biased."

"You think they were there asking for directions?"

"Can't prove *what* they were there for."

The bartender brought fresh drinks. Frank pulled his glass over and took a sip.

"Marty Dimino will be prosecuting," Judd said. "You know his conviction record."

"He's the best, but he's going to need more evidence. Vincent Bugliosi couldn't get a conviction with what we have."

"We have your Aunt Barbara who places them at the scene."

"Yeah, but you and I both know what cops and juries think about eye witnesses. Get ten eye witnesses who saw the same event, and you get ten different versions of what happened."

Frank sipped his drink and stared out at the ocean.

"It's unimaginable that they did what they did without leaving a single piece of hard evidence," Frank said. "They must've been trained by a master."

"The grand jury should decide what we've got is sufficient for charges and a trial."

"Were you first on the scene?"

"No, Graham was there when I arrived."

"How could they do what they did without leaving trace evidence? Forensics couldn't find one fingerprint, or a single hair or fiber that could link any of the four to the crime. On top of that, they all claim they were there asking about a house for sale in the development. So they can't be convicted for leaving footprints."

"We do have something…," Judd said, staring into his glass.

Frank gazed at Judd, waiting for the rest of Judd's statement.

"I didn't want to bring this up until I had to," Judd said.

"You don't keep anything from me about this. Not ever."

"There was a small digital camera found in the den."

"Pictures were in it?" Frank asked.

"Yeah. Shots of your front yard. A '95 Chevy Impala, black, is in the background. There are men in the car, staring at Amy."

"It's them?"

"It's them," Judd said. "We had the photo enlarged and digitally enhanced. The driver is Ernie Gaither."

"Why would you hold back an important photo like that?"

"The camera and digital card are being held in evidence. Look, it's not *that* photo I was concerned about. It's the other shots on the digital card."

Frank stared into his drink glass for a moment.

"Last pictures of Amy and the kids?" Frank asked low.

Judd Kemp never found it necessary to respond to rhetorical questions.

Chapter 5

Judge Harold Spellman's courtroom was packed to capacity with its walls covered by standing onlookers and media personnel. The press wasn't about to miss attending the most sensational criminal trial since the Manson gang murders monopolized the news. It had become a main topic in barroom and office conversations. The Dugan murder trial had achieved media attention equal to the O. J. Simpson trial, and public interest was off the Nielsen ratings scale. Detective Frank Dugan, whether he liked it or not, was on a celebrity level held by top Hollywood movie stars. He was weary of the attention and glad the trial could wrap up today.

The prosecuting attorney, Martin Dimino, stepped over and placed his hand on Frank's shoulder. He leaned close to his ear and whispered.

"Final summaries will be coming up. From there, it's in the hands of the jury," Marty said.

Frank and mouthed a silent thank you. Marty returned to his seat at the prosecution's table on the right side of the room.

Lieutenant Mike Graham, the heavy-set plainclothes detective from the SDPD, drifted by the prosecution table on his way to a seat on the aisle and gave Frank and Marty a thumbs-up.

Ernie Gaither sat at the defense table on the left. Frank saw the other three suspects, Dwayne Pinkney, Scottie Fisher, and Mitch Davis directly behind him in the gallery. He had taken a good look at their raggedy dress and unkempt appearance when they were brought in and interviewed at the station. Today, all four young men wore conservative jackets and ties, their hair trimmed and neatly combed. A *classic real life example of wolves in sheep's clothing*, Frank thought. Uniformed guards surrounded the group with watchful eyes scanning the room often and thoroughly.

*   *   *

Marty Dimino stood before the jury dressed in a dark gray suit, a white dress shirt, and a muted paisley tie. His erect posture and short-cropped black hair showed a sprinkling of gray, giving him an ex-military demeanor. He passed his dark eyes carefully over each member of the jury. After panning past the last juror, he began.

"Four men enter a home, our last bastion of security, an inviolate place, a sacred domain where we share our innermost secrets and our love. Three strange, terrifying men break all the rules of that sanctity, and illegally enter a family's private home. Perhaps, they came for money or whatever they could sell for money."

Errol Malay, the defense attorney, rose from behind the defense counsel's table.

"Objection, Your Honor. Hearsay," Malay said.

Judge Spellman, an imposing man in his forties, shot a look at Malay.

"Overruled," Spellman said. "May I remind the defense, as well as the jury, that summations are not evidence. Proceed, Mr. Dimino."

"Mister Gaither and the three other men, you see here," Marty said, indicating Ernie and the three men behind him, "entered the Dugan home armed with knives, ostensibly to steal—"

"Objection, Your Honor," Malay said, jumping up. "Irrelevant. Only one man is on trial here today."

"Mr. Malay," Spellman said. "If you object once more during this summation, I will *object* to you being here during Mr. Dimino's statements. Make your objections in the body of your own summation to the jury, where you may include rebuttal. I feel like I have to teach law school here, and I, frankly, don't like it."

"Sorry, Your Honor," Malay said, and sat.

Dimino continued.

"This lady here," Dimino said, pointing to Barbara Chalmers in the gallery behind Frank, "has testified that she saw the four men leaving the Dugan home and went over to check on Amy Dugan. What she saw was the horror of watching her brutally stabbed friend dying.

25

Dimino took a sip of water from the prosecution table, allowing his last statement time to have maximum effect.

"Amy Dugan managed to tell Ms. Chalmers that the men wanted jewelry and believed the Dugans were rich jewelry dealers. So the accused, their leader, came to steal jewelry to probably fence for money. But that apparently wasn't enough. He wanted something more. Something decent citizens never imagine, ever, in their entire lives. These men came with lethal weapons, far above and beyond what was needed to pull off a robbery against a single, unarmed woman and two tiny children. No, Mr. Gaither wanted something more. Much more. He wanted blood. He wanted to brutally murder a helpless family, who never caused him one moment's discomfort. Indeed, people who had never laid eyes on him before that fateful day last July. Mr. Gaither and his men wanted to watch a lovely, innocent lady and two small children; one bright-eyed, three-year-old little boy and a pretty little girl of five, die. Here, take a look at them."

Dimino picked up a framed picture of Amy Dugan and the two children from the prosecution table and showed it to the jury. The photo showed a happy Amy and the two children laughing in a beach setting.

"Look at them. Look at those faces, those smiles. Look at the happiness that's there in this picture. Ah, but there's something missing. One face is absent. The smiling and happy face of the photographer. When he took this picture he was happy too, like the subjects in the picture. The photographer is this man here," Dimino said, indicating Frank Dugan sitting behind the prosecution table, "the loving father of those children, and the devoted husband of that beautiful woman. His smile has been removed from his face ... and perhaps from his life.

Dimino paced slowly to the evidence table, picked up a 9x12 manila envelope, opened it and removed a handful of large photographs.

"Now I'm going to show you pictures that are not so happy. You've seen these before, but I want to make them indelible in your minds before you decide the fate of the accused."

Dimino moved close to the jury box and held up one of the photos.

"This is that same little boy you saw in the family picture," Dimino said.

Several jurors were visibly appalled by what was depicted in the photo.

"This is the little girl."

Dimino showed them a different photo.

"It took the county coroner several hours to figure out which child was which."

Frank dropped his chin on his chest and closed his eyes.

"I've known our coroner for over ten years. He's a dedicated professional who has no peer in his field.

After he examined the victims in these pictures, he went out into the street in front of the Dugan home and wept. There are limits to us all."

Dimino pointed to a man in the first row of the gallery.

"San Diego police Lieutenant Judd Kemp here, who led the initial investigation, said the crime scene was so gruesome that several of his veteran men became so physically ill that they asked *not* be sent back into the Dugan house.

Dimino took out another photo from envelope.

"This is that pretty lady in the family picture. After they raped and tortured her, this is what they did to Amy Dugan. It's hard to believe that this was once a person.

Several jurors shook their heads, a few looked away, while others took out handkerchiefs and dabbed their eyes.

"What's even harder to believe is that human beings could do this to someone. And I guess the answer is that no *human* being could. Only *animals,* with no conscience whatsoever could do such a thing."

Errol Malay squirmed in his seat and clenched his fists.

Dimino stuffed the photos into the manila envelope, except one, and placed them on his table. He returned to the jury carrying the single photo at his side.

"They came for jewelry, for money. And, while fully aware of their predetermined course, they committed the most heinous and unthinkable crimes of horror against fellow humans. This is but the first of four trials to be conducted in this case. At present, there is only one man on trial, the man who owned the car identified at the scene. The other perpetrators will soon have their day in court, but for now, we want to concentrate our attention on Ernest Bernard Gaither, or Ernie Gaither, as he's known to his associates. But whether it's one trial, or four separate trials, the State demands justice. Every peace-loving citizen demands justice. Frank Dugan here, as a husband, a father, and a decorated veteran and police officer, pleads with you, his distinguished peers, to, one by one, make it impossible for these four, insufferable individuals to ever cause innocents pain again. To ensure this, we have only one recourse. We ask for the death penalty. We ask that societal cancers be removed. Cut out so they can't reappear and continue to kill. We ask you to make our place in the world safe for our families and safe for little children to smile and laugh again."

Once again, Dimino displayed the happy photograph of Amy and the Dugan children, then stepped to the prosecution table and turned back to the jury box.

"Whatever you decide, I want you to be aware of the fact that this man, Frank Dugan, has already been

29

illegally and cruelly given a life sentence from which there is no return. A life condemned to only remembering his beloved family, loved ones that are never coming back. The State rests, Your Honor."

Dimino sat next to Frank, patted him on the forearm.

"Will the defense make its closing remarks?" the judge said.

"It will, Your Honor," Errol Malay said, rising.

"Proceed."

Malay stepped before the jury. His black silk, double-breasted suit and charcoal shirt sharply contrasted with his fire engine red tie. He smiled at several of the jurors as if they were old friends he recognized.

"Ladies and gentlemen of the jury, the defense wants to see justice prevail in this case every bit as much as you do. Whoever did these crimes has to answer and pay the price for their unspeakable acts. What we don't want is to see innocent people wrongly convicted of something they didn't do, and thereby compound tragedy and wrongdoing with yet more tragedy and more wrongdoing. For then, it is we who become the criminals. Right now, we are asked to consider this case as it pertains to Ernest Bernard Gaither."

Malay strode to the defense table and indicated Gaither with an outstretched palm.

"Mr. Gaither's car has been allegedly placed near the scene of the crime by a solitary witness who claims to have memorized a license plate on a moving vehicle never closer to her than forty to fifty feet and pulling rapidly away. This witness, Barbara Chalmers, the aunt of Frank Dugan," Malay said, pointing her out, "and the next door neighbor of the Dugans, further stated that she saw the four men who left the Dugan house at around 11:30 AM on the day of the crime, yet she was never able to pick out even one of these alleged perpetrators in several police line-ups. We must be certain, when we convict anyone of a crime, that the evidence supports that conviction, and, need I remind you, beyond a reasonable doubt. Therein is the problem with convicting Mr. Gaither, who is on trial for his life and is facing, among other charges, the capital crime of murder. The problem is that there has not been one piece of hard evidence linking him with the crime. Not one shred. There is *enormous* reasonable doubt."

Malay turned his back to the jury and paced across the wide corridor in front of the judge's bench, the index finger of his right hand waggling above his head as he continued.

"The State has produced no motive, not one fingerprint, not one eyewitness to the actual crime upon which you could begin to prove his guilt. On top of this, he has sworn eyewitnesses as to his own whereabouts during the entire day that the crimes took

31

place. Barbara Chalmers has testified that she heard unusual noises and sounds coming from the Dugan house, and when she went over to investigate, she saw four men, one loosely fitting the description of the accused in this case, running from the scene."

Frank looked back at his aunt and smiled.

"She further stated," Malay said, "that she followed them on foot, saw them get into a older model, black Chevrolet sedan and speed away. They *sped* away. But not before, she claims, *not before* she saw their license plate number and memorized it. She claims to have done all that, but cannot positively identify one of the accused men in this crime, including the defendant, Ernest Gaither. Not one. Let me put the question to you, ladies and gentlemen: How would you like to be convicted of murder solely on the grounds that someone frantically misread or misinterpreted your car license number? During this trial, we went to a lot of trouble to show you more than thirty vehicles in this city that fit Ms. Chalmer's recollection of the car, but differ by but a single digit or letter of their license number. Anyone could, under the circumstances, misread a character on a license plate. Any of us. When we took Ms. Chalmers to test her auto recognition abilities, out of ten cars pointed to from forty feet away, she couldn't properly identify the make of the vehicle in seven of the instances. *Seven.* She was wrong seventy percent of the time under ideal and unstressed circumstances."

Malay took a moment to sip water from a glass on the defense table, then continued.

"It's not her fault. Lots of cars look alike these days. Car makers routinely copy each other's designs. Any of us could mistake a Chevrolet for an Oldsmobile or a Pontiac. And, as if dubious recognition weren't enough, the car in question, the one owned by Mr. Gaither, and supposedly seen by this same Ms. Chalmers, was proved to be in a reputable auto shop for repairs at the time of the crimes. If you sat there where Mr. Gaither is sitting, would you like to be convicted of murder based on the evidence shown in this trial?"

Malay was silent for a moment.

"You wouldn't want to be convicted of *speeding* on such shaky testimony. I want each one of you to ask yourselves this question: Is there reasonable doubt? If the answer is yes, acquit this fellow citizen and let's find the real killer, bring in real evidence against him, and serve the real meaning of justice. Thank you, ladies and gentlemen, for bearing this awesome responsibility of judging the life and death of your fellow citizens with honor and dignity."

Malay crossed to the defense table and faced the bench.

"The defense rests, Your Honor," Malay said and took his seat.

Every eye in the courtroom focused on the jury.

Chapter 6

Frank Dugan and Marty Dimino walked the wide hallway in the courthouse, their steps clicking on the terrazzo.

"You did good in there, Mr. Dimino," Frank said.

"Marty, please."

"How long will it take?" Frank asked, adjusting his uncomfortable black tie.

"For the jury to reach a decision? It varies. Guilty verdicts usually come back fast. *Usually,*" Dimino said and glanced at his watch. "Long deliberations usually spell trouble for getting a conviction. This case though, I don't know. Mezza, mezza. I'm not taking any bets."

"I want to be sure they did it," Frank said.

"We all do. If they let Gaither off we'll never know about the other three."

"What do you mean?"

"If we can't convict Gaither, we'll play hell getting indictments against his buddies. The only thing we've got on them is complicity with Gaither. He flies, that's it. They all fly."

"My gut says they're guilty. I've interviewed enough mooks like them. I can feel their guilt when I look them in the eye."

"Don't plan on making jury selection expert your next career."

"Where did they get this Malay guy?" Frank asked.

"He's a little glitzy, but good. Guzman bought him."

"Rico Guzman?"

"Anything stronger than aspirin sold in LA goes through him. He's the Grand Poobah of drugs in Southern Cal."

"I know who he is. We're investigating his operation right now. What's his interest in this case?"

"Those are his boys in here. His street urchins. They lean on people, sell a little, steal a lot. He doesn't want them tempted to turn state's evidence to cop a plea. Could hurt him. So he buys them a lawyer on the rise that the judges haven't learned to hate yet."

A court clerk called to them from the corridor.

"Mr. Dimino, Detective Dugan, the jury's coming back in," the clerk said.

Frank looked at Marty for a read. Marty checked his watch.

"Twenty-two minutes," Marty said and looked at Frank. "I got nothing."

* * *

Silence swept over the courtroom. Everyone was back where they were before the jury left to deliberate. The judge faced the jury.

"Mr. Foreman, has the jury reached a verdict?"

The foreman stood.

"We have, Your Honor."

"Please read the verdict."

"We find the defendant, Ernest Bernard Gaither, on all counts, not guilty."

Bedlam ensued in the courtroom. The suspects, their friends, and Malay rejoiced. Reporters scurried from the room. Frank Dugan and Marty Dimino sat stone-faced. The Judge demanded order, hammering his gavel repeatedly, as if driving ten-penny nails.

"Order in this court! Order in this court!"

The hubbub subsided. People retook seats, voices hushed to murmurs.

"This court is still in session," the judge said. "I realize that passionate beliefs are at issue here, but they will be considered in an orderly manner.

The judge cast his eyes to the jury.

"Ladies and gentlemen of the jury, the court thanks you for your service and consideration in this case."

Judge Spellman turned to the defense table.

"Mr. Gaither, you have been acquitted by a jury of your peers and are free to go. Jurors, you are dismissed. This court is adjourned."

The judge banged his gavel once and the courtroom cleared of almost everyone. Frank remained in his seat while Dimino stood, gathered his papers, and stuffed them into a leather briefcase. Ernie

Gaither and his three friends filed slowly past Frank, looking down at him with derisive smiles.

"Well, I guess they're gonna have to find someone else to hang this broad's murder on," Ernie said to the other three.

"And them two little dorks," Dwayne said.

Frank sprung to his feet and faced them. Marty Dimino dropped his briefcase and restrained him. Ernie stopped next to Frank, faced him, bold in his arrogance.

"Yeah, and them two little ... .kids. We're real sorry about what happened to your family, Mr. Dugan. Real sorry."

Marty tightened his grip on Frank's arms as the four young men strolled away with the detective's eyes burning into the backs of their heads.

"They wasn't kids, Ernie. They was dorks," Dwayne said. "Don't be mistakin' no dorks for kids. You understand what I'm sayin'?"

As the four suspects merged with the rest of the exiting people, Ernie Gaither raised a hand at a chicly-dressed man centered between two trim men at the rear wall.

"The guy in the gray sharkskin suit is Rico Guzman," Marty said, releasing his grip on Frank. "The other two with him are hired help."

Frank eyed the quartet of suspects as they exited the courtroom, followed by Guzman and his henchmen. Frank's glare followed them until they disappeared.

"They call him The Candy Man," Marty said, returning to his briefcase.

"Candy Man?" Frank said.

"Whatever you crave, he's got."

"I've only seen department photos of the guy. Drug business must be good. He looks well off."

Marty stepped to the center aisle and turned to Frank.

"I'm sorry, Frank. I don't know what I could've done to convict that sonofabitch, but I'm taking full responsibility for that. We just didn't have enough reliable hosses to win the race."

"You did all you could," Frank said. "Ball's in my court now."

"What's that mean?"

Frank was silent and stared at Dimino.

"If you're thinking of doing anything on your own, please forget it," Dimino said.

"Forget it?" Frank said. "Forget it? I can't forget it. I see Amy every night. Little Billy and Deborah sitting on my lap. When I try to lose myself in a TV show, or the newspaper, I'll be reminded of them, I'll read about my family every day in the grocery store checkout line. Anywhere there's a gossip rag I see them sensationalized in the media's bullshit captions. No one out there's going to let me forget it, and I'll never let myself forget it."

"The very thing we couldn't make stick against Gaither, a motive, will be bright as California sunshine on your head if you personally claim revenge on those punks. Sure, they might've done it, but you're the one who'll dance if you do anything to them now. If Gaither nicks himself shaving, you could get arrested. Everyone in this country knows how you feel. This isn't a shoplifting case at Bullock's, it's national news, maybe international."

"My life's over, Marty," Frank said. "Over. Got that? They took away the only life I know. They're not going to destroy my life and just walk away."

"Leave vengeance to God, and leave playing vigilante cop to Dirty Harry and Charles Bronson."

"I don't want to live anymore. What does it matter?"

"You want to know why I never committed suicide? And believe me there were times I seriously considered it. You want to know why I didn't do it?"

Frank shook his head.

"Because I knew in three days I'd be pissed off about it. You need to structure some time now. Time to insulate yourself from this. This has been a tremendous blow to you. It's going to take more than these past few months. I know you don't believe it right this minute, but you *will* feel better in time."

Frank stared into space.

"Tell you what," Dimino said, "I'll show you how to pass the next few hours in a positive way."

"Doing what?"

"Knocking down some classy bourbon at Harry's Place."

"How is that positive?"

"After a few of Harry's Wild Turkey Flashfires, I'm *positive* we'll both be unable to say: 'I wish to wash my Irish wristwatch.'"

Chapter 7

The interior of Harry's Place presented itself as a comfortable, old fashioned English pub and smelled of sautéed onions and charred beef. Frank and Marty sat at the bar with opened jackets, unbuttoned shirts, and slack ties. Empty shot glasses and beer bottles sat in front of them.

"I know what you're saying, but our legal system doesn't allow for it," Marty said.

"These thugs have prior convictions running onto five rap sheets," Frank said. "Isn't that different from a man who's never been in trouble?"

"Maybe, but it's usually not admissible to offer in court. Look, there are guys who commit dozens of crimes and then somehow get religion, see the light. I don't know how or why, but they do, and later they get arrested on a bum circumstance, a suspicion, whatever, but this time the guy didn't do it. *Really didn't do it*. Are we going to hang him because he used to be less than a choirboy?"

"No, but that's an exceptional case."

"And how about the reverse? A guy goes through forty years of life without ever taking a paperclip, then boom, he steals a million from the bank vault, or goes to the local McDonald's and starts popping everyone in sight. Never had any prior record. Gonna let him off because he was always a good boy before he broke bad? You've gotta judge each case on its own merit. It's not perfect, but it's the way it is."

Marty rattled a shot glass against one of the beer bottles. The bartender acknowledged the signal with a raised hand.

"Over all, it's a good system," Marty said, shoving the empties toward the inside edge of the bar.

"The system stinks. It lets people who have shown extreme antisocial behavior back out on the street to repeat their crimes."

"What are you gonna do? If you lock up everybody who demonstrates antisocial behavior, you put two thirds of the world in jail. You could arrest everybody in Dodger Stadium when the Giants are in town."

Frank waved a hand in disgust.

"Look, Frank, you're American born and over twenty-five. You don't like the system? Run for office and change it. I wasn't born in the D.A.'s office. I got fed up with being a lawyer who only sets up corporate charters and handles divorces. I wanted to make a difference. So I got into the political ring and slugged it out. When the smoke cleared, I got elected. It was hard knocks. I took a lot of shit. You ever want to get into politics, come see me. I'll save you a lot of grief."

The bartender removed the empty shot glasses and disposed of the beer bottles.

"Give us thirty more," Marty said.

"Coming up, Mr. Dimino," the bartender said.

"Bet he only brings back two," Marty said. "That's the trouble with these trendy new bartenders. Can't count worth a milk fart at a dairy farm."

"How many have we had?"

"I don't know. Two?"

Frank stared emptily across the bar. Marty watched him for a moment.

"Why don't you come home with me tonight?" Marty said. "Sharon'll make us a couple of steaks, we'll hurl back a couple of cold beers, watch a movie ... "

"Thanks, Marty, but I'd better get on home. Amy's got ... "

Frank looked away.

"We'll talk about it later," Marty said, with a pat on Frank's shoulder.

The bartender returned with the drinks.

"Right now there's work to be done," Marty said and raised one of the shots. "Come on, grab onto that Kentucky varnish. Remember, it's only healthy if you drink alone or in groups.

Frank forced a smile and lifted his drink. They clinked glasses, belted the shots back, and took swigs of their beers.

"If you won't come home with me, I want you to stay at my beach house tonight. It's fully stocked with everything you'll need. Beer, booze, coffee. Got TV in the bedroom. Even new toothbrushes. My dentist was a former client. And the bastard thinks *I* charge too much."

"Marty, the department's put me in an efficiency at the Beachcomber until my house is taken off crime scene status. I can—"

"Fuck that tourist flophouse. You stay at my place. There. That's settled."

Frank took another sip of beer and sighed.

"Okay, okay. *Uncle*."

"Give me your keys," Marty said. "We're not driving tonight. Too many cops around."

Frank bunched his mouth and stared at Marty.

"Your keys," Marty said, his hand extended.

Frank slid his keys down the bar where they collided with Marty's beer.

"We'll get through this, Frank," Marty said and signaled the bartender. "Fifty-two more of these, Chuckles."

The bartender shook his lowered head, smiled.

"Do they ever cut you off in here?" Frank asked.

"Yeah, when I tell Chuckles he's pretty."

*   *   *

The taxi drove north on the moonlit San Diego Freeway that paralleled the Pacific's shoreline. As the car curved around La Jolla Parkway to Torrey Pines Road, Marty Dimino directed the driver onto a smaller road that wended its way to a row of beach houses.

44

"It's the last one in this row," Marty said to the driver. "Pull into the driveway."

Marty activated the automatic garage door with a remote control on a key ring.

"Wait here. I'll be right back," Marty said to the cabbie.

Marty and Frank entered the house through a door that connected the garage with the kitchen.

"This is the place," Marty said and gave Frank the house key linked to the remote. "I'll come over in the morning with one of my interns to bring you your car. Help yourself to anything here."

Marty pulled a business card and a pen from his jacket pocket, scrawled a few numbers on the card, and jammed it into Frank's hand.

"It's my cell number and private line at work," Marty said. "Treasure it. I rarely give them out."

"This place is beautiful," Frank said. "Smack on the ocean, no less."

"Yeah, it's what twenty-five years of contingencies, divorces, and retainers will get you. See you in the morning. And hey, no funny stuff, okay. We had a good night. There will be many more of them for you, so keep the faith."

"I'm good. Got your card. Go home."

"Why? Am I beginning to look pretty?" Marty said and bumbled his way out through the garage.

*   *   *

45

Frank patrolled the long hallway and peeked into rooms until he came to one that looked "guesty." He doffed his clothes and flopped nude on top of the bed.

After hours of tossing in and out of sleep and staring at the ceiling, Frank turned on the lamp on the side table and noted the time on his watch. It was 5:07 AM.

Frank eyed the master dresser in the room. A moment later, he found himself rifling through drawers. Inside lay new tee shirts, an assortment of socks, and a pajama set, still in plastic wrap. A brand new package of navy blue swimming trunks stopped his rummaging. He ripped open the cellophane bag and held them to his waist for size. Close enough. He tossed them onto the bed and felt around in his clothes pile and pulled out a Glock 9-millimeter automatic. He sat on the foot of the bed and stared at it until his eyes began to water.

Chapter 8

Frank ambled on the moonlit beach along the water's edge, the cold brine lapping across his feet. He tightened the draw strings on the swimming trunks to secure the loose fit. The surf farther out roared and broke in white froth, the smell of the ocean strong in the predawn breeze.

Frank stopped, stared out at the tiny lights of an offshore ship several miles to the west. His fixed focus blurred and the ship was gone. Something else took its place. A home movie played…

Frank, Amy, and their two children walk along a beachside boardwalk abundant with shops and eateries. Billy, their two-year-old, lags behind and becomes interested in peeking under a pregnant woman's overhanging maternity garment. Neither the pregnant woman, nor the rest of the Dugan family, see him at first. Amy turns around to look for him. She sees what he's doing and alerts Frank.

They try to stifle their laughter as they go back to retrieve him, but it's useless. When they get to him, he's reaching up under the woman's top. The pregnant woman jumps, not knowing what is grabbing at her belly. When she sees that it's a little boy, she smiles in relief, then laughs. Amy and Frank arrive just in time to apologize, retrieve the boy, and hustle him off. Amy pats Billy on the behind, sending him ahead of her where she can keep an eye on him. Their little girl, Deborah, wags an admonishing finger at her brother as he nears his older sister.

The mental scene blurred and dissolved into another series of scenes:

The Dugans are seen buying tickets at the entrance to the Fun House. They all gleefully go inside. The Dugans are seen coming out of the Fun House. The two kids are laughing, but Amy is pale and Frank doesn't abound with joy.

The movie dissolved and another mental movie faded in:

Frank rams Amy's bumper car broadside giving her and Deborah a healthy jolt. Amy grimaces, Deborah frowns and cries. Frank and Billy laugh like mischievous school boys and whisk their car away to find more victims.

The Dugans get into seats on a roller coaster. The ride starts off with a jerk. The roller coaster soon speeds down a nearly vertical section of track, hits the bottom, and makes a sharp right turn. The faces of Amy and Deborah are smiling and exhilarated; Billy looks mortified and Frank ducks his head between his arms, hanging on to the safety bar with a death grip.

At a boardwalk restaurant the family is seated at a table outside stuffing down hot dogs, ice cream, and drinking sodas. Amy takes a big drink of a vanilla milkshake directly from the large cup without using her straw. When she removes the cup from her face, she has a huge white mustache which she proudly displays for everyone.

Amy and Frank dance romantically in an open boardwalk ballroom. The children are asleep on a nearby park bench that faces the dance floor. Frank kisses Amy gently, pulls her close as they slowly trip the light fantastic.

Amy and Frank wearily carry their sound asleep children to their beds in a hotel suite. Moments later, Amy enters their semi-dark master bedroom and crosses to a wide bed. She is silhouetted by the light beaming in from the sliding glass door of the balcony. She wears a sheer nightgown, revealing her shapely body. She slowly lets the gown slide to the floor. Frank watches from the bed. She joins him and they begin to make love in the glow from the moon.

Frank's last mental scene faded to black. His thoughts returned to the present as he stared seaward. Daylight was breaking. He sloshed into the shallow surf, slowly at first, then broke into a run. When the water got too high to plow ahead and stay upright, he dove into the waves and swam toward the distant ship.

Frank stroked for several minutes, stopped, treaded water, and glanced back toward shore. He was far from the beach. He was okay with that. Frank had determined that drowning was the best way to go. The gun would just leave an ugly mess for others. Not his style. No, the sea would claim the former marine as her own, and there would be no need to tidy the remains. Drowning would be the perfect way. He would eventually become exhausted and let himself slip under the waves. He'd be able to hold his breath for a while, but soon his brain would force him to breath, and the sea would fill his lungs. There would be choking at first, but soon he'd mercifully black out as the water displaced his air, and he'd surrender to death.

Frank smiled. He looked forward to being with Amy and the children.

Being an excellent swimmer could prolong things. Frank knew it would take some time for him to wear out, but the water, while cold, felt pleasant in contrast to the warm summer air. He twisted back to look seaward for a moment, before launching into his long swim, and beheld a sight that chilled his blood much lower than the temperature of the Pacific.

Chapter 9

Ominous fins appeared in the distance. Several of them.

Dolphins, Frank hoped.

The reality soon set in. Numerous large sharks were knifing their way in his direction.

Drowning was one thing, but becoming ripped and slashed to death by rows of razor-edged serrated teeth was abundantly another. There was a reason these gray eating machines were the world's most successful predators— not just at present, but since the beginning of their life on earth.

Frank turned east and swam back toward the beach. He glided with long, powerful strokes, careful not to create turbulence and audible splashes in the water. He smoothly slipped shoreward like a silent crocodile, his head shifting from side to side to grab a breath, his eyes barely above the waterline.

The sharks closed in on him before he neared the shore. They surrounded him. Frank continued to stroke his way toward the beach, slowly now, methodically. His heart pounded so hard in his chest he could feel its pulsations in his inner ear.

A massive shark eased over to Frank, maybe twelve feet in length, he judged. It brushed his elbow with its sandpaper-texture body, but didn't attack.

Others in the school did the same thing. They swam inches away, gently bumping him at times, crossing his path, beneath him and beside him. One nudged Frank with the side of its mouth, glistening teeth brushed by an inch from his shoulder, surfacing enough for Frank to see its round black eye.

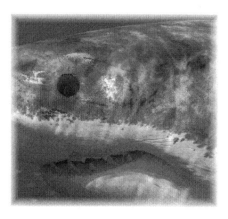

When they gathered the thickest around him, they changed course and headed north, parallel to the coast.

Frank continued swimming toward shore alone.

Death had twice refused to bestow her blessing on him as an orange sun rose over the land.

*   *   *

Frank emerged from the surf and sloshed through the shallows to the dry sand of the beach. He turned and gazed seaward with bewilderment.

"Forget your scuba gear, Mr. Cousteau?" a familiar voice said.

Frank whirled about to face the source.

"If you're heading for Japan you might need some fins," Lieutenant Mike Graham said.

"Hey, Mike. Just taking a wake-up dip."

"I called to see how you were doing, but when you didn't answer, I decided to drop by.

"How'd you know where to look?"

"Dimino called. Asked me to pay the visit."

"Doubting my mental stability?" Frank said, plodding toward the beach house.

"Marty was kinda concerned." Graham said, following.

"When I left him he couldn't make complete sentences."

Frank and Mike entered the beach house. Frank turned on the television in the living room.

"This is an uptown joint," Graham said, taking in the spacious interior.

"Make yourself at home. Only be a minute."

Frank disappeared into the hall.

"Any coffee?" Graham asked.

"Try the kitchen. I didn't make any yet."

In a minute, Frank returned, drying off with a beach towel.

The TV came to life on a morning news channel. A somber announcer spoke on camera.

"The killing of the Reseda youth makes the hundredth in greater Los Angeles this year," the announcer said. "Police officials pledge to increase their efforts in high crime districts, but city lawmakers are in a quandary as to where to obtain more budget money to pay extra patrolmen. The mayor has called for an emergency session of the City Council to address the problem. Many officials say the budget shortfall is statewide."

"No wonder I can't get a raise." Graham said.

Frank went to the guest room, doffed the swimsuit, and redressed in most of his court clothes, minus the tie. He turned his attention to the bed and retrieved his pistol and slid it into his belt holster. Back at the front of the house, he found Mike Graham in the kitchen searching through the cabinets and eventually finding a bag of Starbucks French Roast coffee beans.

"Got a coffee mill?" Graham asked.

"I don't know where anything is here," Frank said. "May be some juice in the fridge."

A ringing phone sounded. Graham pulled the cell from his belt, brought it to his ear.

"What's up?" Graham said, then listened . "Where?" A short pause. "Got it."

Graham ended the call and bolted for the door.

"Senator McAllister's been shot."

"What?" Frank said, chasing Graham.

"Robert McAllister. The U.S. Senator. He's been shot at the marina. I'm outa here."

"I don't have a car," Frank yelled.

Frank ran to the kitchen counter where he'd tossed the beach house key.

"Don't do anything nuts," Graham said, barreling out the door.

"Take me with you," Frank shouted, grabbed at the key and the attached garage remote, propelling the set onto the floor ten feet away.

"Shit," Frank said and scrambled to retrieve the pair, but by the time he snatched them up and scurried to the door, Graham's unmarked cruiser had roared out of the driveway.

*   *   *

Marty Dimino's man brought Frank his Bronco an hour later and he drove to the Beachcomber and changed into his typical detective dress in his hotel room: A navy polo shirt, khakis, and a pair of cross training shoes. He tucked his Glock in its belt holster and drove north on the San Diego Freeway. He tuned the radio to a local newscast, reported by a baritone-voiced announcer:

"Family members say that Senator McAllister was taking his usual early morning walk at the San Diego Marina where his boat is moored, when the attack took place. Authorities say he was shot three times in the upper body by a large caliber handgun. Paramedics administered first aid at the scene on the

55

unconscious senator, and he was rushed by helicopter to the Scripps Mercy shock trauma unit."

The announcer paused for a moment.

"This just in: at this time, the senator's condition is unknown. No suspects and no motive for the crime have been determined. Known in the Senate as a staunch conservative and a strong anti-crime activist, Senator Robert McAllister was home for the current congressional recess after serving more than four consecutive and distinguished terms in the United States Senate. We'll be following this story throughout the day as updates on the senator's status come in."

The announcer paused for a second.

"Coast Guard officials today confiscated more than thirty kilos of pure cocaine while making an inspection of a South American yacht off King Harbor in Redondo Beach."

Rampant crime topped all the recent news stories, not only in California, but everywhere on the globe. Frank felt that crime was going on a military offensive, surging to prove its dominance. He wondered if the underworld was increasing its assaults because it intended to win the war. After all, crime had brought its fight to his own door. Now an important lawmaker had been assassinated. The attacks on 9/11, school shootings, terrorism at shopping malls. Nowhere seemed safe anymore.

Frank saw his face in the rear view mirror. His eyes were like the ones he saw on his marine buddies in Desert Storm before battle. The eyes of a warrior. Now there was another war to wage, another hill to take, another engagement.

Maybe the biggest one of his life.

Chapter 10

Frank parked the Bronco in the driveway of his rancher, turned off the engine, and slid out. He took out a set of keys and slowly walked to the front door. A real estate sign on the lawn advertised the house for sale.

The inside of the home looked like one left by owners who intended to be away for a long time. Frank knew that was partly true. His family would be away forever. The interior remained as it was when he last saw it, but boxes now were stacked everywhere as if a move was imminent. Most of the upholstered furniture was covered with white sheets. Wall decorations and small items were absent from the decor. The rooms in view had been recently painted. The smell of water-based latex still lingered in the stuffy air. Painting supplies and stepladders were scattered throughout the foremost rooms.

Frank began a reluctant, reminiscent tour of the house. The kitchen sparkled like new. Only the refrigerator revealed habitation where a crayon drawing hung on the door attached with a small magnet. The drawing was a child's stick figure of a man, beneath which was printed: "My Daddy."

Frank opened the refrigerator and took out a soda from the sparse offerings inside. He opened the can, took a sip, and wandered out.

The office looked unchanged. The bookcase displayed athletic trophies won by Frank for football and swimming, and framed photographs hung on the walls showing the Dugan family at various ages and holiday events. Deborah, Billy, and Amy dressed like characters in *Star Wars* made Frank ever so briefly smile.

A photo of Amy and Frank hugging at the beach stopped his eye. He picked it off the desk and left the room.

Frank trudged to the doorway of the master bedroom and paused. He forced himself to peer inside and steadied himself against the doorjamb. The room had also been newly painted; the bed, neatly made with a new bedspread. The furniture exactly as it was; his wedding photo with Amy still on the dresser.

He left without going in.

Frank stepped along the hall and entered the children's room. He scanned the single beds, a crib, a dresser, a chest of drawers, and several cardboard boxes. He crossed to the stack of boxes and opened the flaps on one. He reached inside and removed a toy dinosaur, studied it with a pained smile and gently replaced it.

A tightening in his stomach told Frank it was time to leave.

* * *

Frank locked the house, climbed into his car, and placed the beach photo on the passenger seat. Barbara Chalmers intercepted him at the open Bronco door.

"Frank," she said, reaching in, embracing him. "How are you?"

"I'm hanging in there, Aunt Barbara."

Frank slid out and stood facing her. She held him at arm's length.

"You look awful."

"Had a long night."

"I'm so sorry. I did my best to convince them. I saw those men. I saw their car, and I had that license number right. God, they didn't believe me."

Barbara clapped her hand over her mouth, her eyes filling.

"It's not your fault. You did all you could. The trial's over."

Frank kissed Barbara on the cheek and gave her a hug.

"Gotta go," Frank said. "You did your best. You *are* the best. And you're the last of my family now."

"Your father's still alive, isn't he? Back in Baltimore?"

"I don't count that abusive bastard as a relative."

"I'm sorry ... "

"Don't be. As long as I have you, I still have the best of my ancestors…from my mother's Minneapolis side."

"Get along witchya now, love," Barbara said, slipping into a Minnesotan patois.

*   *   *

Frank pulled the Bronco off the road and parked in the lot of a busy shopping center. He jogged over to a newspaper dispenser, dropped in coins, and pulled out a copy. He glanced at the front page above the fold, grimaced, and tucked it under his arm.

Frank returned to his car and skimmed the interior articles in the paper. He put the photo of Amy and him in the glove compartment, and flipped the paper onto the passenger seat. With his hands on the top of the steering wheel, he pressed his forehead against his knuckles. Several moments passed before he snapped open his cell phone and pressed a few buttons.

"Marty, it's Frank Dugan. I need to talk to you right away."

*   *   *

The district attorney's offices were bustling with men and women in business dress hustling about from cubicles to conference rooms to various hallways. Frank threaded his way to a large office where Marty

61

Dimino talked on the phone. The DA faced a window that provided a grand view of the city of San Diego, his back to the door. Marty finished his conversation and swiveled in his chair to hang up the phone. He looked up to see Frank standing in front of his desk.

Frank tossed a newspaper on the desk in front of Marty. The bold headline read:

SENATOR MCALLISTER DIES

Frank leaned on Marty's desk and said, "What will we need for you to run for the Senate of the United States?"

Chapter 11

"Charly Stone said she'd consider it," Marty Dimino said, wheeling the gray Beamer 740 through the traffic on the freeway. "She's a busy lady. After she ran my campaign she was hired by the police department. Ran their psychology division. Profiled bad people. Now she freelances doing PR for anyone who wants attention, branding, any kind of positive publicity. You give her straight answers. She already knows what's in your head. She's like a female Hannibal Lecter without the liver and fava beans."

"Where're we going?" Frank asked.

"The Shamrock, across from Hollywood Park. It's an off-duty cop bar in a tough area, so watch what you say about L.A.'s Finest."

"In that area with the legalized gambling?"

"Just twenty-five hours a day. Why? Got a hot tip on a horse?"

"Is Seabiscuit still running?"

"You'd best keep your money in your pocket, pal."

The Shamrock was old, dingy, and smelled like the inside of a beer hooka. Frank counted twenty or more patrons through the cloud of smoke that hung in the air. The clientele was spread out among the stools at the long bar, a few booths, and bistro tables scattered

63

throughout the open room. Mostly men between thirty and fifty, more than half wearing police uniforms.

An attractive woman in her late thirties, business-dressed in a maroon suit and cream blouse, sat in one of the booths. She locked her dark, penetrating eyes on Marty as the two newcomers stepped into the room. Marty tilted his head her way and led Frank to the booth.

"Good to see you, sweetheart," Marty said and leaned close to kiss the woman lightly on the lips.

"You too. You look thinner," the woman said.

"Always the psychologist. This is Dr. Charlene Stone, Frank. The best campaign manager in the business. Charly, this is Detective Frank Dugan."

"Like he needs an introduction. I have a television, a radio, and I subscribe to six newspapers."

"Next you'll tell me your crapper's in the house," Marty said, inviting Frank to slide into the booth opposite Charly.

"Pleased to meet you, Ms. Stone," Frank said.

"Charly's fine."

"The place still looks as medieval as the last time we were here," Marty said and sat next to Frank. "What is it about this joint? Can't be the uptick décor."

"It's a beehive of information," Charly said. "My work depends on a lot of it. Like getting country lawyers behind DA desks."

"Country? Ouch." Marty said.

64

"So what's this about?" Charly asked.

"Frank here thinks I should make a bid to replace McCallister."

"Jesus, Marty. The man's not even autopsied yet."

"It's my fault," Frank said. "I know soon there'll be a lot of hopefuls tossing their hats in the ring for the senator's seat. We need his replacement to be an aggressive anti-crime person like he was, not some joker campaigning for more entitlements and lower taxes."

"And you're on board for doing this, Marty?" Charly asked.

"I'm here to discuss it."

"Where do you want to start?" Charly said.

"What are my chances, and what's it going to cost?" Marty said.

"Right out of the chute, it'll cost you a drink," Charly said.

"Coming up," Marty said and marched to the bar.

"How are you doing, Frank?" Charly said. "I followed the trial every day. When they read the verdict, I threw a Prada stiletto at my TV."

"I'm okay. But I'd be a liar if I told you I'm accepting that verdict."

"You thinking of going after those guys?"

"First, I want to know if they did it. If I can prove they did, well, let's just say you wouldn't want to be them."

"So you're willing to sacrifice yourself to even the score?"

"If need be. I don't see myself with much else to live for."

"I know more about you from Judd Kemp. He thinks you're as good as it gets in police work. You're an intelligent young man with a purposeful life ahead of you. He doesn't want you to waste it on trash like Ernie Gaither. He'll get his soon enough."

"How about Rico Guzman?"

"That'll be a tougher banana to peel. He's got more insulation than the space shuttle."

Marty returned laden with drinks.

"Beers for the boys, and a Gran Marnier in a *snifter* for the lady. Man, your bartender sure knows his Willies," Marty said, setting down the drinks and scooting into the booth.

"Willies?" Frank said.

"People who tip more than 20 percent," Marty said.

"It pays to take care of those you depend on," Charly said.

"So, what are my odds?" Marty asked.

"I'll give you the Cliff Notes version," Charly said.

"Fair enough," Marty said and sipped his beer.

"Marty, you're a popular man in the news media," Charly said. "But so was Al Gore. That doesn't get you elected to public office. You haven't had one minute's experience in national political life. You're going after an office held by one of the most prestigious public servants since Lincoln, and, because all nature abhors a vacuum, there will be, as Frank mentioned, a dozen other prominent people attempting to fill the job left open by McAllister. I don't mean to be so black and white about this, but these are the realities."

Frank stared at Charly during a lengthy silence. Marty scraped the label off his beer bottle with his thumb.

"Any positive notes?" Frank asked.

"Marty's a respected state's attorney with a sterling record. People in southern California know him and like him. People in San Diego County love and trust him. I like him too, but I'm only one vote. The ones coming from those raving liberals in the other big cities my not find him nearly so appealing. Being a toughie on crime will resonate well with those who've been mugged, but the others who've never had a brush with theft, rape, and murder will dismiss its importance. It's going to take a lot of contributions to run a campaign that will give you a real shot at the title. Steven Spielberg lives in this state and may throw in some help, but you're going to need Bill Gates and Rupert Murdoch size coffers to win."

"So, when do we start," Marty said.

"Tomorrow, six sharp. My office," Charly said. "Bring coffee. Lots of it."

Chapter 12

Rico Guzman sat on the patio of his sprawling mansion that overlooked his walled estate in Palos Verdes. Waves from the Pacific Ocean lapped against the rocks and narrow beach far below the mansion's foothill elevation of two hundred feet. The orange ball of the dipping sun silhouetted Santa Catalina on the western horizon. The Bali Hai scene from the film *South Pacific* replayed in his head.

Errol Malay sat across from Guzman at a teak table where they both sipped black Cuban coffee and stared out at the last of the day.

"I've arranged for you to be on the primary ballot," Guzman said. "The recent news will give you a boost, but we'll need a lot more to gain momentum on the others who'll be running."

"McCallister's death is a stoke of good luck," Malay said.

Guzman looked at Malay and smiled.

"Luck seems to always favor those who prepare," Guzman said.

"Anyone know who did it?"

"They have a low rez video of a man who looked a little like Han Solo in a red baseball cap."

"He get rid of the mask?"

"It made a nice fire for a few seconds."

"He should've kept it. Han Solo is a hell of a sight better looking than Mitch Davis."

"Maybe we'll get him a George Clooney one," Guzman said.

"Get your speeches lined up," Guzman said. "Number one on your platform will be a continuation of McCallister's ideas. Play on the public sympathy for a great American. Talk anti-crime, but be prepared to have tough questions thrown at you because of your association with me. Your court win with Gaither won't help you get votes, so tip-toe around issues that draw them in."

Malay said, "I don't think defending O. J. Simpson made F. Lee Bailey look like he was pro-crime."

"If he ran for public office, you'd see how beloved he was to hard anti-crime voters."

"In that case, we'll need a publicity blitz. All that media's going to cost a ton."

"We have that covered," Guzman said and pushed a humidor filled with Cohiba Espléndidos toward Malay.

"Cuban?" Malay asked.

"You must be kidding," Guzman said as he snipped the end off his seven-inch cigar with a gold cutter. "Cuban cigars are illegal in this country."

*   *   *

Frank Dugan stood at a podium in a sparsely filled auditorium. A sign on the front of the podium proclaimed:

MIRA COSTA HIGH SCHOOL
Home of the Mustangs

Large posters contained the promo: "Martin Dimino for U.S. Senate" printed in red, white, and blue. At the top of the poster were the words:

Time to Get Tough
Enough is Enough

A banner over the stage proscenium stated: "Manhattan Beach Parents Care About Government." Charly Stone, Marty Dimino, and Mike Graham sat together in a front row of the auditorium. Barbara Chalmers sat by herself a few rows back.

"The criminal does not receive any real punishment from incarceration," Frank said. "In fact, as many criminals have publicly stated, they actually prefer prison to the outside. Having gone to prison and later released, a parolee has before him two easy choices: to continue his criminal behavior on the outside, trying to avoid arrest, since no one, in his mind, wants to hire an ex-con, or to allow himself to get caught and return to his friends in prison. Few of us have such clear and simple choices in life. If he robs, he has plenty of easy spending money without having to work for it. If he gets caught, he goes back to bed and board with his pals and still doesn't have to do any real work. Not bad, huh? And while many of you may hold to the idea that prison offers rehabilitation, let me stress this: prison is the College of Crime. It's where criminals go to sharpen their craft.

"People who don't want to go to prison, don't go. And people who don't want to go to prison, but get caught in a crime and go there once, don't want to go back. It's the ones that don't care that I'm talking about. The career criminals. The chronic repeaters. The offenders who seem born without a conscience and any sense of responsibility for the acts they do. Let's deal with them now. It's what Senator McCallister wanted to do.

"It's time to get tough. Enough is enough. We have the man to get the job done now, to carry on the good work of Robert McCallister. The man is District Attorney Martin Dimino, the next senator from the great State of California."

What there was of an audience applauded with moderate enthusiasm. Frank's friends in the audience showed more animation in their response. Barbara Chalmers even stood and applauded.

Frank smiled, but he felt like a rookie stand-up comedian in a comedy club, relegated to working the handful of early arrivals before the headliners played to the capacity crowds.

*   *   *

On the floor of the auditorium, Frank received congratulations by a few people from the audience who lagged back, and a handful of his friends. After the supportive group dissipated, Charly approached him.

"Not bad for your first attempt at public rhetoric," Charly said.

"Are you kidding?" Frank said. "I'm a wreck. I'd rather run through hell with gasoline panties."

"It gets easier."

"I never understood why people are so afraid of public speaking. I do now."

"C'mon. Buy me a drink and I'll give you my real critique."

"Can't wait. It'll be like getting beaten half to death, then shot."

*   *   *

Frank and Charly sat across from each other in a booth at the Shamrock, drinks before them.

"We've got a good message, but we've got to get it to larger groups of people. The death of any performer is a small audience, and, as a public speaker, you are going to be a performer. Ask any actor who's worked before a small house. We need heavy word-of-mouth.

There'll be a primary election in two months. Primary winners get financing. I'll try to pick out the front runner against Marty, but for the most part I want you to talk a positive campaign on the issues and to hell with sniping at the opposition. Mudslinging is what candidates with weak positive issues do."

"I'll do little polishing on the speeches between the inconvenience of being a homicide detective."

"Is the department giving you liberal leave?"

"Yeah, Judd Kemp's cleared it with the captain. He's always been a stand-up guy."

"Judd wants you to concentrate on anything positive. This campaign work fits that bill."

"When's our next meeting? We can't keep holding sessions here."

"As much as I'll miss this place, I'll be setting up our headquarters this week. In San Diego for now."

"What's the territory we'll cover?' Frank asked.

"In the beginning, Marty will work southern Cal, I want you up north. They know who you are from the news. They want to hear about you, your personal experiences with crime. Later we switch, after the media blitz. In the end you and Marty will campaign together. A one-two punch to score the win."

"We have a chance?"

"I wouldn't be here if we didn't have a chance. Marty ain't going to be no shoo-in, sugar, but there's a light in the tunnel."

"My life flashing before my eyes?"

Charly smiled and patted Frank's hand.

"Got a little scoop for you. You'll be the reason Marty gets elected," Charly said. "The people will be voting for you."

Chapter 13

Frank entered the La Jolla beach house, closed and locked the door. He stepped into the kitchen and switched on the overhead lights when tiny objects on the floor caught his eye. There were food crumbs around the base of the cabinets. More fell from the space behind a door. Scratching noises carried out from inside the pantry section.

Frank cautiously opened the cabinet door. A small field mouse looked up from the cereal that he was eating and stared at Frank for a second. The mouse skittered for the rear of the compartment and disappeared. Frank closed the door and leaned on his elbows on the counter top.

*   *   *

The shelves in the pet store contained all manner of pesticides. Frank browsed the labels on several rodent-killing products, but returned each to its place on the shelf.

A clerk approached.

"Something I can help you find, sir?" the clerk asked.

"Yes, ... maybe. I've got a mouse in my house. In my kitchen. I'd like to catch him. Not kill him, just catch him and put him outside," Frank said.

"We don't sell conventional traps here, but you may want to look at one of these," the clerk said, taking a box from a nearby shelf and removing its contents. "It's called a Humana trap. It doesn't harm the animal. You just put your bait in here."

The clerk pointed to a specific place inside the trap

"I suggest cheese, or better yet, peanut butter. When he takes the food, the doors at each end close. Then you can do what you want to with the little culprit."

"I like it," Frank said.

Frank and the clerk stepped to the checkout counter where a second clerk rang up a sale at the cash register for a male customer. Frank waited to pay and listened to their conversation.

"Boy, when I saw the prices on those gerbils, I thought my son was crazy for buying that boa constrictor from you," the man said. "Crazier than he already is, anyway. Eight bucks a pop to feed a snake. I was going to go home and choke him with it."

"A lot of people think we sell the regular gerbils for snake feed," the second clerk said.

"What did you say I should ask for next time? Boxing gerbils?"

"Fighting gerbils. They can't live in community with the other gerbils and have to be isolated. They don't make good pets, either, so we sell them for feed. That'll be seventy-five cents."

The man paid the clerk and took a small box from the counter.

"That's a hell of a sight better than them eight bucks deals," the man said and walked to the door. "I swear I'm gonna hafta choke that boy one day. He'll stroll in one night with a sumbitchin' elephant. Mark my words. He'll want me to rent a damn semi and go on peanut runs."

*   *   *

Frank carefully placed the set trap inside the lower kitchen cabinet and eased the cabinet door shut. He left the kitchen and strode to the bedroom. At the dresser, he removed items from of his pockets, placed them on the dresser top, and stared into the mirror. His tired eyes studied the new lines on his face. He massaged them gently, hoping they would disappear. His hands dropped to rub his lower face. Something in the mirror's wider view of the room behind him put a pause on his cheekbone therapy. Frank turned to face the bed.

The comforter on the mattress was moving.

*   *   *

In the middle of the bed, a rolling a furrow in the down comforter rolled from side to side. Frank cautiously approached the bed, slid out a pillow, and slowly pulled back the covers.

A noise emanated from the dark under the comforter and bed sheet, a sound like a tire hissing air through a pinhole. Frank tugged the covers further toward the footboard. The black head of a king cobra lashed out at Frank, barely missing his forearm. Frank reeled and stumbled backward clutching the pillow and fell onto the floor. The huge snake writhed out from under the bedclothes and loomed high on the edge of the mattress above Frank and struck again. Frank barely had time to jerk the pillow between him and the snake's venom-dripping fangs. He quickly folded the pillow around the snake's head, holding it captive, its six-foot tail lashing about the room, slapping Frank more than once.

Frank struggled to his feet, holding the writhing cobra fast in the pillow, and dashed into the bathroom. He threw the snake and pillow over the top of the glass enclosure of the shower.

Frank collapsed on the toilet and tried to compose himself. A second later, the snake wriggled over the top of the shower enclosure. Frank leapt to his feet and tried to get out of the bathroom. The ten-foot snake stood upright on its coiled tail and whipped its open mouth again at Frank, missing him by an inch, shattering the full-length bathroom mirror on the door.

Frank bolted from the bathroom and yanked the doorknob hard to slam the door shut. The pursuing cobra got its head caught between the rapidly-closing door and the jamb. The cobra's head sheared off and flew into Frank's face, glanced off his cheek, and fell onto the bedroom floor, its jaws still snapping.

Frank stumbled across the room and leaned on the dresser breathing heavily.

The phone on the night table rang. Frank plodded over to the phone and grabbed the receiver.

"Hello." Frank said, his voice strained.

"Stick to police business, Mr. Dugan," a male voice said. "The DA doesn't need your help."

"Want to tell me who this is?"

"In time, Mr. Dugan. For now, quit campaigning ... or join your family."

"You sonofabitch—"

The phone went dead. Frank slammed the receiver onto its cradle and crossed to the chest of drawers, pulled open its drawers, and checked for any more surprises. He charged into the walk-in closet and searched everywhere in the small space. No jungle killers, no tarantulas, no scorpions. He emerged from the closet. Anger took charge of his demeanor. The footboard of the bed bore the brunt of a karate-style kick

"Goddamnit."

The phone rang again. He rushed to it, snatched the receiver.

"You kiss my ass, you chickenshit muthafucker."

"I'm game, but it's tough to do on the phone," the voice of Charly Stone said.

"Oh, my God. Charly, I'm so sorry."

"Bad day?"

"So far, a very large cobra in my bed, a threatening phone call, and I have mice."

"Now give me the bad stuff."

"Wait me a minute. I haven't checked the rest of the house."

"Seriously, a cobra? I have to give it to them. That's original. You okay?"

"I'm good. Don't tell PETA. I Killed the snake."

"My timing's too perfect. I called to tell you that Guzman's backing a candidate for the senate."

"Who?"

"Well, since Hitler was unavailable, he's putting his money on Errol Malay."

"The defense lawyer at the trial?"

"The same smug bastard," Charly said. "Call Marty, Judd, and Mike. Let them check out your place."

"I'm okay. I don't need— "

"I'm not going to waste my time trying to get some macho knucklehead to help me get Marty Dimino in the senate, Frank. You came to me for advice. Now I want you to take it. Call Marty Dimino, Judd Kemp, and Mike Graham right now, or get yourself a new campaign manager."

There was enough silence on the line to pass a freight train through.

"All right, all right. You win. I had a mother, you know."

"How do you feel?" Charly asked. "Do you want to go on with this?"

"More than I ever wanted anything in my life."

"Good man. I'll be over later. And, Frank …?"

"Yeah."

"Don't forget to brush your teeth and say your prayers."

Chapter 14

Marty Dimino spoke before a crowd of people in a park.

"The cost of maintaining a single inmate in our present prison system is approaching a staggering $50,000 a year. Most law-abiding Americans don't make that much money a year. We've got to draw the line somewhere. Imagine that money going into our health care, into higher education to offset the outrageous costs to put our children through college, or into better and more efficient sources of energy. It's time to get tough on this drain on our tax dollars.

The sizable audience applauded.

*   *   *

Frank Dugan spoke before a large, filled-to-capacity auditorium. A banner above him welcomed all to the Los Angeles Convention Center.

"The thugs that broke into my home and killed my family I'm sure were multiple offenders. They likely had prior convictions going back to their juvenile days. They were out loose on our streets, plotting their next treachery among decent folk. I say put violent and recidivist criminals away for good and away from us."

The crowd roared its approval.

"How are you going to do that?" a man in the crowd shouted.

"We're working on it," Frank said.

*　　*　　*

Marty Dimino stood before a packed crowd at a cavernous sports arena. Jumbotrons captured him from every angle and displayed larger-than-life videos of him as he worked the predominantly Hispanic attendees.

"We're not curing our crime problem, only temporarily storing it. The physical appearances of these laughably *correctional* confines are eyesores to all America. I don't know about you, but I'm tired of looking at prisons. And now they want us to pay to build more? With *your* hard-earned money. Enough is enough. *¡Basta es basta!*"

The huge crowd chanted the phrase in a deafening collective voice.

"*¡Basta es basta! ¡Basta es basta! ¡Basta es basta! ¡Basta es basta!*"

*　　*　　*

At a major college graduation, Frank spoke from an elevated platform in the football stadium.

"The number one problem in America today is not the War on Terror or foreign aggression. It's crime. The chances of one of you being harmed by a foreign power is extremely remote. The chances of you or your loved ones being victimized by our own criminals is not only possible, it's likely. It's a sad commentary to report that we can now walk more safely in the streets of Beijing than we can in our own major cities. And here's the real crime: the cost of dealing with these criminals who live within our own borders could be used for your children's institutions of higher learning, for tuition, fees, books, and housing. Oh, that money is going for institutions, all right. Institutions we didn't want to purchase. Institutions we were *forced* to purchase. I say we've had enough.

Resounding applause, cheers, and whistles exploded from the audience.

*　　*　　*

Frank and Charly, dressed in coats, walked to their cars parked next to each other on a nearly deserted lot. The cool night air contrasted dramatically with the warmth of the day and caused Charly's cold hands to seek the comfort of pockets.

"What do you plan to do with these chronic offenders you keep railing against?" Charly asked.

"Not sure," Frank said. "I'm working on it."

"I keep hearing that, but, so far, I'm not getting back any good answers. You've presented the problems for everyone to clearly see. Now you'd better counter with some solutions."

"I know this much. Hardened repeat criminals don't belong where decent people live."

"How're you going to stop them from coming back into society?"

"I don't know yet," Frank said, climbing into his Bronco. "Get into your car."

Charly slid into her Jaguar sedan, closed the door, and rolled down the driver's window.

"Lock your doors," Frank said.

"Well, will you look who's turned into a mother hen."

"Save the smart mouth. Just do it."

She locked the doors and started the car.

"'Night, Charly," Frank said, cranked his engine and drove off.

Charly stared after him as he disappeared from the lot. When she drove only a few feet, a loud screeching noise broke the night quiet coming from her car's engine compartment. Charly stopped the car, turned off the motor, and climbed out. She opened the hood and peered inside.

"A gentleman shouldn't leave a pretty lady alone in a dark parking lot," a deep Southern voice said from behind her.

Charly spun around to face the voice. The source was indistinct in the darkness, but she could see that it was tall, a man moving closer.

"It sets the stage for crime, know what I mean?" the masculine voice said.

"Yeah, I do."

Charly withdrew a small automatic pistol from her coat pocket and pointed it directly at the shadowed head of the stranger.

"Get your hands up, assbreath," Charly said.

The stranger raised his hands high.

"Ho. Wait a minute, Charly. It's me," the voice said, the accent gone.

The stranger moved into the light, revealing Mike Graham.

"You a-hole. You think you're funny?" she said, lowering the gun.

"Holy shit, Charly, I didn't mean to scare you."

"Scare *me*? Check your shorts."

"Peace, Charly. I just wanted to tell you about what we found at your boy's place."

"My boy? His name is Frank."

Graham smiled at her annoyance. "We didn't find any more surprises like that snake, but we didn't find any suspicious prints or solid clues, either. They got in with lock picks. Wore gloves, it looked pretty pro. We're checking the reptile houses at the zoos to see if they're short one large-type king cobra."

"I didn't mean to be rough, but I don't consider dark parking lot jokes funny. Stick to daytime pies in the face."

"I'm really sorry," Graham said, staring at her gun. "You got a permit for that thing?"

"Yep. Marty talked me into getting one when I took on this campaign."

"Probably a good idea. Hanging out with Frank appears to be kinda dangerous."

"So they tell me."

"You know how to use one of those?" Graham asked.

"You almost found out."

Charly got into her car, restarted the engine. The screeching noise repeated for a moment, then changed to loud chirps.

"Your Fan belt needs adjusting," Graham said over the noise.

"I can't hear you. My fan belt may need adjusting," Charly said and drove away, leaving Graham standing in the deserted lot.

Chapter 15

Frank lay on his beach house bed reading a newspaper. A strange sound repeated several times, then stopped. It seemed to have come from the front of the house. Frank's stared at the bedroom door. He gripped and withdrew his Glock from under the pillow and listened. The noise repeated. Frank carefully slipped off the bed, took a small flashlight from the night table drawer, and tip-toed through the hall in his bare feet. He didn't turn on the flashlight, but sidled along the wall to the living room in the dark, feeling with his shoulder as he moved.

As he neared the living room, he waited and listened. The scratching sound radiated throughout the house. Frank's ears directed him to the kitchen, perhaps to the door to the garage. He stealthily stepped toward the sound. The sound stopped.

Frank crouched low as he passed through the doorway into the kitchen, the counter and floor cabinets shielding him. He made his way over to the garage door and flattened himself against the wall. He checked the readiness of the gun in his waistband, aimed the unlit flashlight in front of him, and grasped the doorknob. The knob slowly turned, the flashlight clicked on, and he pulled open the door to the garage. A camouflage poncho and hat hanging on the back of the door were caught in the flashlight beam as they flew into Frank's face.

Frank slashed at the swinging poncho with the flashlight, drew his Glock and pointed it at the offending garment, his trigger finger tightening. A heart-pounding second was enough to stop him from squeezing off the shot as the reality of the situation set in.

A clattering noise snapped Frank's head toward the garage floor, his gun pointed where his eyes searched for the source. A mop in a bucket had toppled from a low shelf near the door. He lowered the gun, exhaled fully, and let his muscles relax.

The original noise sounded again. It was coming from the kitchen cabinet where he'd set the mousetrap. Frank moved two steps over to the cabinet door and flung it open. He shone the light into the cabinet. In his trap was a brown and white field mouse.

"Next time I call Orkin," he said.

*   *   *

Frank carried a plate of lettuce and cheese onto the beach house deck. He crossed to the mousetrap sitting on the beachside railing and pushed the food through the wire mesh.

"Chowtime, Willie Sutton. You gotta get a job, pal. This robbing and freeloading has got to stop. If I let you go around here, in two days you'll be back in my kitchen pulling another job, won't you?"

Frank bent low and close to the mouse, now shredding the lettuce with rapid chews.

"Go ahead. Stand on the Fifth. Don't incriminate yourself. I understand."

The warm breeze off the ocean vibrated the leaves of the two ficus trees in their planters. Frank checked the sky.

"No rain in sight, Willie, so I'll leave you outside to enjoy the air. Watch out for cats and hawks."

Chapter 16

Marty Dimino's BMW pulled to a stop at a traffic signal. As Marty waited for the light to change, he glanced into his rearview mirror and noted the two men in a late model Mercedes who'd rolled directly behind him. The man driving the sedan wore light gloves and dark glasses. The passenger in the sedan stared at his lap and busied himself with something below Marty's line of sight.

The light turned green and Marty drove off, the sedan keeping pace behind. The Mercedes followed Marty through the city streets. Every turn Marty made, they seemed to copy. Marty sped up and made three intricate turns to see if they were truly coming after him. The Mercedes matched each move of the BMW and its every attempt at evasion. Suspicions confirmed.

Marty decided to take the upcoming ramp onto the 5 freeway and try to outrun his pursuers. He floored Beamer, which roared to 75 miles an hour. The Mercedes tailgated at equal speed, the beamer darting past numerous vehicles as they swerved in and out of the fast-moving freeway traffic. The pursuing sedan approached Marty's left rear. The man in the passenger seat of the car pointed a gun barrel out of his window at Marty and let loose a burst of automatic gunfire. The bullets riddled Marty's car, missing him by inches. Marty accelerated more and barreled onto the right shoulder of the freeway, but the unrelenting sedan kept pace with him and appeared to jockey across lanes looking for a new angle of attack.

A motorist, broken down on the right shoulder, stood next to his car as Marty rounded a curve and sped toward him. Marty yanked a hard left to avoid the stranded man, but clipped the trailer of a semi in the right lane of the freeway in the process. The terrified motorist vaulted over the jersey wall next to the shoulder. The clipped truck caromed into the chasing sedan, slowing them both. Marty saw an exit flying up on the right and took it at high speed, scraping the retainer wall as he broadslid his BMW 740 onto the twisting ramp. He glanced in his mirror and cursed at seeing the Mercedes charging behind him, careening into the concrete wall, then righting itself as it squealed after his Beamer.

The chase went on over surface streets as the two cars ran red lights and stop signs, leaving a wake of crashing vehicles and scurrying pedestrians. Marty managed to put needed distance between his car and his aggressive tagalongs by maneuvering around a large box truck. Marty tore through a side street and checked his mirrors. The Mercedes had disappeared.

* * *

The men in the Mercedes, having lost sight of their quarry, slowly patrolled the streets studying every alley and avenue. After backtracking the neighborhood, they caught a glimpse Dimino's distinctive BMW on a side street. The car was parked near the curb, the driver's door fully open. The vehicle looked abandoned. The Mercedes driver made a slow turn and cautiously rolled toward the seemingly empty car.

The two men scanned the area looking for Dimino as their car pulled behind the BMW and stopped. They saw city work vehicles and a lunch wagon dispensing drinks and food to the workers, who were congregated around the open-sided service vehicle. In the middle of the street, an open manhole with accompanying warning lights, caution striped sawhorses, and a Day-glo yellow safety fence appeared to be the subject of the service work. Nothing else was near the open manhole except the BMW, fifteen feet away. A few pedestrians walked the sidewalks, a merchant busied herself arranging flowers in front of a small floral shop, and civil engineer-types in shirtsleeves, ties, and hardhats conferred near a city pickup truck.

A man in a hardhat made notes on a clipboard near the back of the open food truck. He was partially concealed by the van's open rear doors. The two men in the Mercedes got out of their car. The driver, the larger of the two men, approached Dimino's car, withdrew and pointed his pistol into the back seat as the smaller man carefully opened the rear door of the car. Nothing inside but a briefcase on the seat.

They inspected the open front seats of the car. Nothing there, either. The small man gestured his partner to look into the open manhole. They both stared into the dark abyss under the street. They checked to make sure no one was watching. The small man directed the large man to descend on the ladder into the street. The big man showed reluctance, but the small man made his order more emphatic with his gun. The larger partner complied and disappeared into the street. The small man looked around, then followed.

Both men reached the bottom of the sewer, stepped off the ladder, and slogged through the ankle deep water flowing in the subterranean tunnel.

"Son of a bitch," the big man said, shaking the filthy sewage from his designer shoes.

"He's in here someplace, so stop with the shoes," the small man said. "We got work to do."

The two men sloshed along in the tunnel. Rats scurried atop the tunnel's electrical conduits and occasional concrete ledges and made chirping noises as they fell in and paddled in the water.

"They don't pay us enough to do this shit," the big man said.

"Dark as hell in here. Don't suppose you got a light on you?"

"I don't smoke."

*   *   *

Marty stepped out from behind the rear door of the open food truck, removed his borrowed hardhat, and tossed it in the bed of a nearby pickup with the clipboard. He strode to the Mercedes and climbed behind the wheel. The car keys were still in the ignition. He started the car and drove it a few feet, crashed down the sawhorse barriers, and parked directly over the manhole.

Several workmen who witnessed the act, glared at Marty and rushed over to him as he slid out of the sedan. A man with "Leo" penned in black marker on his white hardhat planted himself in front of Marty.

"Hey, bub, what do you think you're doin'?" Leo said. "Practicin' your parkin'?"

"There are men down there. They have guns. They mean to kill me."

"Oh, sure, pal," another worker said. "They're terrorists. We get 'em here all the time."

The workmen laughed.

"I'm Martin Dimino."

The workers stopped laughing and stared at Marty. Other people from the street trickled into the gathering.

"That's Martin Dimino, the State's Attorney," the woman from the flower shop said. "He's the guy in all the news. He's running for senator."

"I'll be damned. It's him," Leo said.

"I need your help," Marty said. "Two men just went down that manhole looking for me."

"There's only one other way out of there," Leo said, then turned to the workmen. "Get some of that short pipe over there."

The men jogged over to a stack of 3-foot lengths of galvanized pipe and each grabbed one.

"They have guns," Marty said.

"Hell, Mr. Dimino, these are real men here," Leo said. "A couple of assholes with guns'll barely be a few minutes entertainment for my guys. How do ya want 'em? Dead, maimed, dismembered?"

"Just turn them over to the police," Marty said as he got in his car. "And thanks."

"Don't mention it," Leo said. "You go on about your business, sir. Okay, boys, let's get on down to number seven junction and take us some battin' practice. Keep the tunnel lights off. Two of you hang back here in case they pop up under the Mercedes. God knows, they ain't gettin' out that way."

The majority of the workmen charged down the street whooping and hollering like cowboys on a cattle drive.

*   *   *

96

The two hit men trekked aimlessly through the sewer. Overhead drain grates offered a few rays of broken light as they appeared every twenty yards. They came to a large, open area where several huge pipes intersected. Dark passages gaped in several directions. They considered making a change of course, but dismissed the idea and continued plodding on straight ahead.

"I can't see shit," The big man said."I think we lost the sonofabitch."

"I think *we're* the ones who're lost," the small man said.

The small man felt a cold, hard object at the back of his neck. He froze where he stood.

"But we're not," a voice behind him said. "Drop the guns."

Two splashes echoed in the tunnel. One of the workmen pointed a flashlight in the hit men's faces.

"If you dudes are lookin' for the Bronx subway, it's east of here about three thousand miles," a workman said.

The small hit man began to make out the faces of four workmen in the scant illumination from the flashlight. He saw that they only had pipes for weapons and nodded at his larger cohort. They both dropped low and made frantic stabs for their submerged pistols.

"Big mistake, pal," the nearest workman said.

It was the last thing the small man heard before the intense pain in his head blacked him out.

Chapter 17

Frank sat in a director's chair on the deck of the Dimino beach house with his back against the building. Near him on the deck's top rail was the Humana trap with the captive mouse. A coffee cup and a cordless phone were on a side table next to Frank as he stared fixedly out at the horizon where the ocean met the sky.

The phone rang and Frank picked it up.

"Hello."

"Your man gives great evasion, Detective Dugan," the voice of Rico Guzman said. "I like competence in an opponent."

Frank kept the phone to his ear, but gave no response.

"To get where I am I had to use a measure of competence, myself."

"Spare me the success story, Guzman. What's on your twisted mind?"

"I can tell from your tone you're not going to make this easy. I spend a lot of money convincing people to make wise choices."

"I've been doing the same thing ... for free."

"I'll get to the point," Guzman said. "Tomorrow is going to be a big day. A *muy* big day. I want to make one last appeal to you to get your candidate to withdraw from the senatorial election. Name your price and I'll pay it."

"Now you're talking. Leave that shoot-'em-up stuff for Wyatt Earp."

"Agreed. So what's the number?"

"My price is simple. I want every one of you felonious goons safely out of reach. Can you cut me a check like that? The day you pay that price, I'll get Martin Dimino to retire from politics."

"In that case, Dugan, I'll see Dimino in hell."

"Save yourself some time, Guzman. Look for him in Washington."

Frank ended the call and ambled over to the mouse.

"Okay, Willie Sutton, I just got an idea what to do with you."

Frank lifted the trap and peered at the mouse at eye level.

"If I was going to continue to give you room and board around here, I wouldn't have gone to all this trouble to capture you, would I? By the way, you are going to vote for Mr. Dimino tomorrow, aren't you?"

* * *

The setting sun glistened off the ocean as Frank powered Marty Dimino's eighteen-foot center console boat toward one of the numerous small islands off the coast of California near Long Beach. Oil well pumps operated steadily on several of the islands behind

100

wooden facades made to look like buildings from the perspective of the shore. Other islets only contained high grass and shrubs with an occasional palm.

Frank gently beached the boat and jumped out carrying the mouse in the trap and a filled grocery bag. He put the mousetrap on the island's grassy bank and dumped out the contents of the bag. Packs of vegetable seeds, a gallon water bottle with a drinking spout like ones sold in pet stores, and a variety of grains and vegetables. Oats, corn, carrots, and potatoes were strewn on the ground. Three ceramic doggie food bowls lay among the other items and Frank gathered them up and placed them at different spots on the islet. Frank taped the water bottle to a pointy stick that he shoved into the moist earth to support it and spread out the vegetables. He stabbed numerous holes in the soil and made furrows, opened the seed packets, and distributed the seeds everywhere he'd created openings in the ground. Finally he opened the Humana trap and released the mouse. The mouse didn't scurry off, but sat and looked up at Frank.

"Well, Willie Sutton, this is home now. Enjoy the food and the crops when they come up. When the water runs scarce, eat these dandelions that are growing all around here and you'll be okay. When it rains, the doggie bowls will capture fresh water for you."

Frank clambered back into the boat and pushed himself off with a boat hook. When the boat drifted to a safe depth, he cranked the outboard. He took a long thoughtful look at the beautiful red sun setting behind Santa Catalina Island, then turned back to the mouse before he revved the 125 horsepower Evinrude to full throttle and sped away.

"Have a good life, Willie Sutton."

On the trip back, with only the drone of the motor to insulate his thoughts, Frank launched into a bit of introspection. He wondered if he was, quite simply, going crazy. He had just placed a mouse on an islet with food provisions for a year, and given it instructions and helpful hints intended to make its solitary life survivable. He chatted with the mouse as if it were a person or a beloved pet. Never before in his life had he done such a thing. Truth be known, he was aware that a hawk could swoop down and make dinner of Willie, and that would be that. *Am I losing it?* he thought. *Has the death of my family put me over the top?* Frank wasn't sure of the answers to those questions.

Time, the healer of all concerns, would have to tell.

*   *   *

Frank opened the garage door of the beach house with the remote and entered the unoccupied cavity in darkness. He shuffled toward the door to the kitchen and fumbled for the light switch on the wall next to the door, but nothing happened. He made his way back to the garage doorway and surveyed other houses in sight to determine if the electric outage was throughout the neighborhood, but every house he saw had illuminated windows and full arrays of lit outdoor lamp posts and floodlights.

Concern swept over him. Frank cautiously moved to the kitchen door and stopped to listen for any telltale sounds coming from inside the house. Nothing.

From the light coming in the garage from outside, he could see a small flashlight lying on the workbench. He picked it up and flicked it on. Its batteries were on their last legs, but it cast enough light to be useful. He slowly turned the brass knob of the kitchen door and pushed the door fully open. Dark and quiet inside. The circuit breaker box was in the pantry off the kitchen. Frank decided to go there and see if any breakers had tripped.

The four strides it took to reach the pantry passed across the wide opening to the living room. Frank swung to his right to aim the weak yellow beam from the flashlight toward the larger room. The flashlight flickered and went out. Frank smacked the light against his palm, but the batteries had given all they were going to.

Frank knew there was another flashlight in the end table by the sofa. A single soft ray of light from a neighbor's outdoor floodlight spilled into the room and weakly projected a thin amber line on the carpet. Frank used it to guide his way toward the sofa.

"You've made this all so complicated, Frank," a man's voice said from the darkness.

Frank quickly turned toward the voice. A deeply shadowed figure sitting in a chair in the living room stood up. The beam of light from outside fell across his face. It was the face of Mike Graham.

"We wasted all that time and energy on that stupid cobra and those two morons from Jersey," Graham said. "If you want to get a job done right, do it yourself, eh, detective?

"Like cleaning up a crime scene before anyone else arrived?

"Yeah, like that," Graham said. "Gaither didn't leave much, but I did have to clean Amy's nails."

Frank's rage taunted him with thoughts of making a try for his Glock, but he knew old school police tactics, and was certain Graham had him covered with an untraceable firearm. Sanity took over and Frank decided on a different tack.

"What do you want from me? Marty Dimino's going to get elected whether I'm alive or not. In fact, you'd be stupid to make a martyr of his biggest promoter."

"That's not what Mr. Guzman thinks."

"And you figure he's the brain of the century?"

"I'm pretty sure he's a millionaire and the rest of us are not."

"So life's merely based on a bag of dirty money? You were a good cop, Mike. Got a nice pension coming, and you could easily get cushy work consulting after you retire. Why throw it all away like this?"

"I can be Guzman's number one man. Have anything I want now, not years from now."

Frank shook his head. He realized the hard sell to get Graham to accept a legitimate rationale was circling the drain.

"You covered up everything, didn't you, Mike? The murders, the break-in here. I never suspected."

"Rico pays so much better than the police department."

"Now what?"

"Don't be naive, Frank. I gotta take you out. You're starting to cause us problems. Rico knows you're after him big time—"

"Rico Guzman flatters himself. He is not my only enemy. It's all men like him. All men like Ernie Gaither. I want every one of them put far away, out of reach. And I just added you to the list."

"Well, good luck with that."

"I'll take all the luck I can get," Frank said.

"I was gonna zip you and your campaign manager the other night, but you got away too fast and she got the drop on me. Bitch. Very paranoid broad, that one."

105

Graham stepped fully into the ray of light, revealing a pistol pointed at Frank.

"Let's leave your hardware here on the sofa."

Frank removed his Glock from his belt and tossed it on the sofa.

"Both pieces," Graham said.

Frank bent down and removed the small .38 caliber revolver from an ankle holster and tossed it near the Glock.

"Now let's take a ride over to the marina," Graham said.

"Same place you had Senator McAllister shot?"

"Not far from there. Senators are powerful people, but it can be a dangerous profession when they get too tough."

Graham motioned to the door with a waggle of his gun. Both men stepped through the door to the garage, Graham an arm's length behind.

"You drive," Graham said. "And should your driving get reckless, I'll take you out earlier than planned."

"Where to?"

"The marina."

"*Where* in the marina?

"Your boat."

"My boat?"

"Guzman's idea. Wants it to look like an accident. Sure as hell ain't my idea. I hate water. I don't even drink the shit."

106

"I haven't used the boat in a while. Batteries may need a charge."

"We'll cross that bridge when we come to it. Got your boat keys?"

"Always," Frank said and jangled the set in his pocket.

*　　*　　*

Frank and Graham parked at the marina, climbed out of the car, and marched down the pier toward Frank's boat tied at the deep end of the pier. They arrived at Frank's twenty-nine-foot Boston Whaler Outrage and jumped aboard. Frank removed the mooring lines, shoved off from the dock, and cranked the twin Merc engines.

"How much power does this boat have?" Graham asked.

"Four hundred fifty horsepower from twin Optimax Mercs.

"Head out to sea. And keep it steady," Graham said, clutching the gunwale.

Frank wanted to get the boat going fast as it could to keep Graham's attention constantly on his anxiety while on the water. But he could make it appear to be a thoughtful concession.

"I'll put her on plane to keep the ride smooth."

The boat pulled away from the marina and made way to the open Pacific. Frank pushed the throttles forward to attain the boat's full speed of nearly fifty-five knots. Frank saw Graham nervously studying the rapidly diminishing land, and soon, he knew only the lights of the shoreline would be visible. Frank noted Graham's preoccupation with the dwindling coast and watched him steady himself by clutching the transom. While Graham concentrated on his nervous footing and darted glances sternward, Frank availed himself of the opportunity to secretly pull out the engines' choke. The motor began to sputter and, in seconds, stalled.

"What's wrong?" Graham said.

"We're out of gas."

"What? You didn't check it before we left?"

"Hey, pal, I'm just the victim here. I leave planning to geniuses like you and Guzie."

"Jesus," Graham said, panning the shoreline. "We gotta find another boat with gas. Maybe the Coast Guard."

Frank pulled back the throttle. The boat glided to a rocking stop.

"The Coast Guard? What are you going to tell them you're doing out here?"

Graham swiveled his head to look out into the darkness to the west. "How the hell am I supposed to get back in?"

"We're drifting out to sea, man," Frank said. "How's your backstroke?"

"I don't like this. I don't like it one fuckin' bit."

Frank sidled to the bow gunwale while Graham gripped the rail near the transom, continuing to survey his nerve-racking situation. Then Frank dove overboard into the black water and swam toward the shore.

"Stop, you sonofabitch! Stop!"

Frank slipped underwater. Four shots popped from the boat and small splashes hit the surface near Frank.

"Don't you leave me here alone on this fucking boat, goddamnit!"

Frank surfaced and backstroked a distance away and watched Graham frantically search the aft area of the boat and finally grab a flotation ring from the side of the cabin. Graham hugged the ring and jumped into the water. Frank rotated to the crawl position and gently stroked shoreward, twenty yards ahead of the audible thrashes of Graham.

The distance widened as Frank smoothly swam on. Graham fired two more shots at Frank's bareley visible wake, but the bullets plunked into the water wide of their mark.

Shore light spilled out onto the breakers and Frank could make out the definition of the marina and the business signs on the shore. Screams coming from the sea behind him broke the quiet of the night.

Frank looked back to see large sharks breaking the surface and attacking Graham. His body tossed into the air like a wet mannequin. More screams, then Graham was violently yanked under the surface as the big fins swirled all about where he'd been. In seconds, the water quieted and the only evidence of the violence was a drifting flotation ring on a patch of sea foam.

Frank dragged himself onto the warm dry sand of the beach and rested. Once again, Frank pondered why the sharks had avoided him, only yards away from a man they'd just shredded into bite-size chunks.

Later, Frank planned to call the Harbor Police and have then retrieve his drifting boat and bring it back to the marina. Unless Graham took them, the keys would still be in the ignition and the boat had plenty of gas. He would contact Judd Kemp and file a report on the incident with Graham. There would be an investigation and the media would be all over the story like fire ants on a honeycomb. But the upsides might be the increased public awareness of murderous acts perpetrated by even those sworn to uphold the law, and the added support voters might give to Marty Dimino's anti-crime senate race.

Nearly dying can have its plus sides, Frank thought.

Chapter 18

Large posters taped to the walls around the office of the Dimino political headquarters depicted their candidate and his popular campaign slogans. Charly Stone tried to hear on the phone over the din of loud cheering and rowdy crowd noises that boomed into the room from beyond the office door.

"Please send a unit to his house," Charly said. "He's got to be in trouble or else he'd be here. Call me here as soon as you know something. *Anything.*"

She hung up the phone and cast worried looks toward the office door as a tremendous cheer roared outside. Charly grabbed her purse and headed for the noise.

*   *   *

Charly jostled her way through the crowd to the elevated podium with its nest of microphones. An illuminated election results board provided the backdrop for the stage. The vote tally next to Dimino's name flashed, indicating the projected winner. He'd been elected by a considerable margin. A clock on the board indicated the time of 10:08 PM. Charly raised her arms to quiet the cheering throng of supporters. The noises gradually subsided enough for her to approach the mikes .

"It looks like we've done it," she said.

The crowd roared its approval.

"Our man of the hour, Martin Dimino, *Senator* Martin Dimino, will be here momentarily. Please enjoy the champagne that's being uncorked in the East Room. It's a celebration of the members of our society who want law and order. We celebrate you ... all of you."

The crowd reacted again with generous applause and whistles.

"Enjoy our victory. Thank you all for your support, your faith, and, most of all, your money."

The crowd laughed, then converged on the opening to the East Room as Marty Dimino entered the room. The throng applauded throughout his march to the stage where he embraced Charly, then faced the spacious hall, filled to capacity.

"The victory this night belongs to every person who wants real justice for the victims of crime. This victory belongs to you, and I will thank you every day as I vote your will on the issues that come before me in Congress. Tonight we will celebrate, tomorrow we go to work. Tomorrow it will be time to get tough."

Marty pointed to the East Room and the mass of people migrated in that direction.

A campaign official in the crowd caught Charly's eye and in pantomime asked her: "Where's Frank?" Charly forced a smile and shrugged.

*   *   *

Charly impatiently pressed buttons on a desk phone and waited for a connection. She glanced at a wall clock in the office. It indicated 11:25. Loud crowd noises erupted outside the office. She jammed the receiver onto its cradle and hurried toward the commotion.

In the main hall, Charly panned the mob flowing toward the entrance, but she couldn't see what had captivated their interest. She dragged a chair from a banquet table and stood on the seat to improve her view. From her higher perspective, she stared at the subject of the hubbub. Frank Dugan stood in the doorway. He looked like he'd been caught in a downpour and rolled in sand. His dirty clothes clung to him like wet toilet tissue and his tousled hair spiked out in all directions. The crowd cheered wildly and rushed to him as if he'd just pitched the winning game of the World Series.

Frank struggled through the hugs and fist bumps and inched his way to the podium as people shook his hands and clapped him on the back. A teary-eyed Barbara Chalmers embraced him motherly.

"I've got news for you," Barbara said. "About the house. I'll call you tomorrow. Promise."

At the podium, he turned to take a good look at the election results board. It showed the time as nearly 11:45 and Dimino's winning margin with 95 percent of the precincts tallied. He turned back to the crowd. The cheering subsided as he docked himself into the array of microphones.

"We began this campaign those many weeks ago with a single voice; a single theme: there's too much crime in America. We wanted to stop it before it smothered all of us and our children. Enough is enough, we said. Well, I'm not as well dressed as I would've liked to be, but I'm living proof that crime will no longer prevail against us. They've taken their best shots and now it's our turn."

The crowd reaction was deafening.

"You guys with the black hats? You'd better saddle up and get out of Dodge. The good guys are pouring through the passes of America."

The crowd responded with thunderous applause and cheers. Frank held his arms high in a gesture of profound victory.

Charly stood in the opening of a side entrance to the hall. She stared at Frank, whose eyes ultimately locked on hers. Frank dropped his arms, beamed a broad smile her way, and winked.

*　　*　　*

Marty Dimino and Charly Stone got chauffeured to Marty's beach house in an unmarked sedan. Police cars and policemen surrounded the house. Two official-looking men in suits greeted and escorted them into the house.

"I appreciate all this, gentlemen, I really do," Marty said to the two men, "but I can handle things from here."

"I'm Special Agent Balfour," the taller suit said, then directed a hand toward the man with him. "This is Special Agent Collins. We have orders to stay with you, senator."

"Whose orders?" Marty asked.

"High up, sir," Balfour said.

"The director?"

Balfour paused and glanced briefly at his partner before speaking.

"The president, sir."

Chapter 19

Frank and Judd sat across from each other in a booth at a coffee shop. Judd stared out the window at the first evidence of morning light, while Frank stirred his coffee more than necessary.

"I can't figure why I haven't heard from Barbara," Frank said. "Said she'd call. About my house."

"Your house?"

"It's listed for sale. Barbara's handling it."

"She an agent?"

"Used to be. Still licensed, so I'd like her to get the commission."

"It's barely daybreak. She'll call. She was there last night well past midnight. We talked for a while. God, how she loves you. Like she loved Amy. Man, the campaigning she did for you and Dimino. Nothing short of amazing. She's probably exhausted from all the excitement and went home to bed like a normal person. While we're on the subject, "Iron Frank," you've got to get more sleep."

"Iron Frank. Sounds like a rusty hot dog," Frank said and sipped his coffee. "I guess my official duties as campaign manager are over. Now you're tucking me in?"

"When's the last time you got seven hours sleep?"

Frank stared out the window at a truck collecting the trash at the curb.

"Just like that. It's over. Like yesterday's news."

"Far from it. I'm anxious to hear the plan you and Marty want to hatch in the penal system."

"Yeah, that's going to be a tough one to pull off."

"An island? Really?" Judd said, raising an eyebrow.

"A rather special island."

"Didn't Gilligan try that?"

"Not like this one, he didn't."

"You know, if this crazy idea fails, you might have to update your résumé."

"Then I'll be dead too. Professional death is scarier to me than any other variety. All I ever wanted to be was a good cop."

Frank watched the pick-up man at the back of the garbage truck jump on the bumper and signal the driver with a wave of his hand.

"Wonder what garbage men get paid," Frank said.

Judd added and stirred more cream in his coffee.

"Think guards are going to want to commute to an island?"

"The guards I have in mind will work cheap and love their job."

*   *   *

117

Frank poured himself a scotch from the beach house bar and hit a button on the remote, making the TV come to life. His cell rang and he muted the TV and looked at the caller ID on the tiny screen. It was coming from the phone in his rancher in Coronado Estates.

"Hello, Barb. Been waiting for your call," Frank said, swirling the scotch in his glass.

"An eye for an eye, detective. An eye for an eye," the voice of Rico Guzman said.

The phone went dead.

Frank set his drink on the bar and bolted for the door.

While driving, he called both of Barbara's phone numbers, but got no answer at either. In thirty minutes he pulled in front of his house, jumped from the car, and ran to the front door. He pulled out the Browning Hi-Power automatic he'd switched for the Glock, turned the doorknob, and the door swung open. Inside, he scanned the rooms, one by one, but encountered nothing out of place. He holstered his gun and punched a button on his cell.

"I'm at my rancher," Frank said. "Got a call from Guzman. It came from the phone in this house."

"Why didn't you call me before you barged over there into God knows what?" Judd Kemp said.

"I wanted to save time in case the bastard was still here."

"How's the place?"

"Nothing's been disturbed, but the front door was unlocked. Not like Barbara to leave the place like that. I tried to call her. Got nothing."

"See if she's next door," Judd said. "Maybe she knows something. What did Guzman say?"

"He said, 'An eye for an eye, detective. An eye for an eye.' And hung up."

"Want me to send over my guys?"

"No. I'll lock up and go, and I'll check with Barbara right now."

"Let's get together later for a drink," Judd said. "The Shamrock."

Frank ended the call and plodded to the hall bathroom. He gazed at his weary face in the vanity mirror and contorted and pulled at his face to flatten the puffiness under his eyes. He stepped to the toilet, poised to unzip, but something caught his attention on the far side of the room. A dark pattern didn't seem normal behind the translucent shower curtain. He withdrew his automatic, snicked off the safety, and moved slowly toward the shower, never taking his eyes off the image inside that he couldn't identify through the blurry plastic. He slid the shower curtain aside with a rapid sweep of his hand. Frank pointed the gun directly at the dark shape.

"Oh, God. No," Frank murmured as he sank to his knees, clinging to the edge of the bathtub.

The body of Barbara Chalmers hung from the showerhead, her Nile green dress covered in blood coming from the deep gash across her throat. Her eyes stared blankly at Frank, her hands turned palms out like in a painting of a Michelangelo saint.

Chapter 20

A gathering of people surrounded an open gravesite. Frank, Charly, and Marty stood prominently among those in attendance. A minister read from a Bible.

"None that go unto her return again, neither take they hold of the paths of life. That thou mayest walk in the way of good men, and keep the paths of the righteous. For the upright shall dwell in the land, and the perfect shall remain in it. But the wicked shall be cut off from the earth, and the transgressors shall be rooted out of it."

The minister closed the Bible.

"And so take peace, dearly beloved Barbara, in the knowledge that your life was upright and good. And that now you walk with Him that knew no evil, but only good, in fields of peace and through gardens where even the flowers never die nor depart."

The minister made a gesture for the casket to be lowered, and then to Frank, who came forward to the grave's edge and scooped a handful of the newly turned earth.

"They can't take any more away from me, Barbara. You were the last and the best I had to give. 'Get along witchya now, love.'"

Frank spilled earth onto the casket, the remainder he tucked into the side pocket of his black suit.

The people slowly dispersed. Frank walked away from the gravesite and strolled up one of the roads running through the cemetery. Charly watched him, but didn't follow. Marty Dimino strode after Frank. They walked together quietly for a moment, then Marty broke their silence.

"Aren't Amy and the children buried up this way?" Marty asked, pointing ahead on the tree-lined lane.

"Yeah."

Marty stopped their walk with a hand on Frank's coat sleeve. Frank halted but held his forward direction.

"I'm your friend, Frank. Friends see things in others that they can't see themselves. Let me tell you what I see. You can walk over that rise ahead and step forever back into the past, or you can turn around and go back and walk into the future with folks who care about you. Your life's not over. It'll never be over 'til you say it is."

Frank turned to his friend.

"Let's go home, Marty."

*   *   *

The Shamrock bar hosted a drinker on almost every stool and the lounge area teemed with patrons, mostly men. Frank, Charly, and Marty occupied the same booth where they originally had discussed Marty's senate campaign.

"You know what?" Frank said. "You two should formally celebrate our victory by taking a well-earned vacation."

"I've got to get ready for the United States Senate," Marty said.

"You don't have to post there for three more weeks. Grab a plane. Get outa here. Enjoy yourselves."

"I'll think about it," Marty said.

"What about Guzman?" Frank said.

"Got nothing on him. He's insulated like the Pentagon."

"A guy can go around killing people while we sit and suck eggs. My aunt was put in a cold, dark hole in the ground today while her killers laugh and scratch."

"We promised we wouldn't do this tonight," Charly said.

"She's right," Marty said, raising his drink. "To better times ... and justice."

*   *   *

Marty Dimino freshened his coffee at the beach house with a hot pour from the kitchen pot. Frank sat on the sofa gazing out at a fishing trawler chugging south across the beachfront outside.

"Just a few miles out that window is what we need," Marty said, taking a seat in a recliner near the sofa.

"Tell me about it," Frank said.

"Back in the thirties, a millionaire named Sanford Prescott claimed and purchased an island directly off Santa Barbara. Maybe a hundred miles west."

"Who owned it?"

"Mexico, originally, but in 1850, when California became a state, it was ceded to the U.S. The government was too busy with more important matters than fooling with a speck of sand way the hell out in the Pacific. Like getting fresh water to our big new state, among other pressing issues. After Pearl Harbor, the military toyed with the idea of making it an ordnance testing site, but it was too remote, too hard to protect and supply, and too overgrown with jungle. And so it sat for years blowing in the currents, sprouting coconut palms, and baking in the sun."

Frank sipped his coffee and leaned closer to Marty.

"Then this Prescott guy comes along. A Howard Hughes type. More money than brains, self-indulgent, and loving the ladies."

"He wanted the island for sexual getaways?"

"Not exactly. He wanted to make it into a resort. Build a hotel, put in swimming pools, staff it, and make money while he scheduled a tryst or two every few weeks."

"This guy married?" Frank asked.

"Oh, yes. Very married. Unfortunately to the source of most of his income. A Vanderbilt girl, with a jealous streak you could land a jumbo jet on."

124

"I never heard of a resort island off our coast."

"Because the resort never happened. Sanford Prescott settled for building a villa and using it himself for entertaining. He did, however, put in a large salt water swimming pool."

"With a whole ocean to swim in?" Frank said.

"Ah, there is the exact reason it was bad for his resort, but could be ideal for our proposal. The waters around that island happen to be a mating and feeding area for the fiercest sharks known to ichthyology."

"Could reduce overhead for guards."

"A human can be compromised and bribed. Try that with a hungry hammerhead or a peckish great white," Marty said.

"So what became of Prescott's villa?"

"A lot of interesting incidents occurred there in the 1940s. We have a strong hunch as to what may have happened at the place."

Marty rose from his chair and paced the room.

"The bodies of two people were found on the island. Decomposed badly, but identifiable. A woman named Rose Elmont, found shot in the head in a bedroom, and a man dead on the beach from a gunshot to his chest."

"Prescott?" Frank said.

Marty nodded.

"Been dead for over a week. When relatives on the mainland expected them back, and they were days overdue, they called the Coast Guard and the police."

125

"Who killed them?"

"Good question. Mary Prescott was among the missing, and so was Rose Elmont's husband, Stanley. Certainly people of interest."

"Where was their boat?"

"Their sixty-foot mahogany cabin cruiser was found in fifty feet of water west of the island. A large caliber revolver was on the boat with two spent cartridges. There was evidence of a fire onboard. She sunk and its two survivors tried to launch the dinghy, but couldn't get it free from the stern davit. It was still connected by a single line to the big boat on the bottom. Best guess? Since their bodies were never found, Rose Prescott and Stan Elmont likely drowned and were later eaten by sharks. Hopefully in that order."

"What happened to the island?"

"The inheritors of it wanted nothing to do with it and donated it to the state of California. Other than being an occasional curiosity to blood-lusting visitors, nothing has ever been done with the place. The villa is still there, although in serious disrepair and missing parts from the weather, vandals, and souvenir collectors."

"Any squatters?"

"Insatiable sharks have a way of discouraging that."

Frank pushed off from the sofa and ambled over to the picture window facing the Pacific.

"Will it be big enough?" Frank asked.

"I've been there. I surveyed it to see if there was any evidence I could use to reopen the case for murder. The island is over thirty-two square miles. Four miles by eight in aspect. Shaped like a fat boomerang. Plenty large enough for our prototype."

"Natural resources?"

"Not bad. Fresh water from highland streams, coconuts, edible plants, and fruit trees that Prescott planted. And chickens. Lots and lots of chickens."

"Prescott bred chickens on the island?"

"They sure as shit didn't fly there." Marty said.

Frank stared hard at Marty.

"I want to see it."

Chapter 21

Frank sat outside the beach house and stared at the breakers as the tide rolled in. He thought about Willie Sutton, the field mouse, and wondered how he was acclimating himself to his new environs. Scenes from his earlier visit to the pet store popped in his head like short television clips.

One of the pet store clerks held up the Humana trap.

"The doors at each end close. Then you can do what you want to with the little culprit."

A second clerk stepped into the picture.

"Fighting gerbils. They won't live in community with the other gerbils and have to be isolated."

The small island off Long Beach came into view. *Frank set the mouse free on the island.* His words from that day returned.

"Well, Willie, this is home now. Enjoy the food and the crops that come up later on ..."

Frank revved the boat engine and sped away.

"Have a good life, Willie Sutton," he heard himself saying.

A pet store clerk came back into focus and chanted, " ... they won't live in community ... .and have to be isolated ... they won't live in community ...

and have to be isolated ... they won't live in
community ... and have to be isolated ... "

The voice trailed off as Frank broke from his dreamlike trance and glanced at the deck below his right shoulder and saw a pair of fashionable high heel shoes. As his eyes moved upward, Charly Stone's stare bore down on him.

"You okay? I've been standing here for over a minute. You seemed to be in another world."

"Yeah. For a moment, I was. Sorry."

"Maybe you should install an alarm system for this place?"

"I don't think that'll be necessary."

"I mean, I just walked up to the back of your chair and could've popped you in the head, if I were so inclined."

"Yeah, I got a little lax there for a minute," Frank said, rising from his chair and facing the house.

"Rico Guzman's not going to go away because the election's over," Charly said. "He'll try you again."

"I figured without his pocket cop, Graham, he'd back off for the time being."

"Don't count on that. He's got lots of torpedoes in his sub. Men who would take any job for a mere pat on the back from *El Jefe*."

"I'll be more vigilant. I promise."

"Marty's going to Washington this month to get sworn in. He's going to have Senator McCallister's crime proposals dumped in his lap. The anti-crime campaign he waged to get elected is going to top his agenda. Got any cannon fodder I can give him to help the cause?"

"You mean like a miraculous new weapon against the underworld?"

"That would be well received, I'm sure."

"I have something I've been working on that may light a fire under our legislators."

"Any idea of a timeline on that?"

"Soon. What I have in mind will either hit the wall and stick, or make me wish I was never born."

Charly lowered her sunglasses and stared at Frank.

"Going to let me in on this plan?" she asked.

"If you can take a couple of days off, I'd love for you to accompany me on a little trip."

"Where are we flying?"

"No flying," Frank said. "Sailing."

"Charly raised an eyebrow and said, "Sailing … as on a cruise ship?"

"A little less large."

"How less?"

"Maybe a thousand feet less."

"You want me to go sailing with you in a dinghy?"

"I finally sold my house and my Boston Whaler," Frank said. "Made out okay. Took out a few bucks and bought a forty-foot Irwin sloop in Playa del Rey. Not new, but Irwin's a fine manufacturer and it's in like-new shape. Doesn't appear like it was used much."

"Well, you know what they say about the two happiest days you own a boat—"

"Yeah, I know. The day you buy it, and the day you sell it."

"Now the big question: you know how to sail this not-much-used sloop?"

"I learned to sail on the Chesapeake Bay and in the Atlantic off Maryland. I'm a pretty damn good sailor."

Charly ambled toward the narrow walkway next to the house. She turned to face Frank.

"I'll go, but I wear only the best life jacket money can buy, and you'd better have a marine radio and disaster gear onboard. Even the best equipped boats can get into trouble. Even experienced men like Ed Smith."

"Who's Ed Smith?"

"The captain of the *Titanic*."

Chapter 22

The July sunrise promised a warmer day than the breezy cool morning had brought to the Playa del Rey marina. A pleasant 84 degrees had been predicted on Frank's cabin radio as he stepped to the short gangway and cast his glance down the pier in time to catch Charly Stone striding her long legs along the quay toward the stern of the sloop. He watched her tilt her head to the aft section where the sleek vessel displayed a single word in dark blue lettering:

Esperanza

Charly had decked herself out in khaki Bermudas, a yellow tee, and blinding white tennis shoes. A red sweatshirt clung to her back with its arms tied around her neck. Dark sunglasses, a designer shoulder bag, and a golfer's crush hat gave her that celebrity-in-hiding mystique. Her shapely tan legs drew Frank's eyes and reduced his estimate of her age by a decade.

"Wow," Frank said, "I'm going sailing with a movie star."

"If I drown, I want to look my best when they recover the body," Charly said as Frank took her free hand and guided her onto the aft deck of the boat.

She surveyed the boat's layout. Her eyes dwelled a moment on the open cabin companionway.

"Is the potty down there?" she asked.

"And so much more," Frank said. "A galley, bunks, and even a salon with a TV."

"You can get TV at sea?"

"Well, this one's not exactly equipped for *that* at the moment. But we can play DVDs."

"Watching a good movie can make floundering in a typhoon so much more bearable."

"Charly, Charly, how you do go on."

Frank handed Charly a life jacket.

"Put this on," Frank said. "One size fits all."

Charly futzed with the straps on the foam-filled vest until it fit her snugly.

"And where *do* we go on?" Charly asked.

"That way, about a hundred miles," Frank said and pointed northwest.

"Drop me off at Santa Catalina. I'll catch you on the swing back."

*   *   *

The waves lapped against the gently heeled hull as the *Esperanza* cut smoothly through the dark blue water of the Pacific, her wake a ribbon of frothy white. At the helm, Frank kept the boat steady on the wind and noted on his instrument panel that they sliced through the gentle swells at better than seven knots.

"You asked me a while ago," Frank said, "what I was going to do to keep hardcore criminals from coming back into society. Well, I've finally got an answer: an island."

"Marty mentioned an abandoned island out this way. Shrouded in a famous murder tale. Once owned by these zillionaires… the Peacocks?"

"Prescotts. Although I'm told there *are* peacocks running wild on the place."

"Okay, you've got yourself an island paradise for the little reprobates. And I get to go onshore with you to check it out and make suggestions for the architectural design."

"It's too dangerous. You stay on the boat. Marty said the water's so shark infested that, even after all these years, no one's ever offered to buy it. You go in the water there and you're not a bather, you're an appetizer."

"What about you?"

Frank stared out at the horizon for an uncomfortably long moment. Charly moved closer.

"Sharks don't bother me," he said low.

"You mean you're not afraid of them?"

"No. They scare me plenty, but for some weird reason, they don't attack me. They've come up to me in the water and touched me; brushed right against me, but never hurt me. It's like I'm one of them. Maybe my smell. I have no idea why."

"That's the most bizarre thing I ever heard. Think it's your cologne?"

"What kind of world do I live in? People want to kill me and sharks are my friends?"

"Do we have to anchor the boat and swim to this place?"

"We could go in on the inflatable lifeboat," Frank said and turned on the auto-pilot.

"How far in? Inflatable sounds a lot like bitable," Charly said.

"Marty said the Prescotts built a pier for their cabin cruiser. Had to be in deep enough water for us to dock to. If it's still there. It's been a long time and many storms ago."

"How deep do we need?"

"Five feet under the keel is our absolute minimum," Frank said.

135

"Deep enough to force one to swim."

"Even three or four feet wouldn't allow you to wade in safely."

"Why not?" Charly asked.

"Most shark attacks on humans occur at that very depth."

*   *   *

Frank studied a chart, then panned the distant ocean, his hands shading his eyes from the glaring sunlight. Off the port bow he spotted a thin strip rising above the horizon. He checked his chart plotter next to the wheel.

"Land ho," Frank yelled into the companionway.

Moments later, Charly emerged and joined Frank at the helm.

"We're here?" Charly said.

"About an hour out, if Marty's co-ordinates are correct."

Frank dropped his eyes to Charly's feet.

"You bring anything hardier than those designer tenners?"

"You mean like mountain boots with spikes?"

"A pair of cross trainers would do."

"Got 'em in my bag, sarge."

Charly watched Frank staring at the sunlit ocean ahead.

"How far?" Charly asked.

"I judge it's ten miles."

"Suppose someone's living there?" Charly said.

"Like unfriendlies?"

"Yep."

"We'll have to take care … and this," Frank said and patted the Browning on his belt.

"Where's mine?"

Frank ignored her question and prepared to put the Irwin on starboard tack as the wind picked up.

"Ready about," he said, then yelled, "Hard alee."

The sloop rolled as the main boom swung to the opposite side, shuddering the boat with a jolting thunk. Charly extended an arm to the side of the cockpit, grabbing for a support strut of the bimini to steady herself.

"Sanford Prescott built his compound on the opposite side of the island," Frank said. "Seems stupid to me. Takes another half hour to get around to it."

"That where we're going?"

"Yeah. I want to see what a few million bucks could buy back in 1932."

"I'll go below and change my shoes," she said, steadying herself. "If I can make it there without going over the side."

* * *

Fifty-five minutes later, Frank dropped the sails, scrambled back into the cockpit, and engaged the inboard engine to make just enough headway to maintain steerage. The island sat ahead less than 300 yards. Charly scanned the beaches with binoculars. After struggling to use the heavy glasses over her designer shades, she ultimately abandoned the sunglasses. Frank scribbled figures in a notebook, and took the wheel.

"We'll circle the island, check the depths, and hunt for that pier," Frank said.

"Nothing's stirring in my view," Charly said. "No pier in sight."

The *Esperanza* chugged around the island from a hundred yards out with Frank monitoring their depth as they went. The gauge showed an erratic range between twenty and fifty feet below the keel. At halfway around the island, on the west shore, Frank spotted an object protruding from the beach.

"Check the far left ahead," Frank said to Charly, pointing. "Looks man-made."

Charly trained the binoculars where Frank had indicated.

"Well … it looks like what *used* to be a pier," Charly said.

"We should be able to better determine its condition on a closer pass."

They motored closer until the damaged pier lay no more than seventy yards away. The weathered lumber was ash gray, and what had been a level walkway of about eighty feet was now spiraled into the water below like a twisted braid of thin sticks. Only the few feet anchored near the land stood erect and walkable.

"Water's deep here," Frank said. "Good reason to chose this site. We may be able to get close enough to use what's left of the pier. Got to be careful we don't get fouled in debris underwater."

"I don't see any sharks," Charly said, studying the water between the boat and the beach.

"Trust me, they're there. They have Ph.Ds in stealth."

"You sure?" Charly said, her eyes narrowed.

"There's a white cooler aft of the cockpit coaming with chum. I thought we could catch our dinner if we decided to go fishing. Scoop out a ladle and dump it off the stern. I'd clip that cockpit tether to your life jacket or at least tie a mooring line around your waist."

Charly ducked out from the bimini, looped a line around her waist, and tied it off with a bowline as Frank looked on.

"Where'd you learn to tie a bowline so efficiently?" he asked.

"Been around boats all my life."

"Never would've known that from that act you put on when you sashayed up the pier, all Hollywood."

"I wanted to establish a few ground rules."

"So, you've been around boats all your life."

"But never around sharks," she said.

Charly opened the cooler lid, picked up the ladle, and dipped into the maroon goo sloshing inside. Frank watched as she stared at the bloody stew she held and made a face like a kid served a plate of raw liver.

"Toss it off the stern," Frank said.

Charly knelt and poured the chum into the shimmering mirror of sun-bright water at arm's length and watched the bloody ragu of fish chunks and entrails splash and disappear beneath the surface. In seconds, the water erupted with violent sprays as conical noses and jaws with pearl white teeth burst above the surface, their bites snapping at the savory tidbits. Charly stumbled to her feet, reeled backward, and jettisoned the ladle, which danced across the stern deck.

"See any sharks yet?" Frank said, facing forward, suppressing a grin.

"Jesus," Charly said. "I may need that potty."

"We'll sail around the island and get a look at the shoreline. I'll bring us back here to go ashore," Frank said, keeping a watchful eye on his passenger.

"Can't wait to hit those beaches," Charly said, holding firmly onto the gunwale with both hands, her eyes on the rickety vestiges of the pier.

"You're only going to hit them if, and only if, that pier is sound enough to use."

"Christ, I feel like I'm with Bogie on the *African Queen.*"

Frank throttled up the forty-four horse Yanmar inboard and powered to deeper water, then set the sails for an exploratory pass around the island.

"Marty said this was eight miles long by about four miles wide," Frank said, "but it looks enormous when you see it like this. No more than thirty-two square miles. I was concerned that it would be too small for a large population of convicts."

"Manhattan Island is only thirty-four square miles," Charly said, "and has more than a million and a half people."

"That almost settles that question."

"Why 'almost?'"

"In Manhattan, they can build upward to the sky," Frank said. "Here, we'll be staying a lot closer to the ground."

Moving around the island, Frank took in the beauty of the tropical hideaway with its long white sand beaches, green coconut palms, and mountainous terrain rising far behind and above the shoreline. On the east side, the center of the island angled inward like a giant plump boomerang making for an ideal harbor site for the prison's primary buildings and landing piers. The two wings sprouting from the center angled eastward for three to four miles on each side, creating protection from damaging winds coming from the north or south. The site would have easy shipping access, economical inmate transfer from

the mainland, and shelter for the naval ships that
would be guarding offshore.

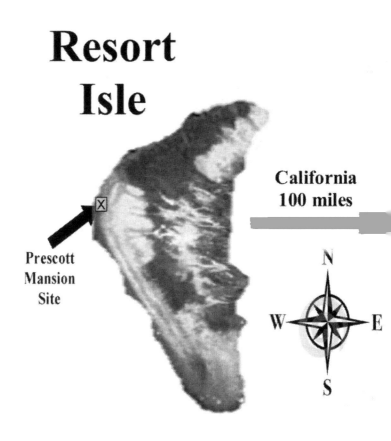

**Resort
Isle**

**California
100 miles**

Prescott
Mansion
Site

N

W ——— E

S

After the *Esperanza* circled the boomerang-shaped
island counter-clockwise and returned to the damaged
pier, Frank puttered in toward the beach with a careful
eye on his depth. When the gauge read ten feet, he

reversed the engine until the boat stopped making headway, scurried aft, and dropped and secured an anchor off the stern to keep the boat from drifting shoreward. He stared at the pier only five yards away. The few pilings that survived rose above the walkway by several feet and were embedded in the white sand below the surface. The good news was that they were the diameter of telephone poles and, unlike the walkway planks, still looked solid.

"Close as we dare go," Frank said. "This is low tide right now. We'll have deeper water soon."

"We're still several feet from the usable part of the pier," Charly said. "What's the plan?"

"We throw a hook onto the pier and pull ourselves over and tie up."

"That pile of shit going to hold us?"

"Only one way to tell. How much do you weigh?"

Charly gave Frank a narrow-eyed stare.

"Less than you, big boy."

Frank pulled out a line with a grappling hook from a storage locker and slung it onto the pier. It grabbed onto a vertical piling and Frank tugged the line taut and tested it for solid resistance as he eased the boat alongside the pier. The foam rubber boat fenders rasped as he secured the sloop to the piling, then looped another line over the jagged remains of a seaward piling near the stern. The pier groaned with the gentle wave motion bobbing the boat, but seemed to hold.

Charly hoisted her bag onto her shoulder.

Frank dug into his pocket and pulled out a Beretta .25 automatic and handed it to Charly.

"Take this," Frank said. "Just in case."

"Thanks," she said and tucked it in her bag.

"You do know how to use that," Frank said.

"Get serious. Guess what I stuck in Mike Graham's face?"

Frank pointed to the pier. "You first."

"Why should I be the test dummy?"

"If I go first and fall in, who's going to save me? You? The other way around, with me on the boat with access to equipment, will play out a lot better."

"Why the hell didn't I press for Catalina?" Charly said and stepped onto the starboard gunwale, bracing herself with a shroud from the mainmast. She gingerly extended a testing foot toward the pier and touched upon one of the few extant planks that seemed supportive. She pushed downward with the exploratory foot, tapping the weathered wood like it was pond ice to determine its safeness for skating. The plank stayed in place, firm. In a single motion, she lightly balleted to the pier and hugged a nearby piling like it was a treasured loved one.

Frank followed her lead, noting her choice of landing spot on the pier. There were now about ten yards of pier to traverse before they could set foot on land. The planks were an erratic maze of uncertain soundness, with large sections where many planks had

144

decayed or fallen away. Moving carefully in a zig-zag pattern ultimately brought them to one last jump onto the sandy beach.

Charly dipped into her bag, withdrew a silver flask, and unscrewed the cap.

"You're having a drink?" Frank asked, his left eyebrow raised.

"I'm betting there's no bar on this island. So here's to ya," Charly said, saluting Frank with the flask, and then took a generous swig.

"I shouldn't have let you chum those sharks."

"No biggie, but I'll never watch *Jaws* again."

Chapter 23

A wide walkway of brick pavers led from the pier to Prescott's hacienda-style mansion a hundred yards inland. The remains of the storm-ravaged building stood tucked inside a palm tree line bordering the beach. Much of its multi-levels were gone. What roof that remained had lost most of its half-pipe Spanish tiles, which lay shattered beneath the eaves. The glass from the windows was almost entirely gone, with only glistening traces dangling from their mullion frames, most of which had blown inward, likely by decades of violent winds.

The stucco exterior displayed open fissures and road map designs of cracks. Slabs of the adobe-colored veneer sprawled on the portico and on the sides of the building. What little paint remained, curled away from the naked wood that once hid beneath its ecru finish. Round support timbers, weathered and rotting, jutted out from the open frames of the walls and lay ashen where many had collapsed. Scrub vegetation dominated the grounds, with an occasional hibiscus begging for attention with colorful red blooms and tropical michelias pleasing the senses with their sweet perfume.

Frank and Charly paused at the steps leading to the elevated portico and studied the shambles of what had once been tropical elegance.

"Go inside?" Charly asked.

"Not a good idea," Frank said. "This place is two nails away from complete collapse."

"Then let's see what's out back."

The two carefully skirted the building and found themselves standing on the edge of a filled swimming pool, sixty feet long by thirty feet wide and bordered in hand-painted ceramic tiles.

"All that beautiful blue ocean and Prescott still needed to build a pool," Charly said.

"Looks like he piped in the ocean," Frank said, pointing to a round opening on the bottom of the pool's deep side. "Used the tide to drain and fill the pool. Clever."

"Bet he installed that heavy-gauge screen down there to keep out aquatic visitors."

"Yeah. The pipe's large enough to allow a dolphin in."

"May want to keep this place for the new arrivals," Charly said.

"This section of the island faces due west. The inmates will be based on the east side."

"Why?"

"Easier access. It'd be impractical to have to travel to the opposite side of the island. Not sure why the Prescotts built on this side."

"Silly, unromantic lad," Charly said. "For the sunsets."

Frank waved off the comment.

"Hardened cons can do without lovey sunsets."

"Won't they have access to the entire island?"

"I guess, but the main complex should be built on the east side, which is four miles away through tough-looking jungle. Why would anyone want to claw and climb their way through that kind of terrain when all their needs are supplied on the east face?"

"Have to want something bad on this side … or want to get away from something."

"I'm sure the island's evolution will be interesting," Frank said and wandered around the pool to the back of the once-improved lot. A spade lay on the ground in front of an open utility shed. Rusty picks, mattocks, and other garden tools covered the floor of the small building. Frank grabbed the spade and headed for the edge of the overgrowth.

Frank paced the perimeter of the grounds, booting aside coconuts that lay strewn in abundance everywhere, and swatting at the weeds in his path with the spade. At the far left, where the jungle abutted the cleared area, Frank stopped and bent over to examine something on the ground.

"If it's money, it's mine," Charly said.

"Can you come over here?"

Frank watched Charly step an erratic pattern through the weeds that ended a few feet from where he squatted.

"Got a camera in that bottomless bag of yours?"

"Yes," Charly said and fumbled through the depths of the bag and withdrew a digital camera. "Here."

Frank took the camera as Charly moved in closer.

"Kodak moment?" Charly said.

Frank pointed to the ground beneath his knees. Charly moved in front of Frank.

"Any idea what did that?" Charly asked.

Frank bid Charly to move in even closer to get a better look. In the damp sandy soil lay a fresh footprint. A footprint like no other Frank had ever seen. Large, reptilian, like a long hand, with five claw marks scribed deep into the soil. Frank figured out the camera controls and took a flash picture of the print. He moved to a different position and snapped another shot, then moved in for close-ups.

"Place your hand next to the print," Frank said.

Charly squatted and did as Frank asked as the camera flashed several times.

"Have we stumbled onto Jurassic Park?" Charly asked.

"It's a kind of crocodile, I think," Frank said and stood.

"Why is there only one footprint?"

"The soil everywhere else is bone dry and hard, except for this low, damp area. Probably where rain water settled."

"Think what made it is nearby?" Charly asked, rising, her head swiveling in all directions.

"Looks fresh," Frank said and made an attempt to capture the print with the spade, but the muddy impression disintegrated the moment he tried to lift it from the soil.

Charly's eyes scanned the nearby jungle and stopped at bright blue and green colors in the shadows of the palms.

"There's something under those palms," Charly said and groped around in her bag and pulled out the pistol.

They both inched toward the brightly-colored object. Frank fondled the automatic on his belt.

"It's a peacock," Frank said. "A male, or what's left of him."

"How do you know it's a male? You major in ornithology?"

"The word 'peacock' is a clue. The females are peahens and are not nearly so colorful."

The fan of feathers glowed in iridescent teal blue, gold, and green around a design of multi-eyed patterns. The creature's head was intact, but the central carcass was hollowed out, leaving only rib bones.

"You guessing your croc-a-thing did this?" Charly asked.

"Be my prime suspect."

"Well, Marty told you about the peacocks, but left out the crocodiles."

"I know this is a big place, but I haven't seen evidence of any chickens yet. Marty said they were everywhere."

"You know it's been years since Marty saw this place. Cold be super-croc worked his way through the chicks and is now moved on to the peacocks."

"Like all these coconuts," Frank said as he made a sweeping gesture with his arm, "those chickens need to be here as a fallback food source. If they've been decimated, we'll bring more in, but we need to find this predator and eliminate him. And any of his relatives. The sharks are one thing, but they stay in the ocean. This bad boy could be a constant danger anywhere on land. I'm not sure that's part of the deal."

"So you imagine this remote island is going to magically transform the meanest, cruelest, most deranged, and out-of-touch-with-reality misfits into penal utopians."

"I have no idea how this is going to play out. I want criminals of their ilk put where there's no return to civilized society. If people like the ones who killed my family want to kill each other, that's their choice. If they decide to play nice and honor rules and regs to live together in a semblance of harmony, then I'm okay with that too. Just so they do it here."

Frank hiked toward the front of the ruins of the mansion.

"It'll be dark soon," Frank said. "We'll rack out on the boat tonight and leave in the morning."

"About the sleeping accommodations…"

"You'll have your own little stateroom."

Charly smiled and fell in behind Frank as they filed back to the beach and the shabby pier.

Before they mounted the pier, they both looked back at where they'd been.

"You know I was hesitant to come along on this venture, but I'm glad I changed my mind," Charly said.

"I appreciate your company," Frank said and turned back toward the *Esperanza* as the orange sun met the horizon behind the silhouetted boat.

"See why Prescott put the mansion here?" Charly said, clambering onto the pier.

Frank followed Charly's footsteps as they light-footed it across the untrustworthy planks toward the boat.

"He was a sex-driven lady-killer who knew the value of atmosphere," Frank said as he leapt from the pier, then helped Charly safely across onto the boat.

"Tomorrow you'll get one last look at your happy internment camp," Charly said.

"You're pretty sure this idea is going to end up badly, aren't you?"

"There's a book I think you should read. Ask your librarian for: *Lord of the Flies*?"

Chapter 24

That night, Frank broiled the salmon filets he'd brought along, and added a tasty oil-and-wine vinaigrette salad, crusty French bread, and a palate-pleasing Berringer pinot grigio. After dinner, Charly sat in the cozy candle-lit salon while Frank served glasses of Bullit Bourbon. They sat across from each other and sipped their drinks. No one spoke for several minutes as they listened to the gentle waves of the incoming tide washing along the hull and collapsing on the sandy beach.

Charly stared at Frank, who studied a chart on the table between them.

"How are you doing?"

Frank looked up from his chart, his eyes studied hers for intent.

"It's been almost two years," he said. "I have my good days."

Charly nodded her approval.

"How about you?" Frank asked. "What's next for you?"

"Work-wise?"

"Love-wise."

Charly laughed.

"I have my eye on a guy," Charly said and danced her eyebrows.

"Yeah? Do I know this lucky man?"

"Quite well."

Frank frowned and stared at the overhead.

"You've lived in his house way more than I have," she said and polished off her drink.

"Marty Dimino?"

Charly smiled.

"Son-of-a-bitch. When did this happen?" Frank said, placing his arms on the table and leaning toward her.

"I fell for Marty when I ran his campaign for DA, but he was married."

"He still is, isn't he?"

"She left him when he decided to run for the senate."

"He never said a word. Have you ... um ... been dating?"

"Have I *slept* with him?"

"None of my business, certainly," Frank said and took a final swallow of his bourbon.

"Let's just say we've *known* each other. And when his divorce is final, we plan to go to the next level."

"That's fantastic, Charly. I can visit my two best friends in one place."

"Hell, that won't be any different than our get-togethers at the Shamrock."

They both smiled, but soon Frank's happy expression faded and he stood.

"I hope you have the love in your life that I had with Amy."

"That's a beautiful wish, Frank. Thank you."

Frank slid out from behind the table and walked aft.

"I can't say that my marriage was all Disneyland and *Jerry Maguire*. Being yoked to a cop isn't easy. My work was always number one."

Frank stopped at the door to the stern bedroom and pushed it ajar a few inches.

"So many times," Frank said, "Amy was there, right next to me, but with my work heavy on my mind, I didn't see her then ..."

Frank opened the door fully, stepped inside, and disappeared into the darkness.

"I see her now," Frank said in a whisper and gently closed the door.

*　　*　　*

The dawn light made long shadows over the *Esperanza* as she lay off the west shore of the island. Frank had pulled up the anchor, cast off the mooring lines, and was powering the sloop gently astern, away from the decrepit pier and the shallows near the beach. He brought the boat about to head out to sea.

Charly climbed to the cockpit from below with cups and a thermos of hot coffee.

"When we circled this island, I spotted a dot of land north of us," Frank said. "I tried to find it on my charts, but nothing was shown in that area. But I know what I saw. I want to swing over to it and look it over before we set course for Playa del Rey."

"Fine by me," Charly said. "Why the interest?"

"It might be more ideal than this island. And maybe no mystery crocs."

"Is it close enough that inmates could reach it from here?"

"Facing naval gunboats and sharks, I doubt that anyone could go far before being stopped or killed. It's about five miles away. Not exactly a couple of laps in the pool."

Frank handed Charly a pair of binoculars and pointed the *Esperanza* north.

"The place I saw may be too small," Frank said. "I'm surprised I even spotted it. It's in this northern area," Frank said and swept his arm from left to right in a four-foot arc. "While I steer the boat, see if you can get a fix on the island with the binoculars."

"Aye, aye," Charly said and elbowed Frank in the ribs.

"I'll try to get us there as fast as I can," Frank said.

"You can't exceed, in knots, 1.34 times the square root in feet of the waterline length of your boat."

"Jesus, woman. You *do* know about boats."

"Since I was old enough to trim a jib sheet."

The strong steady wind kept the sloop cutting the water at her top speed of over seven knots. After forty minutes, Charly stopped sweeping the horizon with the binoculars and fixed her attention straight off the bow, as best she could, on the rolling and pitching deck.

"I may have it," Charly said, "if it would just stop bouncing all over the place."

Frank stood next to Charly and squinted where she pointed. He took the binoculars, raised the glasses to his eyes.

"That's it." Frank said. "We'll be there in another few minutes."

The island grew larger with each passing minute, and while it was considerably smaller than Sanford Prescott's island, it was similar in vegetation and narrow sandy beaches.

"I want to go around her to see the entire shoreline," Frank said. "Maybe find a spot where we can anchor in close and take a serious look."

As the *Esperanza* circled to the opposite side of the island, an entrance to a large lagoon revealed itself, widening deep into the land.

"Looks like we've found our entryway," Frank said and turned the wheel to port and headed straight for the narrow opening.

"We need to switch to the engine and drop the sails," Frank said.

Charly immediately dropped the mainsail without any prompting. Frank engaged the engine, making slow headway into the lagoon, his eyes constantly darting at the depth gauge.

"It's deeper here than I would've thought," Frank said. "Could you take the wheel and keep an eye on that depth gauge, please, while I scan the shoreline?"

"Hey, I know my way around boats. My father owned a lovely Chris Craft, which we practically lived on every summer."

"Every time I peel a layer off your onion, I find out more new and amazing things."

Charly took the helm.

"Twenty-five feet," Charly said.

Frank knew that twenty-five feet translated to at least twenty feet under his keel, a comfortable depth, but unchartered water could hold surprises. The mysterious lagoon seemed to comprise most of the island with only a crescent of narrow land around it.

"I'm betting we're over the mouth of an old volcano."

The *Esperanza* crossed the middle of the huge lake of dead calm water and putted on toward the far bank, opposite the narrow mouth of the lagoon.

While Frank took a moment to take in the surrounding terrain, a loud alarm sounded. He charged to the cockpit and looked at the depth gauge. The water beneath the boat had dropped to fifteen feet and was rapidly falling.

Frank put the transmission into reverse and throttled up the engine. The boat continued forward for several more yards before it slowed. Abruptly, the vessel groaned to a stop that pitched the bow downward. The engine strained, but the *Esperanza* wasn't moving astern. Frank stared at the depth gauge and grimaced. They had run aground. The starboard gunwale rolled gently toward the surface of the dark water.

"We've hit the bottom," Frank said and silenced the shallow water alarm, then punched the clear plastic of the dodger surrounding the cockpit. "Goddamnit."

"What do we do now?" Charly asked. "Kedge off?"

"Normally, we could try, but this boat has a winged keel."

Frank knew the stubby structures that extended laterally on both sides at the bottom of the keel, created a large amount of surface area to embed in the bottom.

"We'll make the attempt, but if the bottom is as muddy and soft as I imagine, it'll be futile."

"How about the tide?"

"That would be a good thought, except look around at the shore. No high water marks. At low tide we'd see evidence of the high water line on shore objects, like rocks, foliage, and beach debris. I see nothing like that. We're already at high tide. When the tide goes

160

out, we'll be in even harder aground. And depending on the tidal range, we could be left lying on our side."

"Call the Ocean Auto Club?"

"We call the Coast Guard," Frank said. "If that fails, we'll have to activate the EPIRB."

"What's that?" Charly asked.

"The Emergency Position-Indication Radio Beacon, but we can only use it if all other means to get help fail. We'll try to kedge off first."

After a failed attempt to use the dinghy to carry the heavy anchor out off the stern, set it in the bottom, and try to use the winch to pull the boat free, Frank gave up and put in a radio call to the Coast Guard in southern California.

"This is K3VLS, the sloop *Esperanza* out of Playa Del Rey, California. Our position is: Latitude 34 degrees, 6 minutes, 19.573 seconds north …"

Chapter 25

The mall between the Capitol and the Washington Monument provided grassy expanses where visitors spread blankets and enjoyed refreshments and lunches in the unusually warm sun of October. Among them, Senators Marty Dimino and Kate Nelson, a woman in her mid-fifties, sat on newspapers and sipped coffee from paper cups.

"Your biggest opposition will come from Monfreda of New York," Kate said. "He represents a huge constituency that works in corrections. He's also got a lot of clout on several important committees."

"Who else?" Marty asked.

"Well, Marty, you've stirred up quite a hornet's nest. You're proposing that we dramatically change a prison system that's stood for two centuries in America. Throw a dart into the Senate and you'll likely as not hit an opponent of your idea. They'll have reasons that range from greed and selfish interests, to fear and civil rights. You're trying to set a precedent for how we establish punishment. Not to mention that several of your detractors will likely throw up the tried but failed ideas attached to Devil's Island type penal colonies."

"The French, and many others, directly supervised and mistreated their inmates. My system provides for no direct supervision. Low labor costs to the taxpayer. No building expenses to house correctional officers. The inmates will govern themselves."

"Or kill each other."

"That's completely up to them," Marty said, slapping the newspaper with his free hand. "At least there'll be no more guilty consciences about capital punishment. The inmates control their own fate. We want the chronic and violent offenders out of our society. We want to put them where there's no return, and we're willing to trade them a sense of freedom they never will have in conventional lockups, especially supermaxes."

"Hey, I'm a fellow Californian and I'm in your corner. You've got to convince those people in there," Kate said, pointing a thumb toward the Capitol.

"Thank God you're here to help me, Kate. I'm so green at this."

"My first term was a nightmare. I wanted to win over everyone and change the world, but I didn't know how to fight. Twenty years later, I've learned the rules of congressional infighting. Now I only want to conquer little pieces of the world, one tidbit at a time."

"All those seasoned senators in there you could hang out with ... Why pick me?

"Honestly?"

"Yeah. I'd like to know."

"You're quite the celebrity in these parts, Mr. Hollywood DA. Big national trial publicity; part of a two man war on crime; gets elected to the U.S. Senate first time out, over dozens of other strong candidates; thwarts assassination attempts. Who could resist a guy who does all that? You're hot news. Man bites dog. You're Indiana Jones around here."

"Get out," Marty said and took a swig of his coffee.

"Okay. That's all bullshit. Happy now?"

"No. The truth."

"The truth is all I just said. You looked like a lost soul and I'm a sucker for a homeless lawyer with a fresh idea on prison reform."

"Now we've got bullshit."

"Maybe it's sex, Marty."

Marty rose, extended his hands, and pulled Kate to her feet.

"I've already got a girl. Come on, we've got to get back in there for the debate and the vote."

They strolled toward the Capitol.

"If the vote should go against you, don't be discouraged," Kate said. "Amended bills come up again and again."

"It's got to pass now. We need new laws right now. By next year thousands of more innocent people will be victims."

"Whoa, boy. This bill isn't going to stop crime dead in its tracks."

"It'll sure as hell put a crimp in its those getting out to repeat it."

"I hope you realize that even if your bill is met with open arms, the process to become law can take months."

"I'm okay with that. We need time to get a consensus from more of the major prisons. Our experiment right now will include only the state of California. But we need the government to put in the major funding for the preparations, and we're going to need it to get the navy and Coast Guard to control the island's perimeter, medical care, and supply shipments."

"Just saying … Patience is a virtue one should learn not to despise. I think somebody famous said that."

"Sounds biblical."

"Maybe from Proverbs."

Marty stopped and turned to Kate.

"Were you serious about that sex remark?" he asked.

"For God's sake, Marty, Look at me. Do I look like Julia Roberts? Besides, my last sexual experience practically scared me to death."

"Honestly?"

"Yeah. And I was alone at the time."

Marty looked to the heavens and grinned. Kate took him by the arm and guided him toward the Capitol steps.

Men and women filled the desks and seats in the
Senate chamber's semi-circular lower floor. Visitors
watched from the gallery high above, many pointing
at people and items below their view. Klatches of
people talked in the aisles of the floor, while others
milled between seats.

Austin Bigelow, the vice-president of the United
States, serving as president of the Senate, sat at an
elevated central podium and called for order. Marty
Dimino sat next to Kate on one side of the curved
rows of desks. People took their seats, and the outer
chamber doors noisily closed. The cavernous room
quieted.

"When we recessed for lunch, we were in floor
discussion on Senate Bill S4148 sponsored by Senator
Dimino of California," Bigelow said. "By way of
review, this bill proposes that the Government of the
United States investigate for funding a thirty-two
square mile island in the Pacific Ocean that lies
approximately 100 miles northwest of Los Angeles,
California. The island, called Prescott Island, and
presently owned by the State of California, is being
offered to the United States for 140 million dollars.
The purpose of this purchase would be to establish a
generally unsupervised penal island for adjudicated
criminals fitting the parameters and degree of criminal

166

sentencing outlined before you on page seven of the bill. I now open the floor for the continued discussion of this bill."

Several senators signaled to be recognized by the chair.

"The chair recognizes Senator Charles Byron of South Carolina," Bigelow said.

"I have a few questions that I would like Senator Dimino to answer, if he kindly will," Byron said, standing. "Number one, sir, if there's to be no supervision on this island, why call it a penal institution? Why not call it what it appears to be, Club Med West?"

General laughter broke out in the chamber and subsided.

"If the Chair please," Marty said, "may I respond to my colleague from South Carolina?"

The vice-president nodded.

"The whole concept of Prescott Island is to get recidivist criminals out of our society and, at the same time, cut our present astronomical correctional supervisory and maintenance costs. The island will be constantly surrounded and monitored by as many as four U.S. Government warships. I've been to the island, senator, and the water around it is so heavily infested with man-eating sharks that I seriously doubt that many inmates will attempt an escape. And even if they did try and somehow managed to avoid the sharks, there's no inhabited land for a hundred miles.

Not a favorable scenario for escape, I'm afraid. By comparison, no inmate has ever been proven to have successfully escaped from Alcatraz, which is just over a mile from shore."

Dimino consulted a paper on his desk.

"The other benefit of the island experiment will be, hopefully, the removal of any further need or discussion of capital punishment in this country, a controversy that still rages in many of our state courts. Capital criminals will go to Prescott Island. What happens to them after that will be determined by the community of inmates. The important result of this isolation shares one similarity to capital punishment: it prohibits the perpetrator from ever repeating his crime in our society."

"Further questions, Senator Byron?" Bigelow asked.

"Nothing further."

Byron sat and Senator Daniel Grant of Florida raised his hand.

"Senator Grant," Bigelow said.

Grant stood and stared at Marty for several seconds. Marty returned his gaze.

"Senator Dimino, how are these inmates going to survive on this island? Are there enough natural resources to support life?"

"There are ample fresh water sources, fruit bearing vegetation, coconut palms, thousands of chickens and other game fowl, and arable soil to plant crops. Also abundant fish."

"Yes, I believe you mentioned them," Grant said. "Ones with large, sharp teeth. We have them all around my state of Florida, but I'll be damned if they keep a soul from coming and going as they please in our waters."

General laughter flooded the chamber.

"How big is this island?" Grant asked.

"It's the size of Manhattan Island, New York."

"I guess that will do," Grant said and retook his seat.

Marty remained standing and said, "There are other varieties of food fish there as well. That's why the sharks congregate there in such numbers. It's a feeding and mating area for them and many other species. In addition to the resources that nature provides there, we will supply certain other needed items such as tools, seeds, clothing, building materials, medicine, and the like. A senate investigative committee and experts in the field will file full investigative reports and make final recommendations. And while this gracious provision of needed supplies may seem costly, it pales in comparison to what we spend currently on our prisoners. At an annual cost of $40,000 to $50,000 per inmate, what I propose will cut that by more than 75%."

A wave of murmurs filled the chamber.

"What happens if the inmates need a doctor?" Grant asked.

"Our initial answer was that the inmates better pray a doctor gets life and is sent to the island."

Gentle laughter trickled through the floor and gallery.

"But we knew we'd better rethink that," Marty said. "We will provide a hospital ship nearby with fully qualified medical personnel and surgeons. Sick inmates will be transferred to the ship by a small launch which will pick them up at the end of a long, covered pier. Only persons requiring medical attention and their transporters will be allowed on that pier, and wheelchairs and gurneys will be available for conveyance. Other inmates may bring the sick to the end of the pier, but then depart before the launch will be sent. All medical treatment will be administered on the ship with guards on duty."

"Sounds like better treatment than many of our poor get right now in our depressed areas," Grant said.

"Make no mistake, this is not to be a tropical vacation spot," Marty said, "but if the inmates pool their efforts, cooperate with each other and work hard, they can survive in the sunshine as restricted but free men. If they squander their time and resources, they'll likely not do well. Everything they need to provide a decent way of life will be there on that island. The choices will be up to them. We intend to fully train them to succeed."

The vice-president nodded to another senator.

"The chair recognizes Senator Jacoby of Illinois," Bigelow said.

"How about communication? Will they be allowed newspapers, TV, radios, and the like?"

"No newspapers whatsoever," Marty said. "Further, no mail, no magazines and, of course, no telephones or computers. But our original model provides for closed circuit television, which will air digital TV shows and movies. They will be given only a communication link with the presiding ship for medical emergencies. Studies have found that liberal inmate communications have directly led to criminal activity on the outside, like witness intimidation, retribution, and the transfer of contraband. Many current street leaders continue to control their gangs and crime families through the simple use of a telephone. We're cutting that perk out."

"That seems a bit severe, senator," Jacoby said. "May be a hard sell to these prisoners, who you've said will be voting on trying out your project."

"This is to be a maximum punishment and security facility. It's far better than what many inmates endure presently in supermax prisons: twenty-three hours in a cell every day with one hour outside in a high-walled court where they might get a glimpse of sunshine. There is to be no return to their former society. The absence of communication with the outside world that they once knew will help to keep their focus on their new life and not on the constantly torturing ideas of escape or scoring special accommodations from the outside. These are people who have lost their chance at rehabilitation. The sooner other would-be criminals realize the fact that there's no coming back from Prescott Island, the sooner we can more safely walk our city streets and countrysides."

"Who will go to your island?" Jacoby asked.

"Initially, those with no chance for parole in their remaining lifetime will go to the island," Marty said. "Any present prison inmates, or those with any former prison record, will go if they are convicted of any further crimes. Even one more. Never-before convicted felons will go if their first offense is a capital crime, a crime of extreme violence, an armed crime, rape, or a crime related to drug distribution exceeding a set amount. The present prisons, as they deplete in population, will be used as military-type rehab centers for first offenders. If a person repeats his crimes or doesn't respond well in the rehab center, he'll likely end his days at Prescott Isle."

Bigelow nodded toward a senator in the first row.

"The chair recognizes the senior Senator from New York."

Kate Nelson leaned over to Marty.

"Look out," she said low.

Senator Anthony Monfreda rose and addressed Marty.

172

"We seem to have abandoned all thoughts and ideals concerning the civil rights of American citizens here. All of a sudden, people don't have any say in what happens to them. I find this entire discussion a little hard to believe. Are we still in America?"

"Senator Monfreda, with all due respect to you and civil rights, people who kill and rape, and brutally maim upright citizens relinquish a great portion of their civil liberties. And just as your freedom of expression ends at the point of my nose, so also do others' rights end at the instigation of heinous crimes. What about my friend, Detective Frank Dugan's wife? What about her civil rights, senator? And didn't their two, little murdered children have civil rights?"

A lengthy silence.

"Two more points," Marty said. "If we don't try a model like this now, criminal recidivism will increase as projected solutions to prison overpopulation begin to allow earlier release times, and even the allowance of parole for formerly life-without-parole inmates. Our public safety problems will increase exponentially, potentially doubling the problems we face now. Inmates existing under supermax conditions, under solitary confinement, many for decades, are dehumanized to the point of abject cruelty. They dream of suicide and feel like dogs kept in kennel cages for endless years. Death is their only reward. Prescott Island will give these men a much different outlook ... and hope."

Marty nodded his thanks to the chair and retook his seat.

"If there is no further discussion, I'd like to put this proposal to a vote," Bigelow said and waited for a response. Seeing none, he handed a document over to a clerk. "Please signify by voice vote as the roll is called."

Marty had already endured one tie vote on his proposal, and he wasn't sure he'd swayed anyone to his side in today's discussion. With the president of the Senate abstaining from being a tie breaker, Marty's gut was in a knot. He hoped Frank was faring better with the government of California. It was going to be a day Maalox and Tums wouldn't touch.

*　　*　　*

The roll call of states in the Senate had come to the latter part of the alphabet as the final names were called.

"Senator Bartlett, Wyoming," Bigelow said.

"Nay."

"Senator Houser, Wyoming."

"Yea."

"That completes the roll," Bigelow said. "Anyone we missed?"

No one responded. Bigelow consulted his voting results.

"It appears that we again have a tie vote," Bigelow said.

"Mr. President?" Marty said, standing.

"The Chair recognizes Senator Dimino."

"Rather than go into another floor discussion and a likely identical tie vote, and since the chair has chosen to abstain from the tie break, with the permission of the Senate, I'd like to propose something highly unusual to settle this deadlock."

"And what might that be, Senator?"

"Since many of these distinguished senators are concerned about the rights of the inmates in this matter, why not let the inmates decide?"

"You would be willing to place the fate of your bill in the hands of the very element that it intends to affect?

"Yes, sir, I would."

"This is most irregular, senator. Give us a moment," Bigelow said and turned to the others seated near him.

Muffled discussion in the chamber filled the air as the vice-president consulted with others on his level. After several moments, he returned to the his seat and attempted to quiet the chamber.

"Order, please. Order."

The talking and chamber noises subsided.

"Senator Dimino," Bigelow said, "if you can obtain a majority vote for your proposal from among the present inmate population of your State of California, which this experiment will initially involve, I'll be the first to consider it a mandate for its passage by this body." Bigelow raised a hand and appealed to the entire Senate. "We need a motion."

"I move that I, Martin Dimino, obtain a vote on Senate Bill S4148 from the entire affected inmate population at present in the state of California. And, further agree, that the result of that vote decide the future of this bill."

"Seconds?" Bigelow asked.

Senator Kate Nelson of California stood.

"Second," she said and looked at Marty, "… proudly."

Bigelow stood.

"By general voice vote, all those in favor of this curious, but very American experiment, signify by saying 'aye.'"

The vast majority of the Senate responded with resounding "ayes."

"Opposed?"

A few voices responded with "nays."

"So be it," Bigelow said. "The motion is carried. Good luck, Senator Dimino. I sense you're going to need it."

Marty leaned over to Kate.

"Why does the vice-president refuse to break the tie?"

"His brother was murdered by a man who is serving a life sentence in Florence, Colorado's

176

Supermax. He feels that any vote from him might be considered biased."

Chapter 26

It had been five days since the Coast Guard had returned Frank and Charly to the *terra firma* of southern California. Frank had intended to stay on his boat at the San Diego marina, but now found himself accepting Marty's forceful offer to continue on at his beach house.

The boat's insurer had flown out to see the grounded *Esperanza* and returned with no solution for getting the nine ton vessel out of the shallow lagoon and back to sea without incurring more expense than the sloop was worth. They decided to pay Frank for the boat's total loss. The amount was a good deal less than Frank had paid for the boat, not to mention the extra radio and navigation equipment he'd purchased that would now spend the rest of its silent days stranded in a solitary location a hundred miles away. Frank mourned the loss, but knew life often handed you lemons. Making lemonade wasn't going to improve his mood about the bad luck.

On a cheerier note, the newly-found coffee appliances at the beach house were working in concert to grind and brew Frank the best cup of java he'd ever drunk. He had scarcely touched his morning lips to his steaming cup when his cell rang.

"Detective Dugan," Frank said, placing his piping hot cup on the kitchen counter.

"Hey, partner," Judd Kemp said. "Got some interesting news for you."

"Interesting, as in the Chinese curse, 'May you live in interesting times?'"

"Much better than that. The boss just got a call from Marty in DC. He wants you to poll the state prisons for candidates who qualify to road test your island idea. On the department payroll."

"SDPD's willing to pay me while I'm hopping around to all these lock-ups trying to convince hard-ass cons they will love life in the palms?"

"The chief thinks this is far more important that collaring repeat offenders a few at a time. You're going to put thousands of them where we don't have to recycle them ever again."

"Why me? I have unsolved cases on my docket."

"We'll take over your workload. Don't worry about it. Did Marty tell you the latest?"

"About getting a majority vote from the lifers?"

"You *do* know about this."

"Again, why me?"

"You're the man who got Marty elected, sport. You're the poster boy for this island project. Who better? Besides, you're a big celebrity. The cons in the joint will love to chat with you."

"Especially the ones I put there."

"They'll love you just the same. They know they're bad boys. Somebody had to bust 'em. But this time you'll be offering to set them free."

"I don't even know where to begin..."

"Pelican Bay," Judd said.

"The northernmost point in the state."

"It's where the baddest baddies live. Marty wants only the worst offenders polled. Guys who only get the stretch their legs an hour or two a day."

"When?" Frank asked and managed to work in a sip9- of his coffee.

"You go day after tomorrow. *More* good news. Corillo's going with you."

"The rookie?"

"Chief wants him to learn from you. And he wants him to watch your back in tight quarters. The guy's built like that Super Bowl linebacker on the Ravens."

"Ray Lewis?"

"Yeah, him, only taller."

"I'm going to need drawings. Projected renderings of the island as it'll look when we renovate it," Frank said. "Can you get me a decent graphic artist today?"

"We'll get you a direct descendant of Rembrandt, if we have to."

*   *   *

The tower overseeing the 275-acre Pelican Bay Supermax correctional complex rose more than twenty-five feet above coil after coil of razor wire atop sturdy, electrified anchor chain fences, ten feet high. Pelican Bay and the word "escape" seldom, if ever, combined in the planning thoughts among its thousand-plus residents, or news stories. Since its creation in 1989, no one had ever left its safekeeping unauthorized, a comfort to the population of Crescent City, a few miles south.

Ironic, thought Frank, that prison names had little if anything to do with what they provided. Very few inmates ever enjoyed solitude in Soledad, and he doubted that anyone housed in Pelican Bay's Supermax ever got a glimpse of a pelican.

Frank and Alex Corillo met with Warden James Griswold in his office and discussed their wish to assemble the inmates and hold a forum in the prison gym or cafeteria. Frank showed the warden the pictures he'd brought in a manila envelope that Alex had carried in. The possibility of speaking to a large group of tough long-timers in one spot got dismissed out of hand by the warden, citing the obvious dangers. That made Frank's job nearly impossible. Doing a dog-and-pony show for every max prisoner in the Security Housing Unit was going to take too much time, not to mention, wear Frank to the bone. The warden suggested a solution.

"We have recently installed a cable television system for the SHU, which we control," Griswold said. "We could put you on a closed circuit airing of your proposal, which will reach every inmate in the unit."

"I like the idea," Frank said, "but I first want to talk in person to the known leaders in the SHU, maybe two or three, at your suggestion. One at a time, of course."

"Can do, detective," the warden said and pressed a button on his desk phone.

*　　*　　*

Frank knew that the facility was separated into two main sections. One half housed Level IV inmates known as the "general population," and included those who had possibilities of rehabilitation and perhaps release someday, while in the other half, an "X" shape configuration on barren ground, named the Security Housing Unit, held the "worst-of-the-worst" prisoners. It was this building that Frank and Alex needed to visit and pitch their alternative life option. Frank was well aware that a handful of gang leaders inside regarded *everyone* as untrustworthy opportunists with ulterior angles. Cops, especially, topped their scammers watch list. It would be the confidence of these men that Frank needed to turn his way. By comparison, putting panty hose on an ostrich would be a snap.

After initial processing, a young guard, who looked like he was born in a workout gym, escorted Frank and Alex into the center hub that connected the four lengthy arms of the X-shaped facility. From there, they followed a long corridor containing six pods of eight cells, eight-by-ten-foot, windowless concrete boxes, lighted only by fluorescent fixtures.

It was here that Frank needed to sit face-to-face with some of the hardest criminals to ever populate a rap sheet, men who killed people for an askance look. But Frank was certain that the key to obtaining a winning vote on the proposal was to sell these kingpins the deal. He wondered where those Canarsee Indians, who sold Manhattan Island to the Dutch, were now when he needed them.

The escort guard introduced Frank and Alex to the officer who monitored and controlled the pod's every activity and cell door.

"I need to speak with a couple of your most-respected inmate leaders," Frank said. "The scariest ones."

"The warden said you were a sensible man," the officer said. "I watched you in the news, detective. You never struck me as being crazy."

"Sometimes you have to grab the devil by the tail."

"Good luck with that."

The officer pointed to one of his monitors showing a man reclining on his bunk, reading a magazine.

"That's Buck Canton," the officer said. "Killed seven people in their mansion in Bel Air."

"Why?" Frank asked.

"Because they were home."

"I'll take him," Frank said. "Who else ya got?"

"Over here is Daniel Crawford," the officer said, indicating a different screen. The man on camera was shaving. "Robbed twenty-seven banks before he had his Nixon mask pulled off by a teller."

"A *bank robber* is in here?"

"He murdered the grabby teller."

"I like him too."

"He's a good choice. Runs all the blacks in the unit and most of everyone else, even though he's gotten religion and preaches every Sunday on our cable circuit. He makes sure all in his congregation fear two things: God and Dan Crawford."

"Let me test out those two," Frank said. "If I need more, I'll stop back."

The officer leaned over to the escort guard.

"I'm going to open Canton's cell first. Be at his door with these visitors when I open him up. Signal when you get to Crawford's."

The escort guard gestured for Frank and Alex to follow him into the austere corridor.

*　　*　　*

Buck Canton, easily six-foot-five, stood when his door slid open and glared at the trio outside his cell.

"It's too early for my shower," Canton said.

"These men have come from San Diego to talk to you," the guard said.

"I didn't lose anything in San Diego," Canton said. "They look like cops."

"We are cops, Mr. Canton," Frank said. "Want to discuss a great opportunity for you."

"Gonna sell me swamp land in Florida?" Canton said and laughed, his foul breath assaulting Frank's nostrils.

"How about we have a sit and discuss it?"

"I had to fire my decorator, but I reckon we can make do with what's here."

Canton took a seat on his stainless steel toilet and pointed Frank to his bunk. Frank sat on the edge of the rectangular shelf that passed for a bed, while Alex and the guard stood at the open door.

"There's a good chance you can spend your days free on a tropical island."

"If you came all this way to bullshit me, you can cart your blue ass outa here and head back south."

"This is not bullshit. Instead of being in this concrete casket you could be in a hammock on a sandy beach watching the sunset and chewing on fresh coconut."

Canton rolled his eyes and smiled.

"What? I get to go there for a week, then turn my body over to an organ harvester?"

"You can stay there as long as you live. Other inmates will opt to go with you. You can govern

185

yourselves, fish in the Pacific, hunt game, grow crops, swim in the ocean, and never, ever see or hear a guard."

Canton laughed.

"What's the catch? Gotta be a catch."

"There is one. You can't ever leave the island and come back here."

"Hell, Ace, I can't ever leave *here*."

"Well, I brought along drawings of what we intend to build."

Frank took the manila envelope from Alex and removed the color sketches of the fully-operational island. Canton looked over the drawings and shook his head.

"This is unbelievable. But I smell a rat," Canton said.

"What have you got to lose, Buck?" Frank asked. "You happy here? You like being in this cell twenty-three hours every day? The closest thing you get to freedom is an hour or two a day out there on the dog run. What's the matter? You afraid of being free?"

"I ain't afraid of shit."

"Then you'll be in favor of this idea when it comes to a vote?"

"Maybe. I don't know …"

"This whole idea is going to be broadcast to the entire population of this unit today, but I need a leader for it to go forward. A man with guts and respect among the inmates. That leader is you. The warden himself endorsed you as the top gun in this facility."

"Old man Griswold said that?" Canton asked.

Frank appealed to Alex.

"What did the warden say, Alex?"

"Exactly the words you just said," Alex said.

"Give it some serious thought, Buck," Frank said. "You're not an animal. You deserve a decent way to live your life. A life in freedom."

Frank stepped over to Canton and extended his hand. Buck rose and shook with Frank.

"They better not want any of my organs on this island," Canton said.

"I can assure you of that," Frank said. "Thanks for your time. We'll be talking to you."

Frank, Alex, and the guard stepped into the middle of the corridor as the guard pressed a button on his shoulder microphone.

"We're clear of 119," the guard said low.

The door to Buck Canton's cell slid closed. The far-away look in Canton's eyes lingered in Frank's mind as they proceeded through the corridor. It reminded him of the longing eyes of animals at a rescue kennel.

*   *   *

Dan Crawford's cell was an exact duplicate of Canton's. Frank stepped inside the cell when the door fully opened. Crawford, a black man of about thirty, rose the nearly seven feet from his bunk and stared down at his visitor.

"I'm Frank Dugan," Frank said.

"I know who you are," Crawford said. "We have TV now."

"I'm here to offer you a way to live out your life on a beautiful Pacific island."

Frank extended the pack of pictures.

"You could start a sweet little church there," Frank said as Crawford pored over the pictures.

"I have a television ministry here."

"The one I propose lets you see your congregation, speak directly to them, bless them by your presence in person."

"You have no idea how much I've prayed for something like this."

"Really? That's an incredible coincidence that here we are discussing the exact same thing."

"What we're discussing is that both you and me are full of the devil's deceiving shit."

Frank dropped his head.

Crawford said, "My people hand me lies every time I encounter them, and yet they profess that they love the Lord, that they are truly saved, and believe unquestionably in God the Father. Then they lie their asses off when it's to their advantage, when it's convenient. And now you come here with this line of crap. Why would I believe anything you say, when I don't believe most of what my own people say?"

"It's about faith," Frank said. "Isn't that what you sell, preacher? 'Now faith is the assurance of things hoped for, the conviction of things not seen.'"

"Hebrews 11. I'm impressed, detective."

"All I'm asking for is a fair look at what we're proposing."

"And why, of all the cons in this maximum security prison, would you be laying this on me?"

"This whole idea is going to be broadcast to the entire population of this unit today, but I need a leader for it to go forward. A man with guts and respect among the inmates. That leader is you. The warden himself endorsed you as the top gun in this facility."

"I'm sure," Crawford said, smiling.

Frank looked to Alex.

"What did the warden say, Alex?"

"Exactly the words you just said," Alex said.

"Your word as a Christian?"

"You have it."

"You'll give us this deal straight? Even the negative aspects? No lies?"

"I'm better than George Washington, Dan. He couldn't tell a lie. I can, but I won't."

"I'll watch your TV show. Good God, it's gotta be better than Brady Bunch reruns."

*   *   *

189

Over the next three months, Frank carried his message to every correctional institution in California that held convicts, who had no chance of ever seeing release. Complete information packets and brochures were distributed to every long-timer or death row inmate in the entire state. Frank equated it with a media blitz, the ultimate real estate pitch, designed to sell the island facility.

The ballots were administered by each prison and carefully overseen by an independent agency similar to the Price-Waterhouse company that handled and maintained the secrecy of the voting on the motion picture Academy Awards. The opportunity for institutional bias could skew the results in favor of passage, since facility administrators and local politicians were heavily in favor of reducing their inmate populations and their attendant soaring costs, which now had crept over $50,000 per prisoner. Strict oversight would be the order for the entire voting process.

By Thanksgiving, the voting was tallied and the majority of the results were forwarded to Martin Dimino in Washington where his senate bill lay, awaiting either a tie-breaking majority, or a defeat, leaving the entire concept of a correctional island dead, perhaps never to be resuscitated.

Frank's phone rang at the Dimino beach house.

"Hi, Marty," Frank said, anxiety in his voice.

"I have most of the voting results. The votes from Pelican Bay are still out," Marty said. "There's a lively debate going on and Warden Griswold has asked for more time. He wanted to know if we'd be willing to come to the prison and answer more questions the inmates have. It might help."

"I'll go, if you go."

"I'll be in San Diego tonight," Marty said. "I'll get us a government plane and we'll leave first thing tomorrow."

"The votes. What do we have so far?"

"We have a defeat. We're minus 897 votes."

"I pitched this idea with everything I had," Frank said.

"I know you did, Frank, No one could've done more."

"With all the negative votes, can we expect the naysayers to accept going to the island if it passes?"

"If we succeed with a winning outcome, only the ones who want to go will get to go. This first wave of inmates could be in the five-to-six thousand range, which is about all I'd want to test in our trial debut."

"Looks like we may not have to worry about that."

"Come on. Put on your best salesman's face for the discussion. They're going to ask tough questions. We need their votes."

"I'm not going to pad it, Marty," Frank said. "I'm laying it out straight."

"Tomorrow, 7 AM at Lindbergh Field," Marty said and ended the call.

Chapter 27

Rico Guzman paced the hand-painted Italian tiles of his restaurant-size kitchen floor. Trails of thick smoke from a Cuban panatela flowed behind him as he moved, filling the room with its pungent aroma. He slapped a folded newspaper against his thigh repeatedly. Ernie Gaither sat at an oak dining table, laboring to keep his sloppily-rolled marijuana joint lit.

"If that cop and his DA friend get this penal island bill passed, the government will hand over several million to bankroll the project," Guzman said, holding up the paper.

"So what, boss?" Gaither said, with the short reefer stuck to his lower lip. "It's for cons with no chance for parole."

"You're not seeing the far-reaching effects. All three-time losers will also be sent there. You and I already have two federal raps on our sheets."

"We did our time, so what's the beef?" Gaither said, snatching the burning roach that had glued itself to his mouth.

"That doesn't matter. One more conviction and we could end up on this coconut colony."

"We ain't into nothin' now," Gaither said. "We stay clean. Send other dudes to do the shady stuff."

"They only have to connect a few dots to come right back to us."

"So, what you wanna do?"

"I'll think of something."

Guzman threw the paper across the room.

"You always do, *jefe*," Gaither said and massaged his sore bottom lip.

Guzman stared out the bay window of the kitchen at the gently rolling sea outside, a view he always found peaceful and settling. Today he regarded it as an ominous, powerful hunter that wanted to trap him in on all sides.

"You're right," Guzman said. "I always find an answer."

*   *   *

Twenty-six inmates seated at tables in the dining room at Pelican Bay wore their toughest faces and burned their eyes into Warden James Griswold as he stood at the front of a room the size of a military mess hall. Helmeted guards lined its perimeter and outnumbered the prisoners two-to-one. Frank Dugan and Marty Dimino sat at a table behind the warden, studying each inmate's body language for signs of indifference, hostility, or alpha leadership. Two men in the special audience stood out above all others in the latter category: Dan Crawford and Buck Canton.

"I'll get right to the point," Warden Griswold said. "Here today is United States Senator Martin Dimino and Detective Frank Dugan of the San Diego Police Department. A few of you have already met the detective."

An inmate in the back said, "Some of us met him long before he came to visit."

General laughter broke out among the inmates, and the warden acknowledged the comment with a terse smile. As the interruption subsided, Frank and Marty unzipped a large art portfolio lying face-down on their table.

Griswold continued.

"As most of you are aware, they have proposed to Congress an alternative method for state and federal corrections. It will primarily concern inmates like yourselves who are here for life without possibility of parole, or sitting on death row. You've requested a chance to speak with these two men about questions you have regarding this innovative and exciting opportunity to serve your terms in the freedom of an island off our coast. I will turn the meeting over to the senator at this time."

Marty Dimino rose and stepped to the first row of inmates.

"I know that you've had a chance to look at and consider what my colleague Frank Dugan outlined for you weeks ago. We understand that you may have questions, and that's why we're here today. To answer them as best we can. Ask away."

A huge man in the middle of the group stood and stared at Marty.

"Suppose I go to this island of yours and decide to break bad and kill me a couple of turkeys that get on my nerves?"

"You can do what you want," Marty said. "Remember, you'll be establishing a completely new society. If you break the rules that your new community sets up, you may have to face the majority who made those rules. They may decide to kill *you*.

The big man laughed. "Yeah, right. That'll be the fuckin' day."

Frank jumped up and took a position next to Marty.

"It was other people who put you in here," Frank said, "and continue to keep you in here ... until you die. If you're so tough, let's see you leave."

Everyone turned toward the big man, who slowly retook his seat.

"Don't ever underestimate the power of the little guy," Frank said, "especially if he outnumbers you. A bunch of tiny army ants could bring the toughest of us to our knees. It was bad judgment and disregard for the rules that put you here. If you go to Prescott Island, you're going to have to play by rules too, but they'll be *your* rules. It's a new chance for many of you. A better chance, I'll wager, than many of you gave your victims."

Murmuring and unrest rippled through the inmates. Frank stared them down.

"You'll find, after four men murdered my family, that I'm not much at mincing words, but I'm also fair. And I don't like a lot of bullshit."

Dan Crawford stood.

"Your literature says we can fish and swim and have a gymnasium, a ball field, and a lot of other nice things. What happens if one group or another of us decides they want *all* that good stuff for themselves? What happens if we have to go to war with each other?"

"My suggestion?" Marty said. "Keep the peace. War has always accomplished one major thing: it kills the bravest and the best of both sides. A war will leave a battlefield of bodies that you will have to deal with, or be no better than pigs that sleep in their own dirt."

Silence. No one spoke or stirred.

"This first group that will be volunteering to go to the island will total a population no larger than the fans that fill a medium-size hockey arena," Marty said. "It's a beautifully workable size to govern and live in harmony. You will be supplied everything you'll need to make your lives pleasant. Not merely bearable, but pleasant. Look at your present quarters, and then look at this."

Marty pulled a brightly-colored picture poster from the portfolio and held it high. The twenty-by-twenty-eight-inch photo depicted a tropical island that one might mistake for a travel ad for Barbados with modern buildings in the background."

The faces of the audience softened, a few even smiled.

"My cell don't have no palm trees," an older inmate said.

"We go there," another said, "we gonna see somethin' like that?"

"*Exactly* like this," Marty said and propped up the poster on the table with its fold-out easel.

"Who going to build them buildin's?" a tall, thin man asked.

"You are," Frank said. "And we're going to provide you with the materials, the instruction, and the tools you'll need to do it."

"How 'bout TV?" another asked.

"You will have closed circuit television with DVD movies at first," Frank said. "Later we may bring in a secured satellite TV link for you."

"So we will have electricity?" an inmate directly in front of Marty said.

"There will be wind generators, solar electric sources, and power supplied by the attendant ships nearby," Marty said.

"Any women?"

"Only on the DVDs and the porn channels," Frank said.

"Look at the bright side," Buck Canton said. "It'll be a great place to be gay."

Marty and Frank exchanged glances.

"What happens if we decide to go for this idea?" Crawford asked.

Frank pointed to the poster displayed on the table. "We all win."

*   *   *

When Frank and Marty returned home to the beach house, there was a surprise waiting. Charly Stone was reading a newspaper in her Jaguar on the right side of the driveway. Marty parked his car at the curb and the two men closed in on Charly's driver side window.

"Thank God," Charly said. "The bartenders are back."

"What's your pleasure?" Marty said and bent over and kissed her, while Frank opened the garage and stepped toward the house.

"No sex stuff until I go to bed," Frank said.

"No sex until I get a drink," Charly said.

"Keep your clothes on," Frank said as he passed through the door. "I'll pour us something tasty."

Frank headed to the bar, set up three glasses, and hunted for the scotch. As he pulled the Johnny Walker bottle from the bar rail, a glinting object across the room drew his eye. He set the bottle on the bar, moved to the sofa, and stared at a metal object peeking out from between the seat cushions.

Marty and Charly entered the room and paused when they saw Frank's frozen stare at the sofa.

"Drinks are at the bar," Charly said, "not on the sofa."

"What is it, Frank?" Marty asked.

Frank plucked a tissue from the box on a side table and used it to pick up an object partially concealed in the seats of the sofa.

Marty and Charly moved in closer to Frank.

Frank held up the gold locket, its gold chain pinched in the tissue.

"It was Amy's," Frank said.

"Jesus," Marty said and began a check of the points of entry to the house.

"Sit down, Frank," Charly said. "I'll get the drinks."

Frank eased himself into a leather chair next to the sofa, while Charly tossed her purse onto a pub stool and busied herself at the bar.

"See if you can find a Zip-Loc bag," Frank said to Charly. "I need to get this to forensics."

Charly hurried into the kitchen. The sound of drawers and cabinet doors opening and slamming shut poured out from the kitchen.

Marty returned and stood in front of Frank.

"No signs of any break-in," Marty said. "No alarms were tripped, no video. Bastards must be ghosts."

"Or will be," Frank said as Charly darted over to Frank with a small plastic bag and held it open in front of him.

"I need to get this to the lab," Frank said, dropping the locket into the bag and rising.

"Before you go," Charly said, moving to her purse, "I have pictures for you from the island."

Marty said, "I'll go over the sofa and the rest of the house to see if there's any evidence of a visitor."

Charly handed Frank an envelope.

"The photos of that animal's footprint are in there," Charly said.

"I'll go see Dr. Kaufmann at the zoo," Frank said. "She'll know what it is."

"See Judd Kemp as soon as you can," Marty said. "He's been tailing our four suspects since trial. May have something to report."

"Next, they'll be charging us for harassment," Frank said. "I told Judd not to do that."

"He's careful," Marty said. "He assured me that they'll never spot the tails. He uses several teams and changes their cars and clothing. Old school pro."

"I got a message from Judd about new evidence from the Huntington Beach jewelry store heist," Frank said. "A couple of the Guzman gang may have left clues."

"Meet us at Harry's tonight," Marty said as Frank exited the room and shot for the garage.

*   *   *

Frank drove to the San Diego zoo and parked his
Bronco next to the reptile pavilion. Inside the
facility's office was Dr. Marta Kaufmann, the
foremost herpetologist in southern California and
perhaps the world. Many of her colleagues had stated
in print that what Marta didn't know about creatures
with scales wasn't worth knowing.

"Good morning, detective," Marta said as Frank
entered her cluttered space. "What do we have this
time? An anaconda that swallowed a material
witness?"

"Nothing as much fun as that," Frank said and
shook her outstretched hand. "I took digital photos of
a claw print and printed them out at my computer. The
actual size was over twelve inches in length. Not sure
what made it."

Frank slid out the photos from a manila envelope
and handed them to Marta. She pored over them for
several seconds and dwelled on a particular one. She
looked up at Frank.

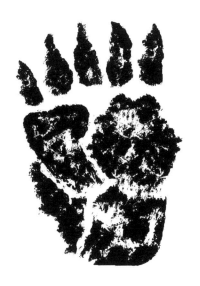

"Where did you get these?" she asked.

"An island about a hundred miles northwest of here."

"The animal that made this print is a long way from home."

"Where's home?"

"Indonesia."

"How did one arrive just off our coast?"

"Good question," Marta said. "I suppose you want to know the facts about this interesting reptile."

"I do. Give me all you got."

"The print in that photo was made by a Komodo dragon, a large species of monitor lizard. A male can grow to ten feet in length and weigh more than two hundred pounds."

"Holy crap."

"It can sprint twelve miles an hour and track a scent more than three miles away. A mature Komodo can dive fifteen feet in water and climb trees to get to prey. It has a particularly nasty bite that inflicts its victim with highly infectious proteins, which will debilitate prey within hours."

"Oh, momma."

"The Komodo typically bites its prey and lets it go. No big fight to subdue it, which might serve to injure itself, knowing the wounded animal will succumb to the deadly saliva in a day or two. It then simply tracks the scent of the decaying or dead animal and makes a meal of it."

"I stood right in the spot where it ate a peacock," Frank said.

"Peacock? What is this island? A remote zoo?"

"It was once a resort a millionaire bought in the 1930s. He built a mansion on it and apparently imported animals that he found interesting to impress his guests. A regular Howard Hughes. The island's being considered as a prison for especially bad convicts."

"If there are Komodos breeding there, your convicts will need to be replenished regularly."

"Suppose there's only one?"

"How big is this island?"

"About thirty-two square miles."

"Then the convicts have a chance. They could kill the Komodo, but they're tough, fast, and wily. And the men would have to be extremely careful not to get bitten in the process."

"The men will have access to medical services," Frank said. "Provided by a U.S. Navy hospital ship."

"If they get bit by a Komodo dragon, they'll need it, and promptly."

"The dragon print was on the opposite side of this island, maybe four miles away. What happens if one of the inmates hikes there and gets bit far from the medical ship?"

Marta handed the photos back to Frank and said, "He gets the death sentence."

Chapter 28

Rico Guzman stood at a bar in his clubroom, a room that easily could have existed in the most elegant hotel in Ernest Hemingway's Havana. He decanted a long pour of Barrilito Especial rum into a crystal brandy snifter and brought it to his mouth and drank half of it.

Ernie Gaither played a solo pool game on a ten-foot mahogany billiard table lit by three shaded lamps lined in a row on a wrought iron chandelier.

A television announcer sat at his anchor desk and spoke directly to the camera.

"The big story tonight is again the latest developments in the penal island bill, which has been passed by the senate, a bill that is directly responsible for the United States being the proud new owner of a beautiful tropical island in the Pacific known as Prescott Island. All presently incarcerated California inmates on death row, or serving life with no possibility of parole, who opt to go there, will be transported to the island next month with the completion of preparatory work and the laying in of provisions. This will be the former resort's first occupancy since 1932."

Guzman drained the last drop of his rum and hurled his snifter at the TV set. The glass missed and smashed against the wall.

"*Chingate*, you fucking shyster lawyer," Guzman said. "Can you believe this shit? A fucking nothing, guinea son-of-a-bitch, and a mick flatfoot who used to put shoplifters in jail for his living, just got a bill passed in Congress that could have me eating coconut tacos the rest of my natural life."

Ernie stopped playing pool and stared at Guzman.

"The senator can't hurt us, boss," Gaither said. "He's got his ass stuck in Washington most of the time. And Frank Dugan is in to his neck with this prison island."

"Can't hurt me? What are you smoking, *pendejo*? Dugan's got the heat on me good. I'm under indictment for drug trafficking and he'll be planning his retirement at the beach. This beach. Not the one at that goddamned resort where I'll be going."

The television announcer continued.

"Our camera crews have not been allowed to film the island any closer than the perimeter of the armada of naval gunboats that encircle it. However, through the use of high-power telephoto lenses, Brad Lester and our on-site unit filed this report earlier today. Brad, what can you tell us?"

A man rising and falling on the deck of a naval assault vessel faced an unsteady camera, the ocean rolling in swells behind his balance-shifting legs. At the bottom of the frame, a super over the shot read:

Brad Lester at our nation's newest prison

"We've been here since early this afternoon, but this is as close as we're allowed to go. The island that has everyone talking lies only a hundred yards to my right," Brad said and gestured for the camera to follow where he pointed.

On the screen, a football field away lay a palm-treed island. Buildings stood inland from the beaches, and supply boats loaded large crates onto an open platform attached to a long, covered pier that extended several hundred feet out from the shore.

Brad continued his report.

"They say that the original exploring Vikings came back to their homeland expounding a wonderful new "green land" to those back home in an effort to glamorize the frozen wasteland so they could expand their world by settling real estate elsewhere. They didn't figure calling it "white land" would sell their idea. The United States will officially name this island behind me Prescott Island, for its former owner, but they have no need to glamorize it with an appealing name. Commensurate with its new purpose, the Prescott family occupancy here was the subject of legendary crime tales culminating in four mysterious deaths back in the 1930s. Deaths that still find their way into modern folklore and many barroom discussions."

The camera switched back to focus on Brad.

"Well, some may call it paradise, while others may label it hell, but whatever you think, it's now part of the USA. It may be Prescott Island to the government, but I'm told the inmates have another name for it. They simply call it 'The Resort,' the new home for thousands of prisoners, currently only from California, but if things go well, it may include convicts from every state in the union."

The camera panned the ocean around the island.

"The pretty blue waters between this Navy assault craft I'm standing on and the island itself are only lovely from the safety of this boat. They are infested with the highest density of man-eating sharks known anywhere in the world. Three lives have already been lost to them in the past few months while armed service people and civilian workers prepared the island for its new tenants."

"As you can see," Brad said, "You could be gazing at a vacation get-away in the Caribbean or south Pacific. Bali Hai comes to mind as I see this beautiful sunset occurring behind the coconut palms from the opposite side of this seemingly tropical Eden. The men who will be the first to populate this eight-mile piece of land may find it hard to believe that this will be their home, without a guard or a warden, and certainly without razor wire and electric fences."

The camera swung back to a full shot of Brad.

"This is Brad Lester reporting from ... "

Brad looks to his right, the camera follows his focus to the island and its swaying palms, now backlit by the orange ball of the sun.

"Resort Isle, America's newest ... prison? Maybe, after all, crime, in a strange way, actually *does* pay."

Guzman pressed a button on a remote control behind the bar and the TV clicked off.

"Time to pay a visit to a senator?" Gaither asked.

"Not yet. But if I get convicted, you make sure you reunite the detective with his wife and kids."

Chapter 29

Judd Kemp and Frank Dugan sat in Kemp's unmarked police car in the department's reserved lot. Kemp produced a 9-by-12 manila envelope.

"The video store clips from the jewelry store only showed the men wearing masks and hats," Judd said, "but the photos in here were taken from video footage shot from a miniature golf concession across the street."

"Why are we just getting these now?" Frank asked.

"The business owner was video-taping his six-year-old son playing putt-putt on the course. He recently got around to editing what he shot that day and discovered the robbery suspects were in the background leaving the jewelry store at the time of the robbery and murder of the proprietor. His tape is time- and date-coded. It's *that* day, all those months ago."

"They wore masks and hats," Frank said. "So what good are they?"

"Take a look," Judd said and handed Frank the envelope.

Frank opened the flap and withdrew several large photos.

"Well, ain't the beer cold," Frank said as he sifted through the photos. "They took off the hats and masks."

"Because they were on the street and didn't want to draw attention."

"It's Gaither, and one of the other guys who was in the courtroom."

"Look in the car parked where they're headed."

"I see two men, but I can only make out the driver."

"We need to work them separately. They'll turn on each other like eaglets in a nest."

"We can't try Gaither again," Frank said and stared out the passenger side window.

"We can sure as hell try the other ones," Judd said.

"Can we put together a case against all three?"

"They'll go down," Judd said. "Bingo, bango, bongo."

Frank studied the photos again, poring over each one as it played out in the escape sequence. He tucked the photos back in the envelope, then stared at Judd, who locked eyes with him.

"I'm not sure I like what I'm seeing," Judd said.

"You know me too well."

"You want Gaither."

"Forget trying the sonofabitch again."

*   *   *

Frank, dressed for sailing in khakis, a white polo shirt, and deck shoes, marched up the wooden boardwalk to the harbor master's office at the enormous boating complex of Marina del Rey. As he approached the office door, a man in his sixties stepped out.

"Been expecting you, Mr. Dugan," the man said.

"You're Captain James Fiske?"

"I am."

"You have something to show me from the insurance company?"

"I do," Fiske said and directed Frank toward one of the long piers that extended out into the bay from the boardwalk.

At the end of the pier, Fiske stopped and pointed at a cabin boat over thirty feet in length. The name, painted in gold letters on the dark mahogany stern, was *Topaz*.

"She's yours if you want 'er," Fiske said. "The insurance company said you were looking for a replacement for your lost sailboat. Well, I figured you might be interested in taking a look at one that could be purchased in the ballpark of what they're willing to pay. Mind you, the owner'd be parting with her at a loss. She's worth a sight more, but he's getting too old to go through all the haggling to sell a big boat, especially these days when boat selling ain't up there with peddling fancy cars in popularity. It ain't a sailboat, but if you'd consider changing your luck on a power craft, well …"

"How come you know about my insurance company's claims?"

"You moored your sailboat here in my marina. I'm the harbormaster of this here marina. Harbor masters know everything about their boats, bowsprit to stern, topsail to keel."

"How old is it?"

"She was built in 1959.

"And you know that because you're the harbormaster?"

"No. Reason I know is, she's mine."

"So you wangled a deal with the insurance adjuster."

"Not a deal yet," Fiske said and squinted at Frank in the bright sun. "That'll be up to you."

"Well, what they offered wouldn't get me anything much better."

"She's a fine boat and would be a good investment. I kept her up for all these years, spit-polished and hand-rubbed, and every year I went under her to remove her barnacles and paint her bottom."

"Why are you selling her?"

"Just got remarried. First wife passed on ten years ago. Loved the water, that one. My new one, not so much. Only water she likes is in a bathtub and a chaser. And I'm getting a bit too old to haul out and go fishing anymore."

"Mind if I go aboard?" Frank asked.

"Certainly not, sir. You go check her out, and if you like what you see, I'll take you out for a spin on 'er."

Frank smiled and took a long stride onto the aft deck of the beautifully-kept mahogany cabin cruiser. The older man followed and unlocked the cabin door. Frank stepped inside and gave the interior a cursory inspection, while Fiske went over more of the boat's selling points.

"She's a Wheeler 34-footer, and'll do about twenty-three knots with her 540 horsepower, twin Crusader engines going balls to the wall. Got everything a person could want, full luxury, I'd say. Air conditioning, complete line of safety equipment, sleeps four, and she'll hold 120 gallons of fuel for a goodly trip without having to stop for a refill. Full galley, got a nice head. Most ladies like that. My new bride, not so much. Got radar, GPS, all the instruments you'll ever need. Engines barely have seventy hours on 'em. She's been loved and spoiled like a cherished daughter."

"*Topaz*?" Frank said.

"My first wife's birthstone."

"I can see the love," Frank said. "She's not a sailboat, but I think I'll take her."

"Sailboat's what got you in trouble, son. May be time to try a nice pampered powerboat."

"You may be right, Captain Fiske."

"Since you're a nice lad, I'm going to throw in the slip."

"Boat slips here are expensive. How are you going to do that?"

"With power comes privileges. I'm the harbormaster, sonny," Fiske said and grinned like Alice's Cheshire cat.

*   *   *

The beach house phone was ringing when Frank entered the door. He rushed to it and yanked the receiver off the cradle.

"Yes?"

"I thought maybe we could make a deal," the all too familiar voice of Rico Guzman said.

"No deals, Guzie."

"Don't be like that, detective, until you hear me out."

"Worried about your indictment?"

"There has to be something you want that I can supply."

"All I want is you and your boys far away in a place where you can't come back."

"Like your fancy resort?"

"That'd work for me."

"Wouldn't you like to know who killed your family? Know for sure who did it?"

"I'm listening," Frank said and sank into the recliner.

"I believe you call it *quid pro quo*. Tit for tat. I give you what you want, and you make sure I don't spend my life on *la isla de tiburones*."

"I'm still listening."

"Well, do we have a deal, or not?"

"Shoot."

"I'm sure you already know that Ernie Gaither and those three other *idiotas* did it, but I'm confirming it."

"Didn't you send them?" Frank said.

"No, no, on the eyes of my mother, I did not tell them to do what they did. They went way beyond what I asked them to do. As I said, idiots."

"You hired the idiots. That makes you responsible."

"Come on, detective. You've had people do things for you that didn't turn out the way you wanted."

"They never killed a woman and two helpless children."

217

"I'm so sorry that ever happened. I truly am. What did I have to gain by killing your family?"

"So you figure this drug indictment is going to go bad for you? Can't your barrister boy Malay get you off?"

"We haven't been close lately."

"That's too bad. I have to admit, he was good."

"But we have a deal now, you and I? So everything's going to be okay."

"Look, Rico, let's get something straight. I pushed for Prescott Island for one reason: to keep convicted criminals from getting back into society to continue their activity. *All* recidivist criminals. It's not just you I'm after."

"How many of them can make life a lot easier for you? How many can remove all your financial worries from now on? You deserve to have a better life than a cop's salary can give you. What do you say? Can we come to a compromise here?"

"Do you remember two years ago when that guy kidnapped the bank president's family and barricaded himself in the their home in Carmel Valley?"

"Yeah. Was in the news big time. You had a long standoff with him. Saw it on TV."

"Well, he wanted a limo, with two million dollars in small bills, to take him to the airport where a private jet would fly him out of the country where he would release his hostages."

"Yeah, I remember."

218

"Not everything was televised and put in the papers. What you don't know is what I said to him."

"You're right. I don't remember that."

"I got in close to him. Close enough to whisper. I promised him everything he asked for, and when the limo drove up, we showed him the money. People were shocked that I gave in to his demands. They cursed me, said I was crazy, wanted my badge. Later, he came out holding a gun on the three hostages and shuffled his way toward the limo."

"Then he fell and all the cops jumped him. Something like that."

"I had ordered a sharpshooter take him out. An ambulance took him away, but he was dead before he hit the ground."

"What's the point here?"

"The point is, I made a promise to him that I had no intention of keeping. I would have promised him the planet Mars, if he'd asked for it."

"So your word's no good," Guzman said.

"My word to lowlife like you is no good."

"I told you what you wanted to know. Now keep our deal, goddamnit."

"Enjoy the coconuts and the ocean breezes, Rico." Frank said and hung up the phone.

Chapter 30

Marty Dimino returned home to do his senatorial state work, of which California had an endless abundance. While the Prescott Island issue still topped every media outlet, the Golden State had other pressing concerns with fresh water resources, illegal immigration, and natural disaster preparation, to name but a few. But recent polls indicated that recidivist crime was the one problem that people feared more than a drought, a worker without a green card, or an earthquake. The "Resort," as it had come to be known among the criminal community, was making final arrangements for its first arrivals in one week, and Marty wanted to be there to observe the auspicious event. From what was being bandied in the news, Marty was certain that everyone in the world would be casting attention on the opening.

Marty hit a speed dial number on his phone.

"Detective Dugan," responded the familiar voice.

"I'm home from the Washington wars," Marty said. "Ready for a trip to the Resort?"

"Couldn't keep me away."

"How are things at the beach?"

"You could use caller ID on your phones."

"It's a beach house with a non-pub number."

"Didn't stop Rico Guzman from calling."

"Caller ID's on the answering machine in the kitchen."

"I'll check it later."

"I see the bastard's back in court."

"Yeah. And if he hasn't poisoned the jury, he may be making the trip to the island with us."

"How tight is the case against?" Marty asked.

"Never tight enough to suit me, but I've got a tip to follow that may put the last nail in his coffin."

"Will you be able to get it into discovery in time?"

"I'll know by tonight," Frank said. "I have a meeting with a guy in La Jolla."

"If you need me, I'll be at Charly's"

"Heard about you, hound dog."

"She told me you tried to feed her to the sharks and scuttled your boat."

"That's why you never can trust eye witnesses—"

"Because they only see what they want to see."

"Bought another boat. Cabin cruiser."

"So you dumped the sluggy sailboat for the insurance and bought one you really like?"

"If you knew how much insurance they gave me, you'd laugh at that statement."

"You be careful. Take back-up tonight."

"Yeah, yeah. Maybe see you later at Harry's?" Frank said.

"If Charly doesn't kill me with affection."

"I'll check the obits."

Frank crossed to the kitchen and scrolled through the caller ID function on the answering machine. The calls from Guzman were listed as "blocked." Frank picked up the kitchen phone from the wall and punched in a number. After two rings Frank responded to the person who answered.

"This is Detective Frank Dugan, San Diego Police. I need to determine the source of a blocked phone number…"

*   *   *

Dwayne Pinkney and Scottie Fisher hunkered low in the dark among power boats hitched to trailers and strut-supported sailboats on the acre of land adjacent to the Marina del Rey harbor. Dwayne peeked out at regular intervals to see when the harbor office closed for the night. He didn't have to wait long.

"The old guy's leaving," Dwayne said.

"For good?" Scottie asked, adjusting the black backpack harnessed to his shoulders.

"He put out the lights and locked the back door. Another minute and we're good to go."

Dwayne stepped out and checked for activity in all directions. He waited until the old man left the area and disappeared in the parking lot a block away.

"No one else in sight," Dwayne said. "Let's get the keys."

Dwayne and Scottie slinked out from their concealment and ambled over to the rear of the harbor office. A shaded lamp on a utility pole shone on a twenty-foot circle of boardwalk planks in front of the office door, then diffused into darkness. Dwayne quietly worked on the back door of the office while Scottie kept watch. Within a minute, Dwayne had the door open and stepped inside the weathered building. Scottie followed and eased the door closed behind him.

The outside light in front of the office illuminated a wall rack with sets of keys that hung on cup hooks. Dwayne scanned the tags on the keys and stopped at a set with "Wheeler" printed on it. He checked outside for any activity, then plucked the Wheeler keys from the rack. Both men exited by the back door and closed it as they light-footed to the long pier a few yards away that intersected the boardwalk.

A the end of the pier, they arrived at the *Topaz* and stealthily stepped aboard.

"Where do we put it?" Scottie asked, shrugging the backpack.

"Under the deck here," Dwayne said and quietly fitted a key from the stolen set into the lock on the cabin. He snooped inside to make sure the cabin was unoccupied.

Seconds later, they were pulling open the engine access hatch and panning small flashlights across the blue V-8 engines. Dwayne knelt on the deck, leaned over, and studied the limited space within the compartment.

"Give me the unit," Dwayne said.

Scottie stuck his penlight in his mouth, unzipped the backpack, withdrew a bundle of wired electronics attached to a brick red block of Semtex explosive, and handed it to his partner. Dwayne hung the package on the port engine, near the feed line from the gas tank on that side of the boat.

Dwayne searched under the cockpit for the wire that connected the depth finder display on the instrument panel above to the transducer in the bottom of the hull.

"Got it," Dwayne said. "Hand me the wire cutters."

Scottie fumbled through the backpack, found the tool, and gave it to Dwayne.

Dwayne scratched an inch of insulation off the boat's depth finder wire and taped his own wire to the exposed copper. He neatly tucked the wires back under the panel and returned his attention to the engines. He set a dial on his analog depth gauge, pressed a button, and installed it beside the port engine with duct tape.

"I hope we're not in water deeper than 900 feet," Dwayne said with a smile.

"Why's that?" Scottie asked.

"That's when this baby goes off. You might say it's an actual 'depth charge,'" Dwayne said and chuckled. "It works on echo-sounding from a transducer that interprets the echoes' timing to determine the depth under the boat."

"Aha."

Scottie smiled and bobbled a few nods, but his puzzled expression looked to Dwayne like he had just lectured him on the relationship between string theory and plutonium nuclear fission.

The two men closed the engine compartment as they had found it, locked up the cabin, and scrambled onto the aft deck, where they furtively searched the pier for any signs of witnesses to their visit. Seeing none, they hopped off the *Topaz* and quick-stepped along the pier to the boardwalk like Olympic speed-walkers.

They re-entered the harbor office, where Dwayne replaced the borrowed set of keys. They reversed their actions, secured the back door and, in moments, were one with the night.

Chapter 31

The Pac-Life Maritime Insurance Company settled Frank's claim and cut him a check with enough money to buy James Fiske's cabin cruiser. Frank had the morning to himself and wanted to take the *Topaz* to San Diego to have Marty's trusted marine mechanic check out his new purchase. The test ride on the boat went smoothly and the Topaz was amazingly responsive for an older vessel. Frank believed Captain Fiske's glowing assessment of the Wheeler, but since it had been sitting at the marina for so many months unused, he thought it best to have it examined by an expert.

Frank got the papers for the boat, his keys from the harbor office, and boarded his new ocean-going transport. He vented the bilge to remove any potentially-explosive gas fumes, cranked the twin Crusaders to throbbing life, and motored out of the marina at five miles-per-hour.

The *Topaz* cut the water smoothly as Frank steered her south hugging the coast and throttled her up to cruising speed of twelve knots. He set the depth alarm at fifty feet, kept her in less than a hundred feet of water, and carefully monitored the depth finder's readings to keep an eye on any rising reefs or hard sand shoals that could claw at the boat's underbelly.

At 11:12 AM, Frank slowed to the San Diego marina's 5 MPH "no wake" limit and idled into Embarcadero Park North and tied up at the long pier. Frank had radioed ahead to Jeff Swenson, the marine mechanic Marty Dimino had highly recommended to check out the *Topaz*. The mechanic stood waiting at the dock where Frank had been instructed to moor his boat.

"Well, I see she made it here, detective, with no billowing smoke," Jeff said. "Always a good sign."

"Took to the water like a porpoise," Frank said and jumped onto the dock.

"A power boat like this is bit different from sailing a sloop."

"I'll say. Lot noisier, but faster."

"Any trouble finding this place?"

"None at all. Your directions were great, and I'm familiar with the Embarcadero."

"I'll take good care of her, Frank," Jeff said. "Have her ready for you in a couple of hours."

Frank handed Jeff the keys.

"Take your time. I'm going to grab a coffee at the Barnacle," Frank said, "then drop in to see a friend at the Coast Guard office."

The long walk to Buster's Barnacle Restaurant felt good, almost exhilarating. A lot of Frank's police work stuck him behind a desk, often sitting, phone-bound for hours. The brisk strides along the quay loosened him up and exercised muscles that had all but lost their endurance memory. He pondered his fitness as he marched at a quick pace toward the business section of the marina. At twenty-seven, he considered himself too young to be going to flab from living a sedentary lifestyle. He wasn't a lie-about, and resolved to work out more, like he did in his baseball days.

After getting his coffee and going back outside, Frank decided to call Rico Guzman, for no other reason than to let him know his "blocked" calls could be unblocked and deciphered.

"Yeah," a gruff voice said on the other end of Frank's call.

"Rico there?" Frank said.

"Who's this?"

"Frank Dugan."

"Oh, the cop with the dead family," the voice said, becoming more recognizable to Frank.

"Mr. Gaither?"

"Yep."

"Get Guzman on the phone, shithead."

"Hey, you can't talk to me like—"

"I'll talk to you like the piece of crap you are," Frank said, his blood boiling.

"He ain't here. He's in court." Gaither said, then the line went dead.

Frank pressed a key on his cell and stuffed it in his back pocket. He sat facing the marina and sipped his coffee as his pulse eased back to under a hundred beats.

The marina Coast Guard office was sub-unit of the larger USCG station a mile away, but Frank had made friends with a chief petty officer there during the murder investigation of Senator McAllister. The chief, Don Berkley, was still piecing together evidence from the fateful day of the assassination and had been a steady supplier of information to Judd Kemp and Frank from day one.

The case was far from closed, but suspicions ran high that Rico Guzman ordered the assassination, trying to remove heat from his drug dealings because the senator was closing in on him like a bad storm.

A photo extracted from a distant marina video cam on the day of the assassination had the resolution of oatmeal and was nearly useless had it not been for the distinctive red St. Louis Cardinal baseball hat the assassin wore.

Rico Guzman kept his 150-foot yacht, named *El Mago*, at the marina, which had been kept under surveillance for months, and well before the murder of the senator. In a review of earlier video footage of activity on and around the yacht, there appeared a man wearing a red cap similar to the one seen in the assassination footage. The man could have been there for innocent reasons, and no weapon was visible in the surveillance video. Nevertheless, he was a "person of interest," which when translated into cop-speak meant "He's probably our guy."

The man in the yacht footage, later identified as Mitch Davis, turned out to be a suspect implicated in the Dugan family massacre. Frank and Chief Berkley "liked" him a lot … for several reasons. If Rico Guzman could protect Mitch from being charged, he would be protecting himself from complicity as well. Now that he was under indictment for drug trafficking, a conviction for any felony would be as good as a murder rap. Any major crime added to his former convictions, would spell a trip to the Resort for life. If he skated on the current charges, he would truly be *El Mago*, The Magician.

Frank approached the Coast Guard office and was met by a chief yeoman sitting outside enjoying the perfect weather.

"Chief Berkley around," Frank asked.

"Out on patrol," the yeoman said. "Be back in a couple of hours."

"Do you know where he's patrolling?"

"Straight out, due west. He's got a lead on a drug submarine. One of those homemade fiberglass jobs that's hard to detect on radar."

"I've heard about them. What's he going to do if he spots one?"

"He's on a chopper with one of our boats nearby. Those subs can't go deep, so once the guys above lock onto it, they'll send out a kill-or-capture craft."

"Sweet," Frank said and cast his gaze seaward. "Maybe I'll go find my friend out there."

"Good luck, sir. Just don't be traveling in a miniature submarine."

"I'll keep that in mind," Frank said, saluted a thank-you to the yeoman, and headed back to the Barnacle for a refill on his coffee.

*   *   *

Jeff Swenson started the engines on the *Topaz* and studied the instrument panel's gauges. Satisfied that all instruments appeared to be working properly, he filled in a preliminary work report and checked all the boxes that pertained to his work thus far with satisfactory marks and notations. He folded the work order and tucked it behind the wheel on the port side of the helm. Then he pulled up the wood cover above the engine compartment that served as a portion of the deck of the cockpit. He checked for adequate ventilation at various points around the compact engine compartment containing the twin Crusader 270 engines. All seemed to be in order.

He knelt, leaned in close, and observed the starboard engine, listening for a smooth idle and watching for any unwanted vibration. Next he did the same for the port engine. Lastly, he leaned his head between the engines to look beneath them for excess water in the bilge. It was there that he noticed something out of place. A foreign device protruded from under the engine, a device he was certain didn't belong there. Jeff leaned in farther, almost toppling, but steadied himself and gasped.

It was a bomb. A big one.

Jeff sprang to his feet, cut the engines, and light-stepped quickly away from the compartment. He leapt from the boat and sprinted down the marina pier toward the concessions.

*   *   *

The time seemed to have flown for Frank as he returned to the *Topaz* and searched for his mechanic. Onboard, he noticed the engine compartment cover lying open, revealing his two blue engines.

"Jeff? It's Frank. You still here?"

No answer.

Frank saw the keys dangling from the ignition and his eye caught the folded paper behind the wheel and removed it. The notations on the paper looked like Jeff had completed his check-up of the boat, but no charges were entered for his services. It struck him as strange, but Frank was considerably more baffled by the open engine compartment.

Must've had an emergency back at his shop, Frank thought.

A few yards down the pier, Frank spied a sailboat with two men working to replace a light atop the forty-foot mast. One man was high atop the mast on a boatswain's chair, while the other steadied its halyard on deck. Frank hopped off the *Topaz* and walked over to the sailboat.

"Excuse me, gentlemen. Have either of you seen the man who was working on my boat?" Frank said pointing at the *Topaz*.

"Matter of fact," the man on the mast said, pointing toward the business district on the land, "he went that way like he was shot out of a cannon."

"He say anything?"

"Not that I could understand," the mast man said. "You hear what he was yelling about, Tim?"

Tim on deck shook his head. "Something about us getting away from the dock ... not sure."

"Thanks anyway," Frank said and lumbered back to the Wheeler.

Before he boarded, he took a long look up and down the pier. Then he stepped aboard and jammed the folded work report in his back pocket with his cell phone. Inside the cockpit, he closed the engine cover and secured it, started the Crusaders to let them idle, and checked his gauges. He then cast off the mooring lines and slowly pulled away from the pier.

After navigating out of San Diego Bay, past the sheltered area of the marina, Frank aimed the *Topaz* west. It was time for a little shakedown cruise, or to use Captain Fiske's words, "put her balls to the wall." The powerful engines roared their approval at being given their head and jumped to its top speed of twenty-three knots, spraying a frothy wake like a jet spewing a vapor trail.

The channel leading off the coast quickly dropped off to over 600 feet as the *Topaz* surged into the open Pacific.

Chapter 32

Jeff Swenson guided the van carrying the San Diego Police Department's bomb unit down the long pier, its siren blaring and strobe lights flashing in dizzying sequence. The van halted next to the slip where the *Topaz* had been. Jeff jumped from the vehicle and shaded his eyes to search the surface of the bay.

"He's gone," Jeff said. "I can't even see the boat. Dear Jesus, he's gone on that floating bomb."

"We've got the Coast Guard on the line," a heavily-padded officer yelled from the truck. "They're sending help from two directions. One patrol is already out there, plus a chopper."

Jeff placed his palms on his knees, hung his head, and hoped he wouldn't hear a distant explosion.

* * *

Frank Dugan saw the Coast Guard helicopter racing straight for him, low over the water. Farther out, a Coast Guard patrol boat pitched and whapped waves as it set a course for his boat. Frank watched them intently as they approached, but a clunking noise beneath his feet distracted him and he throttled down the *Topaz* to a slow speed while he investigated the bothersome sound. He pulled up the engine

235

compartment cover. He dropped to his hands and knees and stuck his head between the running engines. The clunking continued. It was coming from under the port engine. Frank leaned farther in and saw a loose analog depth gauge, flapping against the engine in the compartment. The gauge read 825 feet and rising. Then he saw what it was connected to and made a quick decision. Stop the boat and throw the bomb overboard.

It was impossible to get both of his hands into the tight space, so he reached in with his right hand and tried to remove it, but it had been attached by heavy wires twisted onto the motor mounts. The wires were too tough to untie with one hand. He needed pliers. The dial on the gauge caught his attention as it slowly swept to 850 feet.

Frank dashed to the tool chest as the din of the helicopter roared above him, running with him, the faint shadows of its blades scribing a huge circle on the water and the deck of the boat. Frank looked up, shielding his eyes. A boat horn blared as the 'copter blasted near-hurricane force winds onto the deck. A man on a drop-ladder swung below the hovering chopper thirty feet above him. He held a bullhorn to his face.

"Frank, jump out of the boat!" the amplified voice yelled. "Jump out of the boat *now*!"

Frank gaped at the man like he was a lunatic.

"Get away!" Frank yelled.

The 'copter dropped closer.

"There's a bomb on your boat. Jump out *now*!"

Frank braced himself on the gunwale and squinted at the man with the bullhorn. It was Chief Berkley, coming closer as the helicopter descended.

"Jump, goddamnit!" Berkley screamed through the bullhorn, his voice cracking.

Frank turned to go back to the helm to shut off the engines when a dull thud sounded on the deck behind him. He turned to face its source and a large blur of a man tackled him and knocked them both over the side and into the churning blue water.

The *Topaz* continued on her western course. The helicopter stayed back and hovered over the two men in the water. The Coast Guard patrol boat arrived and two of its crewmen dove in after the struggling men from the cabin cruiser. In seconds, they were alongside Frank and Chief Berkley with tethered flotation devices and towed them to the patrol boat's stern.

The *Topaz* motored on for about another quarter of a mile and then exploded with the force of a bunker buster. The concussive blast was deafening, its shock wave rocked the patrol boat and shuddered the helicopter's prop wash. Pieces of splintered mahogany fluttered down, splashed, and lay strewn over a hundred-yard radius of ocean swells. White chunks of cabin from skyward plunged into the Pacific in every direction. When the smoke dissipated, the *Topaz* was no more. The little that remained of what had been a classic ocean traveler was reduced to thousands of pieces of flotsam.

Crewmen on the patrol boat pulled Frank and Berkley aboard in clutches of strong hands. The Coast Guardsmen propped the rescued men against a gunwale, seawater drained from their drenched clothing.

"I just can't keep a boat," Frank said and blew his nose on his hand.

*　　*　　*

The ensign commanding the rescue boat gave Frank a cell phone. He called Judd Kemp to fill him in on the incident.

The Coast Guard boat ride dried Frank somewhat in the warm air as it sped him to Marina del Rey to get his car. As the boat pulled alongside the visitor's pier, he thanked the Guardsmen aboard and gave Chief Berkley a fist bump.

"You men are the best," Frank said and climbed the ladder to the walkway. "When I was in the Marines, we called you guys 'the Hooligan Navy.' I'll shoot the next sonofabitch who says that."

"I'll shoot *you*, you crazy bastard, if I ever have to beg you off a bomb," Berkley said. "What the fuck were you thinking?"

"I saw the bomb was set for 900 feet. I believed I had time to ditch the bomb and save the boat."

"You can buy a boat, Frank. A life, not so much."

Berkley saluted Frank a goodbye and ordered the patrol boat away. Frank marched for the harbor office.

James Fiske was standing on a step stool, fixing a crooked sign with a hammer and a nail, as Frank sauntered up. Fiske glanced below at his visitor.

"You look like a drowned rat," Fiske said.

"Seen the news, Captain?" Frank asked.

"Nup. Don't watch TV 'til evenin' time. Radio, neither. Got chores to attend to."

"Just as well. TV news is mostly not good."

"Where's the *Topaz*?"

"All over the Pacific Ocean about now."

Fiske stopped his swing to give a nail a whack and turned to Frank, his face dour.

"Something bad's happened to my beautiful boat?" Fiske said, stepping off the stool.

"Someone put a bomb on her. Someone here in this marina."

"Bullshit. No one messes with my boats."

"Stop defending. The bomb had to come from his marina."

"Sweet Mother of God. What's happened to the world?"

"Got any video cameras around this place?" Frank asked.

239

"Yeah. Plenty of 'em. These are expensive boats we keep here. Gotta keep watch."

Fiske shuffled for the office door and stopped before going inside, Frank halting behind.

"When do you figure this happened?" Fiske asked.

"Well, unless you've revived old enemies in the last few days, right after I acquired your boat. I *do* have enemies, old and new."

"The camera recordings go to the main office in that tall building over there," Fiske said, pointing to a high rise a block inland from where they stood.

"Will they let me have a look without a warrant?"

"Hell, yes," Fiske said. "I'll call 'em right now. Go on over there. Top floor. Ask for Maddy Schwartz. She's head of security."

Frank began his trek over to the building and stopped. He looked back at Fiske.

"I'm sorry, Captain," Frank said. "I know she was more than just a boat to you."

"All things die, lad," Fiske said. His eyes filled with redness. "I'm glad she didn't take you down with her, son."

*   *   *

The video tapes covered every angle where a human could walk or enter the marina on any conveyance. Frank requested the footage from the past three days and paid special attention to the night coverage

240

leading to and around the *Topaz*. It didn't take long to see two figures repeatedly in that area with no particular maritime purpose. Two men made constant trips along the boardwalk, in and out of the harbor office, and up and down the pier where the *Topaz* lay moored. An infrared recording from the night before clearly showed the two skulking onto the *Topaz*. One of them toted a backpack. Minutes later, the video showed them jumping off the boat and hustling away. A close shot of the duo widened Frank's eyes. Two faces came sharply into focus, faces burned into Frank's memory forever.

Dwayne Pinkney and Scottie Fisher passed within a yard of a security cam.

Chapter 33

Frank hit a speed dial on his cell. The phone rang twice.

"Detective Kemp."

"It was Pinkney and Fisher who set the bomb," Frank said. "I want them picked up for attempted murder and destruction of property."

"I'll put out the word."

"Do we know where they hide out these days?"

"I have a copy of the court transcriptions," Judd said. "May have an address, but you can't depend on flaky assholes like them staying steady anywhere."

"Pull together what you have and assemble a team. I'll be there in a couple of hours to join the hunt."

Frank ended the call and made tracks for his Bronco.

The early afternoon traffic on the 405 was moderate, making the trip south faster than usual. Frank pulled into the Central Division's lot at 4:17 PM and parked in the section reserved for detectives. Inside the station, he marched to Judd Kemp's desk and found him on the phone. Judd looked up as Frank arrived.

"He just walked in. We'll meet you outside in five," Judd said and placed the receiver in its cradle.

"Where're we headed?" Frank asked.

242

Judd stood. "Canyon Vista Apartments."

"Low rent district. May be crowded with nosies and lie-abouts. Have to warn the unies to keep the curious well out of the way."

"If the two still live there."

"I'd hate to have to throw this into the media to flush them out."

"I put out a BOLO for the Mustang GT registered to Pinkney."

"Love a good car chase," Frank said. "Like being in the movies."

*   *   *

The police caravan of three cruisers and a SWAT van slowed to a stop behind Judd's unmarked Crown Vic two blocks from the Canyon Vista apartment complex. Frank occupied the passenger seat and two plainclothes officers sat in the back.

"We park outside the gate and go in alone," Judd said. "I've got my ear radio set to signal the troops if things go sideways inside."

Judd talked into the wired mike on his ear.

"Everybody be cool, keep back out of sight, but eyes and ears on the target. Frank and I are moving in close. You follow us to just outside the gate. The apartment is number 102, terrace level, second building on the left after you go through the gate."

Judd eased the Ford sedan up to the gate and parked. All four men slipped silently out of the car and quietly entered the housing community. The two plainclothes men skirted the first building and disappeared around its rear.

Judd and Frank adjusted the Velcro straps on their vests and ambled to the front door of the apartment marked 102. Judd tried to peek inside through a picture window on the left of the door, but vertical blinds hung across the window, its slats almost closed. Frank gave a nod to Judd and pushed the bell button. The muted sound of a two-tone bell penetrated through the flimsy door. A moment later, Frank caught the faint sound of the cover being slowly slid off the peephole inside.

"Who is?" a man's voice from the other side of the door asked.

"SDPD," Frank said. "We need to ask you a few questions."

When there was no response for more than thirty seconds, Judd signaled the back-up units. In seconds, the SWAT team stormed the complex and rushed for the door on 102. An officer with a Monoshock Ram charged to the door and with a single swing into its thin wood, splintered the frame and exploded the door inward from the force of the tubular steel weight.

"Police," Judd yelled as three SWAT officers flooded the apartment, closely followed by the detectives.

244

Inside, an Hispanic man of fifty-plus huddled with a middle-aged woman on the far side of the living room, terror in their eyes.

"We're looking for Dwayne Pinkney and Scottie Fisher," Judd said. "Do they live here?"

"No intiendo," the shaken man said. *"Solalmente mi esposa y mi vivemos aqui."*

"Jesus," Judd said and turned to the officers. "Look around. See if there's any sign of them."

The SWAT trio filtered through the small rooms of the apartment and returned in seconds.

"They're not here, sir." one of the officers said.

"Stay here with these two people," Judd said to his men, "while I get a repairman here to replace the door. Manny, you speak Spanish. Tell them we're very sorry. That we are looking for two extremely dangerous men that had this as their address, yada, yada. You know the drill."

Frank's face said it all as he glared at Judd.

"It was the best lead we had, Frank," Judd said as he lumbered out the open doorway.

*   *   *

Back at the station, Frank and Judd stood in front of Captain Jarvis McCann's desk.

"Did it occur to you two to go to the rental office and ask if your suspects lived there? And if not, where they may have moved?"

245

"They might've tipped them. We wanted to catch them off guard, sir," Judd said, his eyes lowered like those of a bad dog.

"Well, you sure as shit caught Mr. and Mrs. Cardenza off fucking guard. We'll be lucky they don't get one of OJ's lawyers and end up owning this police station."

"It's my fault, sir," Frank said. "I wanted grab Pinkney and Fisher before they had time to react to their failed attempt to blow me up. I was impulsive and not thinking clearly. I'm sorry to have caused this trouble."

"This is so unlike you two," McCann said. "You're my A-team, the best cops in copdom. For God's sake, think things out before you act, *please*. I'm sending public relations people over to that apartment to calm this down and maybe give those people some money for their scare. Damn it, if this makes the news tonight, my wife's going to make me sleep in the yard with Bowser."

Frank shifted his eyes to meet Judd's.

"Get back to work," McCann said, "and find those two jackoffs and take them down in a righteous bust so this spectacle today doesn't look as Darwin dumbass as it does."

Frank and Judd filed out of the captain's office and closed his door.

"Where do we go from here?" Frank asked.

"They work for Guzman, who goes to court for sentencing tomorrow. I'm sure he's going up the river for the drug charges, so he won't be coming back. My bet is that Pinkney and Fisher'll be hanging out with Gaither and the fourth musketeer … Mitch Davis. Got to be on Guzman's yacht. I have a surveillance crew keeping tabs on Rico's boat. Let's check their reports."

*   *   *

The crammed courtroom, where Rico Guzman stood before the bench, looked on in silence as Judge Mario Liberto studied documents before him. Frank Dugan and Judd Kemp, in ties and jackets, sat in the back row of the large room, their faces stern, anticipatory.

"This court has found you guilty on thirteen counts of extortion and illegal drug trafficking and distribution," the judge said. "Under the new federal laws of the United States and the Revised Annotated Code of the State of California, I hereby sentence you to Prescott Island where you will spend the remainder of your life. Your sentence is to be carried out forthwith."

Guzman spat at the judge and lunged at the bench.

"Chingate y su nuevo ley," Guzman said as the bailiff and courtroom guards restrained him and pulled him away, forcing him to move toward the

private exit of the courtroom. Many onlookers in the room jumped to their feet.

"I'll be back. No coconut shitheap's gonna hold Rico Guzman. Tell that fuckin' flatfoot back there who did this to get ready to travel. I'm sendin' him to see his family. One way."

The guards dragged Guzman, yelling expletives and struggling, from the courtroom. Judd turned to Frank.

"Time to visit *El Mago*?" Judd asked.

Frank rose, looked at Judd, and nodded. He knew Guzman's yacht now housed the nucleus of Rico's bootlickers. He hoped Pinkney and Fisher were there as he unconsciously adjusted his Browning in its shoulder holster.

Chapter 34

The *Mago* yacht loomed like a mountain among foothills in her 200-foot slip at the San Diego Marina, her ghostly decks deserted in the early morning mist as if she knew in her silence that her master was never coming back.

Frank Dugan and Judd Kemp led a squad of special tactics police to the *Mago's* gangplank and paused.

Judd scanned what he could see above the high freeboard of the stark white yacht. "Looks like nobody's home."

"Criminals plunder and plot at night and sleep in late and tight," Frank said.

"Was that in the academy's poetry manual?"

"First thing they teach you."

Frank pointed to the boat to alert the uniformed group behind him, then mounted the gangplank and headed upward.

Judd followed, with the others close behind. The main deck was deserted and no lights shone from within the bridge windows, or those of any of the visible quarters. Once everyone was aboard, Frank pointed to several cabin entrances, which cued the tactical crew to begin their search for the boat's personnel.

"I'll cover the stern and the heliport," Judd said and ambled aft, his pistol in hand.

Frank stepped forward, but kept his sights on the main companionway. Three minutes passed before two of the tactical officers emerged from the cabin with a groggy man dressed in only a sleeveless undershirt. Frank moved to the new arrival and studied the bloodshot eyes of Mitch Davis.

"Rough night, Mr. Davis?" Frank asked.

"Yeah. I like to party," Davis said, squinting and rubbing his droopy eyelids.

"Where are the others?" Frank said.

"I'm it, man," Davis said. "I'm the chief cook and bottle washer now that Rico's in the can. I guess you can say I'm the captain."

"Well, captain, where's Mr. Gaither, and Pinkney and Fisher?"

"Uh, Ernie's visiting Rico, I think. I don't know about the other two. I been drunk since last Tuesday."

"Officers, make sure this liar stays put," Frank said. "Hook him up to the gunwale rail if you need to."

"Hey, man, you can't do that," Davis said. "I have rights. What's the charge?"

"Indecent exposure and environmentally dangerous bad breath," Frank said and headed for the main companionway to the yacht's interior.

Frank had barely penetrated the cabin's interior when gunshots broke the morning quiet. Frank flew down the stairway toward the sounds and came upon an officer lying on his back clutching his chest.

"Evans, how bad are you hit?" Frank said, bending over the injured man, while darting looks at every part of the main living salon of the yacht.

"Two in the vest," Evans said, his face contorted in pain. "I'll be okay. Two men. One black, one white. Armed with semis. Went through there." Evans pointed to an aft passage. "Go get the bastards, Frank."

Frank straightened and bolted for the opening. Inside the next compartment, a spacious bar and game center, he checked every space that could possibly conceal a person, his eyes sweeping with his drawn 9mm raised to face level. Seeing no one, he moved to the next room, his head on a swivel.

Gun reports sounded from a distance away. Frank scurried for the nearest opening to the sounds. Precious seconds passed before he found the access he needed. More shots popped from above, toward the stern. A stairway on the starboard side of the next room brought him back to the main deck amidships, but he saw no one in either direction. He scrambled to the distant stern where he found Judd Kemp sitting against the transom applying pressure to a bloody wound on his shoulder.

"Where, Judd?" Frank yelled.

"Over the side," Judd said. "Took the Zodiac."

Frank sprinted to the stern rail in time to see the Zodiac and two men roaring away toward the densest part of the marina at flank speed. Though he was sure it was useless, he fired half a magazine at the departing vessel that had managed to put a hundred yards between them and the yacht.

Frank got on his cell and punched in a number to the Harbor Patrol.

"Commander Jessop? This is Detective Frank Dugan, SDPD. We have two men in a Zodiac headed toward the main marina, south. They're wanted for attempted murder of two of my officers. Can you see if the Coast Guard can round them up? I'll join you as soon as I can."

"I'll dispatch a boat right away, detective."

"Sir, be aware, these men are armed and extremely dangerous. Your men are to take every precaution. If they get a clear and safe advantage, take them out with extreme prejudice."

"Aye, to that, detective."

Frank ended the call and pounded his fists on the helicopter shackled to the fantail heliport.

"Goddamnit," Frank said and turned back to attend to Judd, who was now surrounded by many of the tactical officers.

"I'll be okay," Judd said. "Just nicked me."

"Looks like more than a nick," Frank said. "Let's get him medical attention, stat. And make sure the officer vest-hit below gets examined too."

"We scoured the boat," an officer said, "and found no one else. What do you want to do with the streaker?"

"Mr. Davis?" Frank said. "Take him in for questioning. We have nothing to hold him on other than harboring fugitives before the fact, so he'll skate if we charge him."

"Will do, detective."

"Oh, and I'd put some clothes on him before you take him in."

"How about that indecent exposure charge?"

"Did you get a good look at him? Won't stick," Frank said. "Lack of evidence."

*   *   *

Frank and three SWAT officers boarded a 45-foot Coast Guard chase boat designed for speed and armed with a bow-mounted machine gun, headed after the first USCG boat pursuing Pinkney and Fisher. The powerful twin outboards roared their horses and shot the rubber-rimmed speedster through the waves, spraying white water like a hydroplane. Frank and his men hung onto anything near them to stay upright in what was the fastest ocean pursuit Frank had ever experienced.

The lieutenant who captained the vessel radioed the first pursuit boat to get a fix on the Zodiac's position, and bid them success in finding the two men on the run. He signed off and turned to Frank, standing in the cockpit beside him.

"They found the Zodiac beached south of San Diego at Border Field State Park," the lieutenant said over the engine noise, "about one click from the *Playas de Tijuana*. The two men were nowhere in sight, but they abandoned their boat. My guess? They're trying to make it to Mexico across the park."

"Why did they abandon their boat?" Frank asked. "They were less than a mile from the coast of Mexico."

"Not without gas, they weren't."

"We headed there?" Frank asked.

"Aye, sir, fast as this rubber ducky will go."

In minutes, the chase boat pulled alongside the first Coast Guard boat, grounded at the shore of the state park. The Zodiac nearby lay on the beach, the skeg of her outboard dug into the sand.

"Any sign?" the lieutenant asked the officer on the primary chase boat.

"Negative. In the park, I suspect," the officer said.

"We'll take it from here, lieutenant," Frank said. "I don't expect you and your men to hoof it on land."

"We'll stand by here for you, sir. If they double back this way, rest assured, they will not like the reception."

Frank nodded a thank you, jumped into the shallow water, and led the SWAT team toward the wide beach and desert-like ground foliage that extended south to the Mexican border. A SWAT officer handed Frank a vest with a Day-glo yellow cross on its back.

"Figure on a heading south that hugs the coast," Frank said, "but stay in the cover of the a few dunes. They are probably hung over, short on sleep, and scared. They're desperate to escape and will fight it out before yielding. Eyes on anything that moves as we go. The good news is that they frantically rushed to escape their yacht and are likely short on ammo and can only hurl a limited amount of fire."

The SWAT team set their radios to match Frank's frequency and chose short alert signals and adjusted audio levels to avoid broadcasts carrying outside the group.

The four pursuers went inland and spread out across a jagged line that pushed south. Frank donned the Day-glo vest and struck a fast pace ahead of the others to provide an *avant-garde* spotter on the beach side.

A hundred yards southward revealed a shred of white cloth clinging to a Spanish bayonet plant's spike. It was a piece ripped from a tee shirt, still wet with perspiration. A spot of blood on it told another tale: one of the two on the run was further annoyed by a cut on his body, maybe a nasty gash, which Spanish bayonets could easily inflict. Frank held the ragged piece high for the men close behind him to see.

Frank plodded south on a sinuous line that tracked within twenty yards of the beach, while the three

SWAT officers maintained a moving line that stretched farther inland for over three-hundred feet. Heavy sand and low brush slowed forward progress, but Frank moved rapidly ahead by cutting in and out of the soft sand and onto the firmer wet sand near the water.

Within minutes, the border revealed its high, slatted fence and bilingual signs in the distance. Frank knew a pursuit into Mexico incorporated legal entanglements that could negate an arrest under U.S. jurisdiction. He wanted to get to the escapees before they made it into Tijuana. He increased his speed to double time.

Fifty yards ahead, Frank spotted something unusual lying in the weedy grass above the beach, something that didn't belong in any botanical family.

Chapter 35

Frank closed on the object partially hidden in the grass and hit the alert button on his radio. He waited until one of the SWAT officers joined him. Frank noted his rank and the name sewn onto his uniform: E. L. Morton. Both men moved closer and could readily see that the object of their curiosity was a Caucasian man, face-down in the tufts of baked green. He wore a torn, blood-stained white tee shirt. A pistol lay near his limp, open hand.

"Looks like Fisher," Frank said.

"Looks dead," Sergeant Morton said, "but I'll keep my sights on him."

Frank stepped to the body, bent, and checked for any life. He looked back at the officer and shook his head. Lifting the dead man's shirt revealed a bullet wound in the center of his back between the shoulder blades.

"He's shot?" Morton said, lowering his rifle. "Who shot him?"

"Apparently, I did," Frank said. "Took a couple of Hail Mary shots at the Zodiac from the yacht."

"Nice shooting, detective."

Frank rolled the body onto its back.

"Lucky shooting," Frank said, standing. "It's Fisher, all right, but we have another one to catch."

Morton radioed the others on the team and updated them on the status of their hunt.

"They're still in pursuit," the officer said.

"Tell them the runner is the black man."

The sergeant complied and plodded back to his position in the search line. Frank continued along the beach, hugging the low foliage. As he neared the border, his radio beeped an alert. He darted toward his team as his radio crackled to life.

"Suspect is right at the border," the radio voice said.

Rapid shots boomed through the morning air. Sprays of sand exploded near the search line from the bullet divots.

"Taking fire," the radio voice said.

Frank scrabbled through the tangled ground-hugging flora, falling twice to his knees, as he plodded toward the border.

More shots zipped through the grass, striking plants near him with crisp slaps.

Frank kept low and crept on until he reached one of the officers.

"Where?" Frank asked.

"He's moved west. One o'clock," the officer said. "Where the water meets the beach."

"I'm one step from the border, detective," Duane Pinkney hollered. "One step and you can't touch me, you lame-ass flatfoot."

"Give me your rifle," Frank said to the officer next to him.

The officer extended his SIG556 rifle to Frank, who jammed it into his shoulder and sighted toward Pinkney, who waded into the lapping waves.

Pinkney moved into the ocean to his waist and appeared to be considering going around the high fence that extended into the Pacific for over two hundred feet. Two of the SWAT team closed in on Pinkney, rifles at eye level.

Pinkney turned back and fired two errant rounds at the officers who approached, but it served to halt their progress. Pinkney changed course and grasped the high vertical slats that comprised the border fence, apparently planning a climb over the barrier. He scrambled upward for six feet and was succeeding in his struggle to attain the top. A few more scratching and clawing purchases on the weathered wood and Pinkney pulled his head and chest over the top.

A single shot cracked the air. Pinkney's progress halted, then reversed. He slid downward fast, jarring his chin on the top of the fence as he plummeted into the surf of the USA. Pinkney bobbed face-down in the water and never lifted his head to take a breath.

Frank handed the rifle back to the officer.

"Radio the Coast Guard in the Harbor Patrol to come retrieve these two bodies," Frank said. "I'll call the coroner and the morgue. We'll go back with the

Coast Guard and tow the Zodiac in. My thanks to you and your men."

"We could've mailed this one in," one officer said.

"Having qualified back-up makes any individual confident to contribute."

Sergeant Morton said, "Appreciate the good thought, but, detective, you're one dead-eye sonofabitch."

*   *   *

Frank looked at the monitors next to Judd Kemp's hospital bed, keeping a sharp eye for any signs of instability.

"Stop checking my vitals," Judd said. "They're kicking me out of here tomorrow. I'm okay."

"You lost a lot of blood, partner," Frank said.

"Listen, I'm sure Davis is out of custody by now and is busting his ass to tell Gaither not to return to the *Mago*. I had a tail put on both of them, so we'll see where they hole up tonight."

"I have no case against either of them right now, so what's the use?'

"Mitch Davis will throw Gaither under the Greyhound if you tighten the screws on him. He's a punk-ass coward who'll give up his own mother after one swift kick in his frank and beans."

"So you think I should go lean on Mitch," Frank said.

"Duh. Yeah."

"I don't know …"

"Look, ideally we want all that remains of the four that came to your home either on their way to the Resort, or on their way to hell. Plus Guzman. We can't stop our investigation now. I want the whole bunch where they can do no harm to decent people. You think those assholes are going to start doing charity work and attend mass because they skated around the legal system? Give me a break."

"All right, I'll see what I can dig up on Davis."

"If not, make something up. Make it good enough to question him pigeon-in-the-box style. Old school."

"You're right," Frank said as his cell vibrated on his belt.

Frank studied the incoming call, raised an eyebrow, and looked at Judd.

"Detective Dugan," Frank said.

"Who?" Judd asked in a whisper.

"It's Errol Malay, detective. I was hoping we could have a chat about the present state of affairs with Mr. Guzman and his associates?"

Frank muted the phone. "Hard to believe. It's Errol Malay."

"Holy shit. What would he want with you?"

Frank switched the cell to speaker and placed a finger to his lips to silence Judd.

"What's the catch, Malay?"

"No catch. Rico has reneged on his payment to me for handling his legal mess. Promised me a lot, even if he lost his case and had to go to the Resort."

"What kind of promises?"

"Well, for openers, what was he going to do with that big yacht he owns? He's never going to see it again and the money from selling it won't help him in the least."

"He promised you *El Mago*?"

"And his lavish hacienda. He has no relatives that he doesn't hate, and his loyal idiot boys have outgrown their usefulness to him. I at least tried to save him. I'm the closest thing he has to a friend. So why not put his chattel in the hands of a person he knows and trusts?"

Judd Kemp shook his head.

Frank said, "The money from his estate could buy him a lot of escape attempts from the Resort, futile as they might be. If I were he, I'd put my trust in that money more than a give-away to my attorney who let me get convicted."

"There was no saving the bastard," Malay said. "He was up to his eyes in so many mistakes he couldn't buy his way out this time. Even *he* had to know that, delusional as he is."

"So what do we have to talk about? Going to offer me half interest in the yacht to assuage your conscience about my family?"

"There could be money in it for you. A lot of it."

"Money you know well I couldn't accept."

"We place it in a Swiss bank account. Who has to know? When you get tired of being a lawman, you might like to retire to Barbados or maybe Tahiti."

Frank chuckled and Judd had to cover his mouth to muffle his laughter.

"Yeah, I have a whole set of videos of me parasailing in my Speedo above the beaches of French Polynesia."

Judd had to jam his face into his pillow.

"What I want to talk to you about is Ernie Gaither," Malay said. "I have new evidence that you can use to bring him to justice. Evidence that can send him to join his mentor at the Resort."

"Aren't you skirting around client confidentiality?"

"Gaither was never my client, Guzman was. And since Guzman wants to welch on his promises, I don't feel like helping him by supporting his right-hand sycophant so he can dream about getting outside help into Prescott Island."

"Where should we meet?" Frank asked.

Judd wagged a cautionary finger at Frank.

"Guzman owns a shipyard warehouse at the south end of the marina. Ernie Gaither is holed up there. A huge painted sign on it says: 'Seaside Marine.' The main door has a window in it and a light over the transom. A sign on the door says: 'Employees Only.'"

"I'll find it," Frank said.

"What time will work for you?"

"I'll be at the range until seven. I can make it by eight."

"Still working on your craft, even when you've proven today that you're already an expert. I saw the news flash about Pinkney and Fisher."

"The way you get to stay an expert is the same way you get to Carnegie Hall."

"Ah, so. See you tonight, detective," Malay said.

"I'll be there," Frank said and ended the call.

"You're not going there without backup …" Judd said.

"Stop with the nagging. I'm a big boy, momma."

"You're a big boy idiot."

Judd pushed the button on his night table for the nurse.

"I'm getting out of here tonight and going with you," Judd said and reached for his IVs.

Frank grabbed his shoulders and forced him back onto the bed.

"You're not doing anything of the kind. A lot of help you'd be with one good wing. And the good one's not even your shooting wing."

"I feel like I'm partnered with that nutso Riggs from *Lethal Weapon*, I swear to God."

Frank left the hospital at 3 PM and drove to the station to catch up on his messages and to file his reports of the morning activities. The paperwork and interviews with the captain and the media would take him into the evening. An hour at the firing range took him to 7:30 with enough time to make his meeting with Errol Malay.

As he contemplated the appointment with the underground counselor, he recalled words of caution from then President Ronald Reagan: "Trust but verify." With an opportunist the likes of Malay, Frank would be going light on the trust, and heavy on the verify.

Chapter 36

The sprawling Seaside Marine warehouse was lit only by a single interior light peeking out of the windowed employees' door, the parking lot at the water's edge of San Diego Bay empty save for two cars bumpered up to the building. Frank eased his Bronco next to the black Mercedes convertible with the California vanity license plate:

CRTKING

Frank had to smile at the cryptic plate's likely translation: *Court King*. It contained a double meaning. Malay fancied himself a master in the courtroom and also a superior tennis player. At his fee level, he could well afford the training it would take for him to be a contender at Wimbledon, but he contented himself with local celebrity matches, which, because of his fondness for media attention, often made the entertainment news. Big wins in court helped his inflated regard of himself and he never failed to grab anyone with notoriety, who happened to be involved in high profile legal snares. An ambulance chaser who chased Rolls Royce ambulances.

The door to the warehouse opened easily and Frank entered. He eyed the huge open room from side to side. As his head turned from left to center, he felt something hard pressed against his right side.

"So nice of you to come pay us a visit," the unforgettable voice of Ernie Gaither said as Frank twisted his neck toward the speaker to confirm his recognition.

"Where's Malay?" Frank said.

"First we take the gun," Gaither said and yanked Frank's pistol from his belt holster and jammed it into his waistband. "Mr. Malay doesn't like guns in his consultations. Now the other one."

"What?"

"The piece in your ankle holster," Gaither said with his palm extended.

Frank bent and removed the .38 revolver and handed it to Gaither.

"Now, then," Gaither said, "Let's go over here and you grab a seat there in that nice chair in front of the desk."

Frank moved as he was directed, Gaither close behind, and sat.

"Here's a little news flash for you, Mister Gaither. A lot of cops know exactly where I am and are awaiting my call to tell them the highlights of my meeting with your attorney."

"Ooooh. Then we'd best not muss up your hair or we could get in trouble."

267

"So, where's Malay?"

"Just cool your jets. He's comin' soon. Had to take a crap."

Gaither sat behind the desk, keeping his gun aimed at Frank while he deposited Frank's pistols on the desk top.

"Going to miss your boss?" Frank asked.

"For a little while maybe."

"Oh, he's coming back?"

"Just shut the fuck up and sit. What Rico's gonna do ain't none of your affair no more."

Frank made a zipping gesture across his lips with his thumb and forefinger.

"That's right. Keep your trap shut."

Footsteps approached from behind Frank, who slowly turned to see Errol Malay strolling toward the desk. He wore a suit and tie and looked ready to appear in court. An expensive suit and tie, Frank imagined.

"Sorry for the delay, detective," Malay said as he reached Frank's chair.

"I sat him down here like you said," Gaither said, standing.

"Did you get the detective's guns?" Malay asked.

"Yep, got 'em right here," Gaither said and pointed to them.

"You'll understand, detective, that I don't want any gunplay to spoil our chat," Malay said and picked up the semi-automatic with gloved hands and studied it.

Frank noted the gloves with suspicion. He didn't like giving up his Browning, but he knew, without even the .38, things could get ugly.

"A Browning Hi-Power. Been around a long time, but still a fashionable choice. Ernie, please go lock the door. I want to talk with detective Dugan in private."

Gaither scowled and lumbered to the door.

"How was your session at the range?" Malay asked.

"I hit the target once in a while."

"I'm sure you did."

Gaither strode over to the entrance and bolted the door, while Malay watched. When Gaither returned, Malay approached him.

"Hand me your gun, Ernie. We don't need any firearms being brandished about, do we? The detective didn't come here to cause trouble. He's kindly agreed to meet with me to discuss some important things with me concerning Mr. Guzman."

Gaither's expression turned sour, but he reluctantly did as he was told and extended his pistol to Malay, who tucked it into his waistband, along with the Browning.

"Come with me, detective. I want to show you why this building was so important to Mr. Guzman. You come too, Ernie."

Malay disappeared into the blackness of the cavernous warehouse. Frank saw Gaither looking at the .38 on the desk, but he moved to follow Malay

269

rather than pick it up. Frank slowly pulled up the rear, narrowing his eyes to better discern a safe path into the unlit area.

"Over here," Malay said, casting a flashlight beam to mark the way.

Frank stepped cautiously toward the light.

"These are the controls for the two massive cranes high above us," Malay said as he shone his light on a yellow box containing buttons, which hung from heavy electric wires extending upward into the darkness. "These cranes were used to lift and position Rico's mini-subs and extremely fast cigarette boats when they came here for maintenance."

"Drug runners?" Frank said.

"I'm not sure what he used them for …"

"Perhaps water skiing?"

"At 70 miles an hour, I imagine that could be exhilarating."

Malay aimed his flashlight upward to reveal the massive cranes opposed to each other on gear-toothed steel rails.

"The cranes could load the boats into pools and test them within this building without having to reveal their presence outside. Pools like this one."

Malay placed his hand behind Frank's back and gently directed him to a black abyss less than six feet behind them. He cast the beam of the flashlight into the dry concrete pit more than twelve feet below with sheer vertical walls.

As Frank neared the edge, Malay shoved him forward with a force that Frank couldn't counter in time to avoid toppling into the deep void. He landed on his feet, but the speed of the drop made his legs buckle and dash his body forward onto the gritty floor of the pit. His knees and right shoulder took the brunt of the fall and filed pain reports to Frank's brain that nearly blacked him out. In his groggy damage assessment, Frank heard a voice from above.

He knew it wasn't God welcoming him home.

Chapter 37

"Watch out for that pit, detective," Malay said from out of Frank's sight. "You know falls kill more people every year than traffic accidents."

Frank struggled to his feet and moved to the rear of the sixty-foot space to get a better angle of view on the upper floor of the warehouse. As he squinted in the darkness, the main work lights of the building went on overhead. The pit was too deep to see much above its high walls, so Frank slid down against the back of the enclosure and sank to the floor.

After scanning every foot of the dry pool, Frank realized that escape without help would be impossible. The feeling of helplessness that accompanied his predicament depressed him. He tightened his jaw and massaged his aching leg and shoulder and checked to make sure all was still functioning.

It was going to be a long wait until Judd and the police came to rescue him. He believed if Malay intended to kill him, he'd have already done so. But the shove into the pit had surprised him. And Frank hated surprises, even those associated with birthdays.

Judd's warnings blared in his head. Maybe a little back-up wouldn't have been such a bad idea.

*   *   *

Malay called to Ernie Gaither.

"Ernie, come over here. Where I'm standing. I need your help."

Gaither moseyed over to Malay, devoid of enthusiasm in his slow, measured steps.

"Yeah, what do you want?" Gaither asked.

Malay raised Frank's Browning and shot Gaither in both knees. Gaither collapsed to the concrete floor and wailed in agony, blood pouring from the wounds.

"Oh, my God," Gaither grunted, writhing from side to side, clutching his lower thighs. "My God, why, Errol? Why, man?"

Gaither continued to bellow and moan as he attempted to stem the bleeding from his legs.

"What the hell are you doing?" Gaither said.

"I'm tidying up a lot of loose ends," Malay said. "Rico has no further use for his Baker Street Irregulars and wants me to retire them. The detective kindly took care of Pinkney and Fisher, leaving us now with you and Davis to expunge."

"What are you doing to me?" Gaither asked, his voice hoarse, his breathing labored.

"Why, I'm killing you, you useless waste of humanity."

Malay stepped a few feet away and picked up a steel cable and a shackled chain, which he secured around Gaither's ankles. He attached the loop on the cable onto a heavy hook dangling from the crane high

273

above his head. Gaither attempted to cast off the chain, but his feeble kicks only added to his pain and he gave up, flopping onto his back.

"Going up," Malay said, as he pressed a button on the crane control box.

The crane with the hook holding the cable to Gaither's legs whirred high above and pulled upward. With the slack taken up, the crane hoisted Gaither's body from the floor and carried his screaming head to five feet above the floor, where he dangled.

"Now, for the final touches," Malay said, wrapping another chain and cable tightly around Gaither's chest under his armpits.

"Don't do this," Gaither said, his voice weak, flailing his arms at Malay. "Please don't do this."

"Isn't that what Dugan's wife said to you before you murdered her and the children?"

"Guzman wanted them killed. I just did what I was told."

"Well, I'm just doing what *I* was told … by the same man."

"Guzman wants me dead? After all I done for him?"

"He appreciates your loyal service," Malay said and hit two buttons on the control box.

The two cranes near the ceiling moved in opposite directions on their steel rails. The chains binding Gaither tightened as he rose toward the ceiling. In seconds, his body lay horizontal between both cranes thirty feet above Malay. Gaither screamed as the chains pulled in opposing directions. Then the screaming stopped and Gaither's body was ripped apart, his legs swung in a downward arc on one side while his upper torso spun away in the other direction. Blood showered onto the floor below, splattering in patterns as the cables twirled in a pendulous motion. A twist of intestines still connected the body's halves like a drooping clothesline.

"Did you get a good look at that, detective?" Malay asked toward the pool where Frank was captive.

"You brought me here to witness this?" Frank said from the pit. "What the hell are you thinking?"

"I'm thinking that you're going to be my patsy."

"How?"

"Here's your pistol, detective," Malay said, peeking over the edge and dropping the gun with a clunk on the floor below. "Not that it will offer you much assistance. Those walls are twelve-feet high and straight up. There's no door and I removed the nice ladder that used to be here below my feet."

Frank scooted on his haunches to his Browning and examined it for damage and for ammo. It was still loaded and had incurred only minor scratches on the slide from the drop. He checked the action and found that it functioned properly.

Frank looked up and Malay ducked from view.

"Why, Malay?" Frank asked.

"Mr. Guzman has no intention of withering away at your mosquito-infested resort," Malay said, his voice fading. "He doesn't want to return only to find he has a quartet of idiots who intimately know about his numerous drug dealings. Idiots who, upon arrest, could use their knowledge to leverage better plea bargains, more lenient sentencing."

"How about you?"

"Rico Guzman knows I'm beyond reproach. I'm legally bulletproof. Attorney-client confidentiality, all that. And, let's face it, he has to trust someone, particularly a person he believes can rescue him from his beachy prison."

"You know that's impossible," Frank said.

"They told Orville Wright that mass air transportation was impossible."

"What about Mitch Davis?"

"I have a new name for him."

"What's that?"

"Next."

Frank wanted to respond, but ached too much to enter into futile banter with a lunatic who, at the moment, held all the trump cards.

"Nothing more to say?" Malay said, his voice sounding closer. "Here's your other gun."

Frank's revolver scraped down the wall loosely tied to a rope by a single overhand knot around the trigger guard. The gun's rear sight gently touched the floor in the corner farthest from Frank. The rope

276

snapped upward and away, releasing the pistol with a clunk and disappeared over the top of the pit.

"Fine. Goodbye, Detective Dugan. And I do mean goodbye in its most ultimate sense."

"We'll be seeing you, Malay."

"In case you're interested, I'm calling the cops now," Malay said.

"Good," Frank said.

*   *   *

Frank was confident the cops would come and get him out of this concrete deadfall. The cops would come and Frank would tell them what that crazy sonofabitch had done. The only thing that concerned him was the whacko getting off on an insanity plea.

Being held captive was one of Frank's primal fears. The mere thought of losing his freedom terrified him.

In a few minutes Frank knew he would feel better. In a few minutes he would be free. But right now he felt busted up, hurting, and brain-tired to the point of exhaustion.

*   *   *

Mitch Davis knew that it was only a matter of time before he would have to answer for being an associate of Rico Guzman. Dwayne Pinkney and Scottie Fisher had already answered. He watched the news. He saw them bringing back the bodies.

Guzman was gone, but Mitch was never certain that Rico couldn't connect with outside help. Help that he could call on to eliminate any witnesses to his former crimes, crimes the cops didn't even know about. Even vicious crimes they suspected, but couldn't prove, like sucking the police into sending Detective Dugan to Huntington Beach on that jewelry store ruse while he and Ernie Gaither and the gang rushed to Dugan's home to kill his family before he could return. All because Rico got a premonition that Frank was onto his new mini-submarine drug transports from South America. Paranoid fucker.

Well, Mitch wasn't about to sit around that big yacht and wait for them to come again with their SWAT guys and kill him. Errol Malay was creepy slick and made him shudder. He could afford to trust no one. Hell, even the yacht wasn't safe anymore and he couldn't move the boat himself and sail anywhere without a crew. But staying there was suicide.

There was one ace left in the hole. Malay had sent Gaither to the Seaside Marine warehouse for a reason that made no sense. He planned to meet Detective Dugan there, Ernie had told him. "Gonna do him up right this time," he'd said. That whole scenario was fishier than the San Diego tuna market. So, Mitch decided to get himself some insurance. Insurance that

278

he could barter with for his safety, even his freedom from doing jail time.

It was quiet now. No one was in sight, so he unscrunched himself out from the cramped parts room in back of the warehouse. He peeked out the door's dirty window, through the small circle he'd wiped clean. He'd heard Malay drive away and the coast was now clear. The detective had fallen into a deep hole below view, so he felt it was safe to come out. Ernie Gaither sure as hell wasn't going to squeal on him. Now. all he had to do was hot-foot it unseen back to his car three piers away on the marina quay and scram out of there.

Mitch snugged Rico's high-definition video camera under his jacket carefully, like it was his baby. He smiled as he stepped out from hiding.

In a weird way, this is *my baby.*

Chapter 38

A caravan of police vehicles arrived at the Seaside Marina warehouse shortly after 9:30 PM. The doors on a black Chevrolet Suburban flung open on both sides as a uniformed SWAT team jumped to the asphalt of the parking lot and charged to the employee entrance and carefully flowed inside. Judd Kemp emerged from a dark blue Crown Vic, his wounded shoulder aided by an arm sling, and marched to the door where a helmeted officer gave him the okay to enter.

Judd panned the dark expanse of the warehouse, but couldn't see much past a few feet before him.

"Thanks for the fast response," Errol Malay said as he approached the police team from the darkness of the warehouse.

"Where is Detective Dugan?" Judd asked.

"In the boat pool over there," Malay said, pointing into the blackness to their left, "where he fell."

Kemp raised a hand to the officers to hold their positions and headed for the pit, followed by Malay.

"He apparently stumbled into the dry pit in the dark," Malay said.

"Any chance of getting lights on in this place?" Judd said.

"I think there are some switches somewhere in here," Malay said and took a pocket flashlight from his jacket and searched the walls around him. "I'm not very acquainted with this place." He shone his light into the area near the pit and lit the base of a thick supporting column. A panel of electric switches could be seen in the beam. "These might be the ones."

Malay made his way to the column and began flipping switches. The first three he threw did nothing to illuminate the area where he stood, but number four, five, and six turned on the overhead lights. The cranes and their dangling hooks became visible.

A grisly scene appeared before the new arrivals as the dismembered body hung in two pieces from crane hooks that extended to the railed cranes high above. Blood still dripped from the shredded torso and separated hips held aloft, the floor painted in splattered red like in a macabre Jackson Pollack painting. The stern faces of the officers failed to hide their revulsion at the sight.

"Jesus God," Judd Kemp said and dropped his eyes to the floor.

"I heard Mr. Gaither screaming as I pulled into the parking lot," Malay said. "When I got inside, I could barely see him in the dark. I took out my flashlight and saw enough to see him being pulled apart by those cranes up there. Detective Dugan was over to the left. He yelled at me and I pointed my light where I heard the voice. He had his gun aimed at me. Then he stepped toward me. That's when he stumbled and fell into the pit. When I was sure he couldn't get out to shoot me, I called 9-1-1."

Judd crossed to the edge of the pit and looked inside. Frank was sitting against the wall in a corner, his head tilted against the concrete. Passed out with his gun clutched in his hand.

"Frank!" Judd hollered. "Wake up."

Frank stirred and looked around the pit with half-open eyelids.

"How can we get him out of there?" Judd asked Malay.

"I don't know, detective. Maybe there's a ladder or a rope around here ..."

"Look for a ladder," Judd said to the officers. "I want Detective Dugan up and out of there."

*   *   *

Judd sat next to Frank, who lay tilted up in the bed at the UCSD Medical Center. Judd consulted a notepad on his lap.

"Sergeant Boyle drove your truck back from the crime lab," Judd said. "The good news is they found nothing incriminating in your Bronco."

"Did you arrest that sonofabitch?" Frank asked.

"Malay?" Judd said.

"Yeah, Errol Malay, the psycho murderer lawyer."

"I interrogated him."

"And …" Frank said, his eyes wide.

"Frank, your story and his story are vastly different."

"Sure they are. He'll deny everything. Do you think that lying bastard's going to cave to the truth? Lying is his stock in trade."

"He didn't deny anything. He says you did the killing."

"And you believe him? Am I talking to my partner right now? Who are you?"

"Frank, I want to prove Malay wrong in everything he said, but I need evidence. The only real evidence we have is to determine the source of the bullets dug out of Ernie Gaither's legs. If they match your weapon, it won't go well for you with a Grand Jury."

"I told you, he took my guns as soon as I arrived."

"Yeah, you told me," Judd said and stood. "Do you know how many times I've known you to surrender your piece? It starts with a zero."

"This was different. Malay wanted to keep any possible gunplay out of our talk. He took Gaither's gun too."

"We didn't find a third gun. We found you in possession of your Browning and the revolver from your ankle holster, but that one doesn't appear to have been fired."

"I'm telling you, he took my guns, took Gaither's gun, shot him twice with my Browning, and tortured him."

283

"And you saw this?"

Frank tightened his lips.

"I was too far down in that pit. But I heard the shots and I heard Gaither screaming. And when the cranes pulled him up, I saw his body separate. It was like an x-rated scene out of a bad horror movie."

"Here's the problem with that scenario: you hated Gaither and wanted him dead. Malay works for Guzman and defended Gaither. What would be his motive for killing him? And here's another problem. They found GSR on your gun hand and your clothing. Nothing on Malay."

"I went to the range before I came to the warehouse. I go twice a week. Practically everything I own has GSR on it. Malay wore surgical gloves and he had plenty of time to wash himself clean before you arrived."

"We never saw gloves. And where's Gaither's gun?"

"Beats me. Malay hid it," Frank said. "Search the warehouse and look outside."

"If Malay took it, as you say, it sure as shit won't be there now. You never said anything about Gaither's gun when we were hauling you out of that pit."

"Good God, man, I was busted up, dead tired, and sure you'd see what had happened as I did. I didn't put any significance on Gaither's gun."

Judd paced the room.

284

"I'm going to hit the lab. Get the report on the bullets in Gaither."

Judd strode to the door and opened it.

"You're wasting your time," Frank said. "Those bullets came from my gun. I told you they did."

"Then I'm hoping they're too distorted for a match to the Browning."

"You know that hasn't got a chance in hell. They're my bullets. Two were missing from the magazine. We have to prove *who fired them*."

"Frank, you know I'd take a .44 magnum in the chest for you. Come to think of it, I *did* take a bullet for you," Judd said and glanced at his shoulder. "But I'm going to need somebody to toss me a bone on your behalf to be able to help you."

"For now, just believe me."

"I've never known you to lie. I do believe you."

Frank smiled for the first time that day.

"I'll be okay," Frank said. "God didn't spend all His time nurturing me to see me die like a mad dog on a prison island."

Judd said, "I asked the lieutenant sitting outside to wait until I had a chance to talk with you. He was kind enough to grant me the favor. He's here to formally charge you with first degree murder. You're not likely to be given bail on a capital charge, so I asked him to see that you're not put into the main population at the detention center. It won't be the Bonaventure, but it'll be reasonably private."

Frank nodded his thanks. Judd waved a goodbye, exited into the hall, and closed the door.

Frank stared out the window that overlooked Dickinson Street, his eyes focusing on nothing in particular. He knew that proving Malay shot Gaither with his Browning was up there with finding Nessie and Sasquatch surfing at Laguna Beach.

*   *   *

Three jail-celled months went by before Frank got his day in court, for what that was worth. The prosecution seldom receives a slam dunk at trial, and even rarer yet was one where the defense could offer no reasonable doubt, no alibi, and nary a witness on the defendant's behalf. Even character testimony by Senator Martin Dimino and Charlotte Stone carried little to no weight in balancing Lady Justice's scales toward Frank's innocence.

The jury found Frank guilty of first degree murder in less than an hour of deliberation, a record for San Diego County. They didn't have to recommend a sentence of life, either with or without parole, or death, since the new felony laws made that a clear conclusion. There would be no options, no choices: Prescott Island would be Frank's residence until the end of his days.

Marty Dimino visited Frank the day before he was to ship out to the Resort. They sat and talked by telephone across a thick Lexan window. Frank's orange attire added to the despair he tried to hide by keeping a partial smile on his face.

"Judd Kemp said he visited you yesterday," Marty said. "He told me he's not going to give up on your case."

"They honor appeals for Resort Isle convicts?"

"If they find irrefutable evidence that someone else murdered Gaither, I'll make it my personal mission to get you an appeal."

"Have you picked up on the irony of all this?"

"Apparently not," Marty said.

"I'm following the life of James Douglas, an Earl, who was executed in Edinburgh on a device called the 'Scottish Maiden,' which he had introduced to Scotland as a capital punishment method."

Marty looked puzzled.

"He promoted the execution machine for beheading criminals and political rebels, then ended up being executed by his own device. I promoted Prescott Island as the last punishment for capital criminals and now I'm going there myself. Ain't that a gas?"

"The humor in that is lost on me. You don't belong there. You're not a criminal."

"Neither was ole Jimmy Douglas."

"Charlie and I got married."

"No shit. You finally married that doll baby. Congratulations, Marty."

"She's taking all this kinda hard, or she'd be here. Trust that her best thoughts and prayers are with you."

"Never a doubt."

Marty stared at Frank for a long moment.

"I see something brewing behind your eyes … something you're not sharing."

"You see a man you're never going to see again in the living flesh," Frank said, shaking his head. "That's all that's behind these eyes."

"You had the same look when late in my campaign we had to find a spectacular concept to go with our anti-crime platform. An intenseness was in your gaze, and shortly afterward, you latched onto the Prescott Island idea, the perfect answer."

"I wish I had a perfect answer for this situation, but I don't have even a sniff of one."

Marty looked askance at Frank and raised an eyebrow as the guard on duty stepped behind Frank and touched his shoulder. Frank and Marty rose but held their phones to their ears.

"So long, Frank. Keep hope. It will be a comfort to you beyond measure."

Marty hung up his phone, gave a thumbs-up, and walked away.

Frank stared after his friend until he disappeared.

Tomorrow he would be in a place where there were no friends.

Chapter 39

Two navy gunboats flanked the five-hundred-foot LST-1179 carrying the latest band of prisoners scheduled for Prescott Island. Helicopter gunships flew patterns on course with the ship. The twenty-eight men occupied specially designed on-deck, individual quarters, equipped with a bunk, sink, and toilet. Every unit had a window to the sea outside. Of all the possible modes of prisoner transport, a specially-adapted ship was determined to be the most favorable choice. ConAir was out since there was no airstrip on Prescott, and control of a rebellious incident aboard ship posed many better options than those occurring mid-air. A ship could be stopped at any time to deal with any insurrection, not so much for a plane.

Frank Dugan regarded the sunny view of the Pacific with oppressive sadness, even though he believed the placement of the rooms, with their clear views of the ocean, a product of inspired moral genius. From the beginning, he'd felt the passengers on these trips to the Resort should be constantly encouraged to regard their destination as a form of tropical freedom; a vacation from their former concrete and steel incarceration. To that end, the outside sights from the upper deck succeeded, and ranked far superior to being crammed into a moldy hold below decks in a troop carrier, like cattle, blind to their fate. In addition, prisoner problems could be dealt with on an individual basis without overseers having to concern themselves with the dangers of concerted efforts multiple convicts might pose. But Frank hadn't come from long years of imprisonment in a cement box. He had known the freedom of beautiful beaches where equally beautiful people gathered and played. He had known endless days in sunshine and great eateries. These and many more things would be missed, but none as much as his good friends that he loved.

The hundred-mile journey would take most of the day and lunch and snacks arrived at appropriate intervals. Closed circuit television played current movies and hot coffee and soft drinks were served throughout the voyage. It wasn't a Carnival cruise, but it wasn't bad.

Frank's concerns drifted from the current accommodations to what lay ahead at the island. He was a cop who had arrested dozens of the men who'd be in reception when he landed on their private beach. And while he was instrumental in the idea of this tropical isle becoming a reality, he knew men there had no reason to fear further punishment for an additional act of murder, his murder, in particular. Inmates on Resort Isle had only two things to fear: sharks and each other.

*   *   *

Errol Malay could hear the tick-tock of his mental clock counting off the closing hours of his unfinished agenda. The issue of Mitch Davis needed to be resolved. He represented the last person with knowledge of the murders of the Dugan family, knowledge he might use to bargain his way into a cushy plea deal with the California legal system. Knowledge that could drag Malay to a defense table where he might find himself a defendant in a fight for his career and perhaps his life. Mitch could disclose the details of the Dugan murder plan, and well might, since his hero, Rico Guzman, had been stripped of his super powers by the Kryptonite of Frank Dugan.

Malay had visited the *Mago* in hopes of finding Mitch, but the yacht looked abandoned. The typical signs of occupancy were absent. No recently cooked food was in evidence in the galley or in the trash, the ship's air conditioning continued to over-cool quarters where no one dwelled, not even a drop of recent moisture could be found in any of the heads. Only one thing looked out of place: the open safe in Rico Guzman's sprawling stateroom.

The weeks were flying by and Mitch needed to be found. Attempts to reach him by cell phone transferred directly to a canned recording. Mr. Davis was apparently lying low, and doing a fair job of it.

As planned, Frank Dugan had been neatly taken care of. Now only one person posed a threat to his security. With Mitch eliminated, Errol Malay, Esquire would be one rich legal beagle, wallowing in the bounty of treasures that he had the power of attorney over and title to. Rico's paranoia over losing his possessions to the state, should the unthinkable happen and he get arrested, had forced him to trust his legal counselor. Trust him with everything he owned. It was good to be Errol Malay this day, but one loose end needed to be tied up.

Malay called Mitch's cell one more time.

"Hello," said a voice that Malay recognized.

"Mitch, this is Errol Malay, Mr. Guzman's attorney."

"Yeah, I know who you are."

"I've been calling you for days. I have news about Mr. Guzman that I'm sure will interest you."

"What kind of news?"

"Good news. Can we get together somewhere?"

"I have some news too," Mitch said. "Not terrific news for you."

"Oh? Care to share?"

"I'll share all you want, but you might want to keep what I have to say under your hat."

Malay waited. Several seconds passed before Mitch continued to speak.

"I was at the warehouse when you murdered Ernie. Got it all on video."

Malay rolled his lips inward and firmed his teeth on them.

"I took the precaution to send out letters and copies of the tape," Mitch said, "to a few trusted people who have instructions to get the video to the cops, should I turn up missing or dead."

"What do you want, Mitch?" Malay said, his voice grave.

"I just want to be safe … and maybe a few bucks to take me away from here."

"How much?" Malay asked.

"How 'bout two hundred grand?"

"Where do you want to meet to get it?"

"Send it to Detective Judd Kemp in my name. He'll see that I get it."

"And then you'll trade him your video tape for the money?"

"Naw. I ain't inscrupulous like you lawyer types."

The fuck you're not, "inscrupulous," Malay thought.

Two hundred thousand dollars would only be the prelude, Malay knew, and would be followed by more demands from his weak-witted blackmailer. He would agree to this first request, but put every resource he could muster to determine where Mitch was. He couldn't use the police to put out a BOLO on Mitch's car because it might trigger the release of his video tape letters, so global satellite positioning would be first. A criminal lawyer could easily secure a cell

293

phone's location by making it part of a legal investigation. The phone company would help without alerting the cops. Hell, Malay had purchased the phones and phone service provider for all of Guzman's thugs. It was his account and he knew exactly what company to contact. Find Mitch's cell, find him.

Mitch might be bluffing about the video, but Malay would ask to see a sample. What happened after that needed to be carefully planned.

"I'll get the package together today," Malay said and ended the call.

Malay despised anyone having a one-up on him. As much as he hated it, he might have to put Mr. Davis's disappearance on hold, and later put him on ice.

*　　*　　*

The LST could land personnel directly onto beaches, but the stringent nature of the security at Prescott Island made that impossible, so the ship docked at the long pier, specifically constructed to accept new arrivals. Covered in a heavy steel mesh tunnel, occupants on the pier could be seen, but safely contained. The process was rigidly choreographed and overseen by a cadre of naval and correctional officers. A ranking officer spoke to the new inmates as they lined up to disembark and become part of the island community.

"You will step to the pier and walk single file all the way to its far end at the island," the officer said. "There, a gate will open, allowing you to pass onto the beach. Several sponsors will greet and orient you to island life. Listen carefully to what these men tell you. It can make your stay here more pleasurable and seem a lot less like punishment. The choices you make, starting today, will determine that outcome. Good luck, gentlemen."

The gate at the boat side of the pier opened and all twenty-eight men marched to its end at the beach. When everyone stood within the pier's two gates, the entrance near the LST was relocked and the island gate was opened, allowing the men to move onto the sandy beach. Once all were ashore, the beach gate was relocked.

Frank knew about the sponsorship program, since he had instituted it to acclimate new prisoners to how the island veterans had decided to rule their unique population. Dan Crawford was Frank's first choice to establish a viable form of government for the Resort, certain that anarchy would lead to bloodbaths and a total failure of the entire island prison experiment. Dan assured Frank that he would take the lead and have a workable plan in place within a few weeks. Men listened to Crawford and feared his power and reach, a respect that was legendary back at Pelican

Bay. But Frank never expected he'd one day be under Crawford's jurisdiction.

When Frank stepped off the pier and set foot on the beach, several inmates pointed at him and spoke out.

"There's that detective guy who put my ass in Soledad," one said.

"Yeah, I know him too," another said. "Put me in Quentin for *dos equis*."

Several men crowded around him, menacing looks defined their faces. Frank prepared for his first tough encounter, balanced his stance, and clenched his fists.

"That'll be enough of that, gentlemen," a booming voice behind the gathering said. "We have rules of civility here now."

The towering man behind the voice came forward. Everyone in his path parted to allow him passage. It was a barefoot Dan Crawford dressed in khaki Bermudas and a white tank top with a large crucifix printed on it in bold red ink.

"Bet you never figured on me standing here," Frank said.

"You'd've won that bet, Frank," Crawford said. "You men go on about your work. Mr. Dugan and I have business to discuss."

The group gave out a few mumbles, but dispersed peacefully in several directions. Dan smiled at their compliance.

"I promised you a system of order and, so far, it seems to be working," Crawford said. "There are a

296

few hard liners who may give us trouble, but what government doesn't have its Benedict Arnolds and Jane Fondas?"

Crawford looked over Frank from head to foot and shook his head.

"What in the world did you do to deserve coming here?" Crawford asked.

"Honestly? Nothing."

"Yeah, we all use that one. Never seen so many innocent men in one place in my life until I hit Pelican Bay."

"Seen Rico Guzman?"

"Of course. He's one of those rebel types I spoke of, who wants to do things his way without any consideration of the bad example he sets for morale. I've left him alone for the few weeks he's been here because he's new. I may have to tow him in if he doesn't come around soon."

"You're wasting your time, Dan. He's not used to taking orders from anyone. And he's as ruthless a bastard as you'll ever run into. Nothing is beneath him if he wants something."

"What does he want?"

"Now that I'm here, he'll want me."

"As in dead?"

"He only knows his way and killing. We'll be tangling soon. I'm not looking forward to it, but it has to happen."

"You hate having to fight him?"

"I wanted him to be sent here where he couldn't run his criminal activities like the king shit he thought he was in California. I wanted him to pay every day of his life for ordering the hit on my family. Now *I'm* here, and I'm going to have to punish him in a different way."

"You intend to teach this bad boy a lesson?"

"No. I intend to kill him."

Chapter 40

Dan Crawford gave Frank, and the men who arrived with him, a tour of the budding village that had been erected in sight of the long pier. Construction had cleared thick botanical overgrowth and advanced into the jungle for more than a quarter mile, and from side to side on the beachfront for half a mile. Neat avenues of prefabricated housing stretched in rows before large buildings that held supplies, tools, generators, and recreational equipment. A sports field was in its early grading stages with a baseball backstop already in place. An uncovered wooden pier extended into the sea for more than four hundred feet and allowed for fishing the deeper water. Near the open pier, special netting fenced in a large swimming area in the ocean making it safe from the ever-present makos, bulls, and hammerheads.

Crawford pointed to a concrete slab easily three hundred by three hundred feet square.

"The foundation here will soon support our meeting arena and theater."

"This place is a hell of a sight better than where I was," a curly-haired man said. "I never sat in a theater and I never saw a palm tree … or a damn beach."

"We're trying to make it as livable as possible," Crawford said, "but we need every man to pitch in and cut back on the gang machismo and the hate."

The group walked on the white-sand beach. Chickens scurried out of their path as the men plodded toward the water.

"I see you found the chickens … or they found you," Frank said.

"It's like having our own self-replenishing KFC."

"Has anyone explored the rest of the island?" Frank asked.

"Been too busy here," Crawford said. "Maybe next year."

Frank envisioned the western side of the island, the peacocks, the swimming pool, and Sanford Prescott's decaying mansion. One other feature from the other coast slithered through his mind:

A Komodo dragon.

* * *

That evening, the newly established mess hall buzzed with activity as men stood on line to get supper meals from the lengthy buffet. Frank stood with Crawford, looking on with amazement at the orderly fashion the inmates picked up their food.

"The men are assigned meal times in half hour intervals," Crawford said. "It takes a couple of hours to serve all five thousand, but, so far, it's working well."

"How did you manage to get enough kitchen help to work this miracle?" Frank asked.

"That was easy. They get to select the menu and eat first. I have volunteers I haven't even used yet."

"You're more than a mere sponsor here, aren't you?"

"I'm wearing a couple of hats. Spiritual leader, project director, and president *pro tem*. No one else wants to do it."

"Maybe no one else *could* do it."

"I can't do it all. Soon, I'm going to need a lot of management help, especially in the area of discipline. A lot of tough guys from back in the states want to be tough guys here. They have to understand that this unsupervised island life is only going to succeed if we all pitch in and work together. Survival depends on it."

"Supply control an issue?" Frank asked.

"Sure. The biggest. The "me first" element wants to hoard what they can snatch and hide. They want to fashion weapons from tools intended for other purposes. It's in their former prison nature. They can't shake that survival mindset. I have trouble keeping track of machetes and knives."

"How do you discipline offenders?"

"It's right up there with 'How do you bust a buck private?' What can I do to a man who's been sentenced to death stateside? He's free to do whatever he wants here. Who's going to stop him if he wants to kill someone?"

"You have to stop him. Carry out his execution."

"Rolls off the lips easily, but, brother, pullin' it off is another story," Crawford said.

"Get the toughest guys on your side. Reward them for toeing the line and make them your police force."

"They think this island is all about freedom from police and authority."

"If this experiment fails, they're going back to their former prisons. Impress that firmly in their minds. Make it job one."

"And who better for that job than you, detective."

"Oh, crap," Frank said. "Open mouth, change feet."

Crawford smiled and gathered in Frank by the shoulder, his huge hand covering most of Frank's upper arm.

"How 'bout you being our chief of poh-lice?"

*   *   *

Frank wanted to face off with Rico Guzman while he still had his optimum strength. He could foresee that after several weeks on the island his physical resources might be compromised. Prior knowledge of the island could also give him an advantage if Guzman was yet unaware of what lay on the western

302

shore. These were small points, but Frank knew that victory in many an Olympic competition was decided by one one-hundredth of a second. He wanted every edge he could get. His adversary was no pushover. Rico Guzman hadn't risen to the top of the California illegal drug industry by being a pussycat. People who got in his way ended up dead, often by his personal tiger claws. And his physical strength was only exceeded by his mental toughness. Frank Dugan feared few things in life. Rico Guzman was one of them.

A meeting with Guzman needed to be arranged, the sooner, the better. Frank walked from his assigned barrack and searched for Dan Crawford.

Fresh supplies flowed from the pier where men loaded them onto wheeled wagons for others to tow off the beach and take to the island's warehouse. Crawford, participating in the operation, glanced up to see Frank as he approached.

"Mornin', chief," Crawford said.

"Not 'chief' yet, thank you," Frank said.

"It's a job you were born for."

"Yeah, a prison whip master. It's all I dreamed about being as a kid."

"What else you going to do here? Macramé?"

"I need to meet with Mr. Guzman. Can you arrange that?"

"Going right into the buzz saw, eh?"

"It's going to happen, so let's get it over with."

Dan stopped pulling parcels from the pier and stepped out of the production line.

"You know we have rules for this kind of combat."

"I've heard."

"I'll call for a community meeting tonight. I'll make sure Guzman is there."

Frank gave a thumbs-up. It had begun. The countdown to a final resolution with the man who had orchestrated the murder of his family. There would even be an upside if he lost. Frank would again see Amy, Aunt Barbara, and the children.

*   *   *

The local communication system carried the announcement of the meeting, open to all the inmates. Crawford had earlier requested representatives from each faction existing within the community. Each established gang was allowed one member to represent them in a council presided over by Dan Crawford, their uncontested leader. In addition, council members came forward to speak for, not only the blacks, the latinos, and the Muslims, but groups like the gays, the independents, and even the seniors. No special interest group was left out. Council voting depended on a quorum of three-quarters of its members to pass any rules or laws that stood to govern the community as a whole. It would be an attempt at a democratic form of government, and could work if it didn't become too divisive. Proof that their political concept would function and endure over time remained to be tested at the Resort.

No one wanted to see its survival more than Dan Crawford. If it failed, every man on the island would be on his own. There would be war, rampant murdering, and constant anxiety for everyone. Every moment of sleep would be interrupted by a nervous eye panning the bedside. Soon, only a handful would remain. Prescott Island would fail and any survivors would be shipped back to mainland prisons. Crawford constantly warned his public of that *Lord of the Flies* scenario and prayed that they listened carefully.

Most of the entire population on the island attended the meeting being held at the mess hall. Crawford looked of the attendees and knew which ones had come to set up a formative legislature, those who came out of curiosity, and those who looked at it as a form of entertainment. He also knew the ones who spelled trouble. It would be a mixed batch of personalities. His job would be to emphasize its importance to their survival.

Rico Guzman sat at a table to the left of Crawford, while Frank sat at one on his right. Guzman and Frank exchanged glares regularly and then returned their attention to Dan as he stood at a makeshift podium between them.

"Thank you all for coming," Crawford said. "We have tonight what will be a first for the Resort: its first challenge for mortal combat. I have talked with Mr. Rico Guzman regarding his feeling about co-existing with former Detective Frank Dugan of the San Diego Police Department on this island. He has expressed that there can be no viable way to live in harmony with his former nemesis that he's certain wants to kill him. Frank Dugan blames Mr. Guzman for killing his wife and family and has determined that the only suitable justice for Mr. Guzman is death."

A murmur of low voices swept over the crowd. Crawford waited for the vocal reaction to settle.

"We recognized early on the need for rules to be in place for these types of irreconcilable differences. We knew, from our prison days, that hate like this always ended in somebody getting killed. There were never any rules. Often, the victim never had a chance. Here at the Resort, we want to level that playing field, or perhaps I should say, that killing field."

Crawford unfolded a document before him.

"Here are the rules we established during our first week on the island. One: the combatants will be given a single liter of drinking water, a jackknife, and a machete. They may wear any clothes they own, including shoes. Two: the winner of a coin toss will choose between being the pursuer or the pursued. The pursued will be given twenty-four hours to leave our village and disappear into the jungle; the pursuer will stay in the village until the twenty-four hours are up, after which he can give chase to his opponent. Three:

all observers of this contest must stay one hundred yards away from both combatants. A security team of ten men will see that you comply. Any human help given to either party during this combat will immediately be dealt with by our security team who will punish the helper, or helpers, with likely death by being taken out to the end of the uncovered wooden pier and thrown to the sharks. If they can survive that, they'll be allowed to return to the community. This rule also applies to the combatants who might enlist or request any outside assistance. Four: the contest will continue until one or the other, or both combatants, have been killed."

"When does this contest go down?" and inmate in the front row asked.

Crawford looked first to Rico, then to Frank.

Crawford said, "Tonight we'll have the coin toss and decide who's going to stay and who's to go. The two men will be issued their water, knife, and machete. Tomorrow morning, the twenty-four hour lead time will begin. The next day, the pursuer will give chase."

Crawford took a metal disk, which doubled for a baking soda can's lid, from his pocket and displayed it to the audience and then to the two men beside him.

Rico Guzman stood and said, "Just to show I'm a right kinda guy, I'll forget the coin toss and let Mr. Dugan choose his own fate."

The crowd rumbled. Crawford held his arms high for calm.

"Would you like to accept Mr. Guzman's generous offer?" Crawford asked Frank.

Frank stood and said, "I would. I'll be the pursued, so Mr. Guzman will have a clear path into the jungle and won't scratch his pretty legs."

Laughter erupted from the crowd.

"Well, that's that," Crawford said and pocketed his makeshift flipping coin. "Tomorrow at dawn Mr. Dugan will depart and the clock will begin the countdown."

Frank strode to the back exit of the hall and made tracks for his barrack. He would plan how to penetrate the dense flora that would oppose him on his itinerary to the western side of the island. An average person could walk briskly at about four miles per hour on open, flat terrain. Through thick jungle with mountains to cross, a lot less. Maybe two miles-per-hour at best. But to make the west side in four or five hours would still give him time to plan once there. The marines had taught him how to cover his tracks, so Guzman might not pick up his trail for days. In days, Frank could have time to make weapons, even traps, but he was counting on using something much more unexpected than that.

Chapter 41

Errol Malay homed in on Mitch Davis's cell phone. The phone company tracking report found it to be centered in basically one spot overnight.

Chula Vista was a town only a nine miles south of San Diego, a town Malay knew well. His own country club was in Chula Vista. To make location even easier to find, the phone was in an area off the 5 freeway with only one motel, the likely place an idiot in flight might trust as affordable and safely off the radar. Malay was sure that Mr. Davis could pay for his stay with the money he'd availed himself of from the *Mago's* safe, a money hole Guzman often neglected to lock.

The Playa Vista Motel had no *playa* in sight and nary a *vista* of one. The office clerk was a dullard that Malay easily conned into telling him where he might find his nephew for twenty dollars plain. Room 14 was on the lower level and clever Mitch's car sat in the parking space directly in front of it. Malay mused that he could've saved the twenty.

Malay knocked the door of 14. He could hear the TV playing inside and the stirring of human movement.

"Open the door, Mitch."

"I'm calling to have my tapes sent if you don't leave me alone," Mitch said through the door.

"Look, if I intended to do you harm I'd be shooting myself in the head. Your tapes would get sent and I'd get arrested. Think about it, Mitch. You would fare much better by hooking up with me."

"You murdered Ernie."

"Guzman wanted him dead. Ernie had things he could use against him … and you."

"Guzman's on that island. For good. So why kill Ernie?"

"Revenge. Ernie did things that put Rico there."

"I don't know …"

"You have no reason to fear Guzman. You did nothing but help the man."

"He's got no contract out on me?"

"Oh, for God's sake. You've been watching too many mafia movies."

A minute passed. Then the door slowly opened a few inches and Mitch peeked out at Malay.

"What do you want with me?" Mitch asked.

"We have a shitload of property to split up. I can't take it all. My taxes are killing me as it is. You can have half of Guzman's bank accounts, and I don't need that fucking Queen Mary of a yacht."

"I can't sail it. It needs a crew."

"Well, jeez, hire a crew. You're a rich man now."

"For real?"

"Am I coming in or are you coming out?"

"I'll come out."

Mitch slid out between the door and the jamb and sat on the hood of his car.

"That was pretty clever of you to send copies of that video to your relatives," Malay said.

"I didn't want to, but I was scared. I hate involving my relatives in this."

"You know, me being a lawyer and all, I need to see proof before I go to work for someone. I want to help you, but we have to be able to trust each other. If you have a sample of that video, I need to see it before I start sharing a lot of money."

"I can show it to you," Mitch said, "but you know those copies I sent are real. They're out there."

"Of course. I'd like to see the film. Actually, I'm kinda curious to see what that execution of Ernie looks like."

"It was horrible, man. Some bad shit."

"Look, what you don't know is that Ernie was preparing to toss you to the cops too. He wanted all of Rico's money. I was next on his list."

"Yeah? Let's go inside," Mitch said and stood. "I got the camera inside with the original tape."

Both men disappeared inside room 14 and closed the door.

Malay wanted to get that original video out of play, then find out where those other tapes were sent. He'd throw serious money and booze at Mitch until his lips loosened up. A few nice dinners at exclusive restaurants, some expensive duds, and a new sports car should do the trick.

All that remained would be disposing of Mitch's body.

*   *   *

The knife Frank was given was an overgrown Boy Scout knife with several cutting blades, a file, a can opener, an awl, a small magnifying glass, and two types of screwdrivers. It came with a sheath for wearing it on one's belt. The machete also came with an olive drab canvas sheath, paramilitary, and a belt clip. The liter bottle of water was issued with a small shoulder bag for carrying. The machete got an early workout on the kudzu vines and chest-high plant life as Frank hacked his way south. He'd go south first, knowing that Guzman would be keenly watching the direction he headed as he left the village. Frank had no compass, but the sun would help him when the time came to change course to west.

Frank used his trailblazing time to consider what weaponry he could bring to bear against Guzman. A spear was certainly possible, but how about a bow and arrow? That would give him a distance advantage and eliminate close encounters of the first kind. A bow would need a suitable flexible wood and something to use as a string, and the arrows would need fletchings to stabilize their trajectory in flight. He didn't believe

312

yew trees were native to Prescott Island, so the traditional wood choice among the ancients for making bows was out. No, it didn't look good for going all Robin Hood when he wasn't anywhere near Sherwood Forest.

Traps he could do, but traps require that you get your prey to traverse the trap's location, like over a beaten path. No beaten paths here. Didn't look good for path traps either.

A machete or knife fight could go a lot of ways, and even if you win, you could be badly cut up or limp off to bleed out and die later.

Time to go west. Frank studied the early morning sun and traveled in the direction old Sol was heading. He stopped his hacking south and embarked on a serpentine path west, scraping past jungle obstacles to the right, then to the left, leaving no cleared way in his wake. By the time Guzman journeyed out, Frank's trail would be repaired by Mother Nature. By the time Guzman found Frank, he'd likely be one tired *Cubano*.

Another problem entered Frank's busy mind. What if it took Guzman days, even weeks, to find Frank? Frank would have to fabricate shelter, obtain food, and find more than a liter of drinking water that rode on his shoulder. Coconuts could be his salvation and there were plenty of them everywhere. Comforting to know, but after about ten coconuts, he was sure he'd be craving a pizza.

Frank wondered how long this affair would take. A week? Months? Hell, he could scratch himself, get an infection, and be dead by the time Guzman finally got to his cold body.

A simple plan was turning into a complex situation. A situation that produced more fear than any human enemy could instill.

*   *   *

Malay sat at the linen-clad table at his country club and watched Mitch Davis stuff down a fourteen-ounce filet mignon like there was a prize for it. He thought the video tape he'd viewed depicted as damning a testimony to torture and murder as he'd seen since *The Texas Chainsaw Massacre.* Mitch had indeed captured a graphic piece of indisputable evidence against him. But the evening was going swimmingly and Mitch had drunk four Maker's Mark old fashioneds and was jiggling the ice in his drained glass at every passing waiter for another.

Malay planned to tactfully interrogate his charge with subtle queries intended to disclose the location of those dangerous tapes. The question remained, how many copies were out there in different locations? One, two, more? He had to wheedle that out of his toasted enemy, and soon.

When Mitch passed out, Malay would return to the motel and extract the tape from the video camera and replace it with one of the blank tapes in the gadget bag.

Malay seethed at the idea that this was going to be a battle of wits where it was smart versus stupid.

But stupid, so far, was costing more than a Malibu call girl, and wiping the floor with smartie.

*   *   *

Frank made it to the Prescott mansion in less than five hours. Not much had changed since his visit with Charly. A few more Spanish tiles had cascaded onto the yard and more glass had vacated the windows and glinted in small shards on the roof and patio.

There had been so little time to thoroughly explore the place before, but now a more in-depth examination might prove useful in the upcoming clash with Guzman. He stepped lightly as he made his way onto the shaky front porch and then to the entrance, which, when pried open, scraped loudly against the debris lying below the door's wide bottom edge.

Inside the musty smell of aged plaster blended with a pungent odor of mildewed wood. Frank wanted to hold his breath as he scanned the walls and grand staircase, but soon abandoned that idea and resorted to shallow inhalation. The stairs had miraculously avoided the deterioration that most of the house had endured. Their oak risers and treads displayed mission style newness and the Oriental runner was amazingly intact in vivid colors. His eye caught a door under the stairs and stepped to it for a closer inspection. Behind the door stood a stairway leading to a black abyss below that Frank could only imagine was a basement. Maybe a wine cellar, considering the former owner's penchant for the impressive entertainment of his guests. With no light available, Frank opted to visit the lower level later.

Shelter wasn't going to be a problem for this first night, anyway. It would be more than eighteen hours before Guzman would be allowed to give chase. Finding a soft mattress to lie on would be nonexistent. Everything fabric here had fallen victim to moisture, mildew, and critter residency. The hard floor would do, but cutting conifer branches from the nearby landscape could serve to soften hours of hard floor sleeping.

Back outside, Frank circled the house searching for the few pines that grew among the palms and reserved a watchful eye for anything convertible to a weapon. The utility shed still had tools and the spade was right where he'd left it, jammed into the ground by the shed door. He pulled the spade from the soil and surveyed the area. Beyond the pool, he saw what he surely needed.

And it saw him.

Chapter 42

After dinner, and a *crème brulee* dessert for Mitch, Malay ordered two snifters of *Gran Marnier* after dinner drinks. Malay weighed the possibility that the 90 proof liqueur would either make Mitch more garrulous or send him into an alcohol blackout.

"Why did you pay for a sleazy motel when you could've stayed with a relative?" Malay asked.

Mitch's head tilted forward and backward repeatedly and contained bloodshot eyes with lids at half mast.

"Relatives ask too many … um … too many stupid questions."

"You mean your mom and dad?'

"No. Dad's dead. Mom lives up in Costa Mesa. Too far to drive … drunk."

"Does Mrs. Davis need some of this money we now have?"

"Mrs. Davis? No … no. My mom's name is Stukowski. Married a Polack. Stan. Nice guy, though. Doesn't beat her like the old man did."

Mitch took another sip on his GM.

"How about your other relatives who *don't* ask stupid questions?"

"Shit. That jus' leaves my uncle Phil. He's okay, I guess, but he lives in fuckin' Sunset Beach. Talk about a goddamn road trip …"

"He your father's brother?"

"Yeah, but not mean like that bastard my mom used to be hooked up with."

"You going to share any of this money with any friends or relatives?"

"Well, shit, I ain't got any friends. They're all dead. Even my girlfriend dumped me."

"Other relatives?"

"Mom and uncle Phil. That's 'bout it. Hey, can we go grab us a few zees somewhere? My ass is fading, man."

"I understand. Eating can certainly wear one out.'

"You messin' with me?"

Malay laughed.

"No, my friend. I enjoy a person with a good appetite. Hope you enjoyed everything."

"I did. That was some good shit."

Malay signed the check on the table and stood.

"What do you say we crash at the del Coronado?"

"You got the money, honey. I got the time," Mitch said and wobbled to his feet, clutching his linen napkin, along with its matching table cloth. Several items on the table cascaded to the floor.

Malay peeled Mitch's fingers off the tablecloth and guided him toward the door.

"The Hotel del Coronado," Mitch said. "Son of a bitch. Class up the ass."

Malay forced a smile.

"It'll be like a suppository from heaven."

*   *   *

Guzman forged into the overgrown mass of foliage, chopping at the plant life like the sugar cane harvester he'd been in a former life. He plodded on following Frank's original direction with its obvious path, but within half a mile, the clearly visible swath of severed flora ended and he faced a dense wall of scrub palms and vines like a verdant roadblock. It was time to stop and think. *Which way would that cop bastard go?*

A light bulb flashed in Guzman's head. The jungle was too tiring for Dugan to continue thrashing his way, so he decided to take an easier course: the beach. Travel would be far kinder by scuffling through the sand and shallows than fighting the razor-sharp palm fronds and unforgiving lianas. That scenario posed a question: where was he going? Around the entire island? The island was more than thirty miles in shoreline circumference. That would be a lot of scuffling.

Two of the inmates, who had fallen victim to Detective Frank Dugan's dogged investigations and subsequent arrests, made it clear to Guzman that they would relish a chance to kill the nightmare cop who

319

ended their illicit careers. Rico had demurred. He wanted Dugan all to himself, and told them he would slaughter the detective and dedicate the killing to them and all inmates whose freedom had been cut short by the young phenom of the SDPD.

Guzman decided to take the beach route. At least it would be cooler, less obstructed, and a lot more scenic. He would take his time. There was no rush, except for the need to replenish food and water. On many an evening the teenage Guzman had stayed in the tobacco fields and lived off the land. He knew how to find water and how to set a stone-fall trap for a rodent. He could light a fire and even make himself a crude cigar from the tobacco he'd stolen from the drying barns. This island would pose no more difficult living than he'd experienced early in his life.

After all, Cuba was a tropical island too.

*   *   *

Malay plopped Mitch Davis's limp body into his elegant bed at the del Coronado's ocean view suite. The seriously-impaired drunk was asleep before his head struck the pillow.

It was time to recount what had been gleaned at the country club dinner and do a bit of research on his laptop. He discovered that Mitch's mother, age 52, was married to a man named Stan Stukowski, age 60, and they lived in Costa Mesa on Wilson. He was certain that they had one of the tapes he sought. The uncle, Phil Davis, age 54, lived in Sunset Beach on PCH over a surf shop. Stan was a welder and worked in Newport Beach, primarily in the boat yards. Phil was a liquor store clerk in Sunset Beach. That seemed to be the total roundup of Mitch's extant relatives. Breaking in to their homes and finding those two tapes didn't seem to portend any real difficulty for a man with the resources of Errol Malay.

He would travel north in the morning and leave Mitch at the del Coronado with plenty of money, and a note saying he had to depose several witnesses for an important upcoming trial.

*   *   *

Frank stared at the Komodo dragon beyond the pool. Colorful feathers adorned the gigantic maw of the nine-foot reptile, a throwback from a long-ago age where there were no humans. The hapless peacock it was dining on lay below its open jaws, which were lined with too many sharp teeth for Frank to estimate. With the machete drawn and at the ready, Frank hoped his first life-and-death fight wasn't going to occur here and now.

The Komodo returned to its meal, ignoring its audience of one. Frank eased the tension he applied to the handle of the machete. The mystique of this animal had crossed his mind numerous times since his last visit, even when he wasn't fully aware of what its footprint proved it to be. But now, having learned so much about this magnificent hunting machine, Frank wanted him as an ally. No one else on the entire island knew about this creature, a serious advantage to the one person who did. Frank planned on how he could use a dragon to be his friend. It reminded him of a movie about a young boy who trained a dragon, only this one didn't fly.

The element of surprise could be a warrior's most powerful ally. He thought of Pearl Harbor and knew that that was undeniably true.

*　　*　　*

Rico Guzman had circled the south end of the outer island and was now on a northern heading, hugging the surrounding waterline. He kept a sharp eye for any interior activity that could come from the jungle, especially any activist wielding a machete.

The ten or eleven mile trek had consumed more than half of his water. A stop to crack and eat a coconut had delayed him a bit and the overhead sun put him at nearly noon. The rich coconut meat and sweet milk was worth the time, and, after all, what was the rush? Dugan wasn't leaving the island. It was a big place to hike, but not so big that Rico Guzman couldn't find him.

Guzman wondered if Frank Dugan was actively searching for him, instead of lying in ambush, waiting for him to mindlessly cross his booby-trapped path, or charge out from hiding to slash him across the neck with a deadly swing of his machete. He chuckled at the thought of the flatfoot beating him on turf akin to that where he'd been born. The *pendejo* was from Baltimore. What jungle was near Baltimore? Disney World?

As the sun drifted toward the ocean on the west side of the island, Guzman continued to search for evidence of his quarry. So far, he hadn't seen a single sign of human origin. Not a footprint, nor a freshly bludgeoned palm frond. *Nada*. No man could *swim* around the island. It was too far and there were those pesky sharks. Besides, when he'd arrived he'd been informed about the constant aerial surveillance of the island by the U.S. Navy and Coast Guard. He crossed off swimming, but had to consider that the man had somehow navigated across the dense jungle. But thirty-two square miles of jungle, as he'd been told, was a lot of territory to hide a man.

This fight would not be resolved in a day. Guzman decided to pace himself for the long haul. He sat on the trunk of a palm tree that had fallen across the beach toward the water, and planned how he would pass the nights.

*   *   *

323

After confirming that Phil Davis was working in a Sunset Beach liquor store off Pacific Coast Highway, Malay drove the few blocks to the address he'd pulled from the Department of Motor Vehicles. He was amazed at how careless many people were regarding the security of their homes. The lock on the upstairs apartment door opened with the gentle insertion of a credit card. Inside, he found the video tape lying in a dresser drawer on top of socks and boxer shorts. He was in and out in less than five minutes.

Now he knew for a fact that the tapes existed. He exited and relocked Phil's apartment and headed south for Coast Mesa. Mitch's mom and stepfather might present a bigger challenge than his uncle had. There would be two of them. He might have to employ a ruse to get them both out of the house so he could conduct his search, but he had outlined several plans to get what he wanted. A successful attorney always kept alternate strategies at the ready.

Malay knew why he topped the bar association's list of successful lawyers. He had always stayed smart. Being smart never failed him. He'd get his tape, which would nullify Mitch's threat to his career. Mitch himself would be next. Again, all smart moves, smart strategies.

Malay smiled at the mental preview of how he'd dispose of Mitch Davis and write off the twerp's dinner and hotel outlay as business expenses. What good was an IRS concession unless you used it? He could even deduct the cost of the trips to Sunset Beach and Costa Mesa.

Life was good.

Chapter 43

Frank continued his exploration of the Prescott mansion. He found that a narrow casement window in the back of the building provided light for the basement, not much, but enough. The sweaty tee shirt came off Frank's back and served as the rag to wipe the crud off the window. The improvement was substantial and he could see objects in the cellar below. A generous wine rack drew his attention. Rows of wine bottle necks protruded from the wooden shelves. A few could still be drinkable, Frank imagined. A trip back to the door under the staircase might prove beneficial.

The oak treads creaked as Frank took cautious steps down into the cellar. The cleaned casement window allowed him to make a survey of the room. Other than the wine rack, there wasn't much to see, but one object drew his eye. Hanging from a hook on the south wall was a coil of hemp rope, about fifty or more feet of it. Frank wondered why it was there. A further examination of the room revealed the reason.

The wine racks had ropes strung across their length and under the necks of the wine bottles at their shoulders. The half inch diameter hemp was tied off with large knots at the outer sides of the thick oak. The ropes gave support to the downward angle of the bottles and apparently could be adjusted to achieve the desired pitch to keep the corks wet, supple, and swollen.

Frank instantly saw purpose for the find.

*   *   *

At noon, Mitch Davis crawled out from under the soft comforter on the del Coronado's king bed and trudged to the bathroom to flood water on his crusty eyes. He was fully dressed except for shoes and his head ached like he was having a terminal migraine. The medicine cabinet was filled with soaps, bath oils, and shampoos in little sampler bottles, but no medicine. He thought the cabinet was totally misnamed, slammed its mirrored door shut, and jammed on his Nikes. A minute later he was taking the elevator to the bar. Hair of the proverbial dog was what he needed. A lot of it. And he'd charge it to Malay's bill.

Each drink tasted smoother than the one before and soon the throbbing in his temples subsided. Drinking felt good, especially when it included good boozes like Wild Turkey and Makers Mark.

Malay still scared him, but with what he held over the lawyer's head he'd now be a partner with the fancy-fuck attorney. Milk him for all he was worth. Mitch knew he could turn the video over to the cops anytime, but what would that get him? A pat on the back and a thank you? Shit, living on the high side was nice. He and Malay would split ole Rico's pesos and live the life that that Cuban prick used to have.

Yep, he finally had the world by the ass.

*   *   *

Malay parked his Mercedes on Wilson, half a block from the home of the Stukowskis, and punched in the phone number he'd found online on the "white pages." The burner cell phone speaker sounded three rings.

"Hello," a pleasant feminine voice said.

"Is this Mrs. Stukowski?" Malay asked.

"Uh … yes it is."

"Mrs. Stukowski, this is Detective Matthews of the Huntington Beach Police Department. We have your son and need you to come here to take him home."

"Oh, my, what's he done?"

"He hasn't done anything wrong. He was attacked by a gang of hoodlums and roughed up a bit. They stole his car and we have men out tracking it down."

"Huntington Beach, you say? Where is your station?"

"We are located on the South East corner of Yorktown and Main at 2000 Main Street."

There was a long pause on the phone that made a tiny bead of sweat develop on Malay's forehead. Malay had looked up the actual address of the Huntington Beach Police Department just to be safe, but as good as his ruse was, pregnant pauses still produced anxious perspiration.

"I'm writing what you said down," Mrs. Stukowski said. "Yorktown and Main in Huntington Beach. My husband and I are over in Costa Mesa, but we'll be right there."

"Excellent. You drive safely. We'll be looking for you."

Malay ended the call and watched the white stucco house fifty yards up the street. In less than five minutes, a middle-aged woman and man hurried from the house and drove away in a red Toyota of pre-millennium vintage. Malay waited a enough time to hear a Top 40 song on the radio, then drove up Wilson and parked in the Toyota's vacated space. A minute later he was at the back door of the house. It was unlocked. Malay shook his head in disbelief, and stepped inside.

He called into the house, "Hello. Anybody home?" and waited for a response. No response. Assessing where a lower middle class household would keep important documents came down to dresser drawers, desks, trunks, and fire-proof lock boxes. The upper middle class used safe deposit boxes in banks and often had fire-proof containers as well, but the Stukowskis would likely be folks who trusted the simple security of their own home, a foolish reliance, at best.

Malay found the troublesome letter and video tape cassette in the bottom drawer of a lateral file in the den.

With the small parcel stuffed in the back of his waistband under his jacket, his steps were retraced and Malay drove away, mindful that no one paid any attention to his visit.

Now it was time to choreograph the death and disappearance of Mr. Davis.

*   *   *

Gentle currents swirled in the bottom of the pool as Frank tugged on the iron grate, which was larger than a semi's tire. His brain was about to demand a breath when the grate pulled away from the concrete pipe it covered. He shot the eight feet to the surface and gasped, filling his burning lungs with precious air.

He glided through the sea water to the edge of the pool nearest to the mansion, vaulted himself out of the water, and retrieved his machete. The afternoon air was warm and felt good after his cooling dip. He stretched and extended his arms high above his head. It was then that he heard the rustling noises, like dry brush being trampled.

"Good God, there *are* more than one of them," Frank uttered aloud.

Ten yards away, at the edge of the jungle tree line stood six Komodo dragons staring at him, their tails thrashing from side to side. Slimy goo dripped from their mouths.

Frank gathered up the rope next to the pool.

*   *   *

The cool night sky was alive with stars as Malay returned to the Hotel del Coronado. He found their room empty, but spotted Mitch's cell lying on the nightstand, which he tucked into his inside jacket pocket.

Downstairs, he settled his bill at the desk, collected Mitch from the bar, who was two degrees from being falling-down drunk, and drove to Guzman's yacht. The *Mago* would be the perfect place to end the threat of Mitch. Davis. It might be tricky, but Malay would take care of the details. His life had earned him an honorary doctorate in handling details, albeit self-awarded.

Mitch slept for most of the ride, but as the car jolted over the marina's speed bumps, he stirred enough to open his lazy eyes to survey his whereabouts.

"Why are we going to the yacht?' Mitch asked as the Mercedes pulled into its familiar marina space and parked.

"We need to get that boat in shape for sale," Malay said. "A lot of money is sitting unused on the water."

"I have to swab decks?"

"No. We need to take inventory of what will be needed. Later I'll bring in a cleaning crew."

"How much is it worth?'

"Enough for you to live like royalty for the rest of your life."

"All right, man. I'm down with that."

Malay led the way to the yacht and they boarded her, Mitch struggling to mount the inclined gangway.

"I want to see the staterooms that you guys used when you were here. Which one was yours?"

"I'll show you," Mitch said and lumbered into the main companionway.

A few stair steps later, Malay stood in Mitch's quarters, a classic ship's stateroom turned into a living space redesigned by a wayward teen. The mussed bed looked like it had never been made. Empty beer bottles and drink glasses lay strewn from night table to dresser to deck. The smell of stale cigarette smoke and spilled beer permeated the room's air.

"Nice digs, eh?" Mitch said.

"Elegant," Malay said. "Let's head aft to check the fantail bar."

"Can we have a drink while we're there?"

"Absolutely, my friend. Could use one myself."

On the fantail, Malay lit the bar lights and made a straight bourbon drink for Mitch and popped the cap on a Perrier for himself.

"Bottoms up," Malay said, serving the round.

Mitch slugged down the drink and slammed the glass on the teak bar.

"I'll have another, Mr. Barkeep."

Malay complied, filling Mitch's glass the brim. Mitch took a little longer to consume the fresh bourbon drink and stared at Malay with a blank expression.

"There are several large scratches where the Zodiac went over the side. We need to see how much damage needs to be repaired before we put the *Mago* up for sale. We need to replace the Zodiac as well."

"Scratches," Mitch said, slurring the word. "We don't need no stinkin' scratches."

Mitch laughed at his movie misquote.

"We most assuredly don't," Malay said, "but let's take a look."

"Tonight? It's dark out."

"I've got a light, and we'll need to use safety lines."

"What you mean 'safety lines?'"

"You'll see. Let's go."

Malay steadied Mitch as they jostled their way to the deck that formerly carried the Zodiac. It had been secured on the seaward side of the wide deck where mooring lines now lay near the gunwale. A swim deck extended from the stern outside the transom. Malay shone his flashlight on the swim deck, a ladder descent below.

"We need to step out onto this deck to get a good sight angle on the damage," Malay said as Mitch swayed next to him. "Tie this line around your leg for safety. You don't want to slip overboard in this cold water."

Malay extended one of the mooring lines to Mitch, who stared at it like it was a dead snake.

"All right," Malay said. "I'll hook you up."

Malay tied the heavy line around Mitch's right ankle and then tied the other line around his own.

"Okay, now step onto the swim deck ladder with me," Malay said, offering a hand while he tethered Mitch with the line.

Mitch bumbled over the transom, clambered down the ten rungs, and plopped unsteadily onto the swim deck with Malay's help. Malay followed and moved to the starboard edge of the narrow deck and peered up at the side of the vessel. He took a small flashlight from his pocket and shone it on the side of the yacht.

"Take a look up there," Malay said. "You can see the marks."

Malay switched places with Mitch and guided him to the edge with a hand in the small of his back. Mitch stretched to see the boat's side as Malay washed his light on the imaginary damage.

"Get a good look," Malay said, nudging Mitch farther out on the edge of the deck. "We need to make a detailed report to the insurance company."

"Man, it's hard to stand out here … I think I should …"

Malay made one last look around to make sure no other eyes were able to see them, then shoved Mitch into the water, lapping only two feet below the swim deck.

"Oh, God," Mitch said falling, then plunged head-first into the dark bay water.

"Bottoms up," Malay said under his breath.

Malay pulled up firmly on the line around Mitch's leg and held his foot out of the water for more than three minutes. Mitch flailed and struggled violently, but couldn't get his head back above water. Soon all activity below the surface stopped. Malay untied the line and let Mitch's body slip into the blackness below.

Malay returned the two mooring lines to where they had been coiled and hosed off the decks to remove any footprints.

Malay felt certain that when Mitch's body was discovered, the authorities would examine him and find that he had been well past drunk, apparently fell into the water, and drowned. Simple as that. Many cops already knew that Mitch stayed on Guzman's boat, so there would be little suspicion of any foul play.

The Mitch Davis threat: eliminated.

*   *   *

Frank scoured the grounds of the Prescott mansion for anything useful for combat. His sweep of the back yard brought him to something puzzling. He conjured with its meaning and formed a theory.

Apparently Sanford Prescott planned to dig a moat around the property. A four-foot wide ditch, sixty yards long, and more than eight feet deep, curved across the yard a hundred feet from the back of the mansion. It extended to the pool but stopped a few feet short, as if awaiting later connection to the seawater supply from the swimming pool. The walls of the ditch were sheer and slippery-moist from the natural humidity and ground moisture of the island.

Several chickens had fallen into the ditch and strutted about at the earthen bottom in confusion, with no ability to escape. The scene had given Frank an idea, a tactical one the marines would've been proud to use.

He gathered small twigs and grassy weeds.

*   *   *

That night, Frank stayed busy while he felt safe from any visit from Rico Guzman. Tomorrow he'd have to be more on guard. A crude spear had rewarded him with a couple of fish, a pleasant change from the epicurean monotony of coconut meat.

Drinking was a dilemma. He suspected that many of the vintage wines in the cellar were not only potable, but delicious, with their classic labels from French chateau wineries the likes of Lafite Rothschild, Margaux, and Latour. But drinking wine might dull his senses, and alcohol could dehydrate him at a time when water would be as important as air. He'd have coconut milk and pretend it was Bailey's Irish Cream.

Amazingly, the chickens, absent during his last visit, had returned. Survival, concerning food, had blossomed into a tropical feast. The fireplace, where he cooked the fish and poultry, produced minimal smoke, since he'd burned only aged oak balusters ripped from the staircase, and promptly extinguished the fire after use. He was keenly aware that any fire announced itself by wafting its distinctive smell on the airways, but he allowed that he would be alone this first night. Tomorrow might be a different story.

Staying inside the mansion would be chancy after tonight. Tomorrow he'd take his issued tools, plus a bow he'd fashioned from a bed slat and a strand of mattress wire, and seek safer digs. Hickory shafts from an ancient set of golf clubs proved arrow-worthy, and he'd tested his archery skills on a few chickens he's snuck upon as they pecked seeds in a flower bed. Now it was time to look around for a suitable new hideout and a secure place to sleep.

Outside, the sky was overcast. Dark clouds promised rain and he was thankful his heavy work was done. Outside he noticed something else. Two men from the inmate community stood across the back yard. They carried machetes and stared at Frank.

"Paybacks can be hell, detective," the chunky one with a gravelly voice said.

"I dreamed of having a shot at you like this," the skinnier man said. "Every night in Folsom I dreamed of this moment."

Frank readied the bow and loaded an arrow.

"No *Playboy*s and *Hustler*s in the magazine rack?" Frank said.

"You don't reckon for real you're gonna hurt anybody with that piece of shit bow and arrow, do you?" Chunky said.

Frank held his readied arrow pointed to the ground and kept his gaze on the two men. The skinny one began slapping his machete on his palm and marched toward Frank. The stocky man joined in the march and walked on a parallel line with his partner. They moved in lock step for another three yards. Frank held his position.

The next stride made by the inmates landed on what appeared to be solid ground covered with weeds, but it gave way. In one second, the two men plunged into the ground and disappeared. Frank approached the eight-foot deep ditch he'd covered and peered at the men below lying on their backs. The ditch extended for thirty yards in both directions from where the two men lay.

Skinny scrambled to his feet, looked up, and said, "Are you're so stupid, dick, you don't think we can't climb outa here and get at you."

"Tell that to your ditch mates," Frank said.

"What the fuck you talkin' about, asshole?" Chunky said.

From the darkness of the weed-covered tunnel on either side of the inmates slithered two Komodo dragons, their razor-toothed maws agape.

"Jesus, man, what the fuck…?" Skinny yelled as one dragon clamped his jaw on his leg.

The chunky man scrambled to recover the machete he'd dropped when he fell in, but the other Komodo was on him, snapping his saliva-slick teeth again and again on the man's face.

Frank knew that even if the two inmates could muster the strength and ingenuity to escape the ditch, they would only prolong the inevitable. In twenty-four hours the Komodos would follow their infected scent, track them down, and devour them while they were still breathing. Tracking them in that ditch wouldn't pose much of a problem for the giant reptiles.

The screams from the ditch filled the pre-rain air. A third man emerged from the tree line and stared at Frank. Frank recognized him as the outspoken man at the council meeting convened by Dan Crawford.

"Care to join your friends?" Frank asked, pointing to the collapsed vegetation that had concealed the ditch.

"No fucking way, dude," the man said and scurried back into the cover of the jungle.

The noises from the ditch reduced to growls from the dragons and moans from the men. Frank left it at that and headed to the cabana behind the pool. It would provide shelter and give him a wide view of the house and grounds. When and if Guzman found this compound, Frank would fight the battle here on familiar territory.

*   *   *

Daley Foster had not heard from Mitch Davis, going on six days. He had called her at least once every day, and while she had ended their romance, she still cared about him and agreed to accept one of his video tapes along with its dreary instructions. She had tried to contact him on his cell, but her calls went unanswered. Mitch warned her that should trouble befall him, she was to follow the video tape instructions to the letter.

Daley called Detective Judd Kemp at the San Diego Police Department.

"Detective Kemp, this is Daley Foster. I have information for you from Mitch Davis. I understand you know him."

"I do," Judd said. "Where is he?"

"I'm not sure. He calls me every day, but I haven't heard from him for almost a week. He said to contact you if I suspected something was wrong. He left me specific instructions and a video tape."

"Do you know what's on the tape?"

"No, but I know it has something to do with one of your detectives."

"Which detective?"

"The one who was convicted of murder and was on TV a while back."

"Frank Dugan?" Judd asked.

"Yes, that's him."

"Can you come see me at the station?"

"I'll leave now."

"You know how to get here?"

"I know where it is. I went there one night to visit one of Mitch's friends."

"I'll alert the desk sergeant to pass you through."

*   *   *

It was morning of the fourth day. The sun was hidden behind the island, east of where Rico Guzman lay nestled in palm fronds. He slid out from his crude shelter, stood, and danced his legs to increase their circulation.

Two of his days had been spent blazing paths into the brambles and thick greenery. Nothing of Frank Dugan had materialized. Guzman had retreated to the shoreline.

He gazed at the narrow beach to the north and realized that traversing the outer perimeter of the island merely indulged his own desire to take the easiest route. He knew the interior would have to be penetrated if finding Frank Dugan topped his agenda, but he saw something in the distance that piqued his interest enough to walk the sandy strip a few more paces.

Two hundred yards later, he saw the remains of a broken-down, rickety pier.

Stories had floated through his new inmate population about the history of the island, a history that surrounded the Prescott family and their rich patriarch Sanford. The stories centered on the tropical retreat the millionaire had built on the island, but convicts had been led to believe that any evidence of the elegant resort had long disappeared, the victim of many violent storms. But here Guzman plainly could see the vestiges of a man-made pier. And where there was a weather-exposed pier, there could also be a better protected building or two nearby whose condition may have fared better.

Rico paced inland from the pier, up a gentle slope, and encountered a paved walkway. His eyes followed where the pavers led.

They led to a Spanish mansion.

Chapter 44

Errol Malay sipped a neat 18-year-old Glenlivet in his country club lounge and surveyed the new menu the chef had put together for the fall season. A young man with a sexy woman ambled by his table and Malay's prurient imagination undressed her twice before the couple made it to the bar. The pleasant interruption of his menu perusal made him recall something Mitch Davis had said when they'd chatted over dinner at the club. It was almost insignificant, a small, a throwaway tidbit, but Malay didn't achieve his competitive edge by overlooking even the tiniest detail that could prove important.

Malay played back the evening with Mitch. He had purposely guided the conversation to determine Mitch's relatives who might have received one of the video tape copies of the Gaither murder. Mitch had mentioned his mother, his uncle, and something else … *someone* else. A girlfriend that he'd broken up with recently.

Could he have given her one of the tapes?

He had to find her. But how?

Malay rose from the table and rushed out to get to his car. Mitch's cell phone was in the glove compartment. He had meant to get rid of it, but now was elated that he'd kept it. Mitch's girlfriend's number had to be on that phone's call log.

Five minutes later, Malay found numerous calls to "Daley" in Mitch's call log and contact list. He dialed her number.

"Hello," a female voice said.

"Is this Daley?" Malay asked.

"Yes. Who's this?"

"I'm Robert Platt, a friend of Mitch's. I haven't seen him lately and was a little concerned about him. We had plans to meet for dinner tonight and he never called to confirm."

"I haven't heard from him lately, either."

"Maybe you and I can figure out where he might be. Can we meet somewhere?"

"I'm on my way to the police. Mitch left me instructions to contact them if I didn't hear from him for several days."

"The San Diego police? Who are you seeing there?"

"His name is Detective Kem—"

"Who?"

"Look mister, I don't know who you are. Why are you asking me all these questions?"

"I have a video tape he gave me," Malay said, his mind racing to say what he needed to find out where this girl was. "I'm supposed to contact the police too, but I don't think Mitch is in any trouble. His uncle told me he was there last night at his house for dinner."

"So you feel giving this video to the police is premature?'

"Exactly. It could cause Mitch a lot of trouble."

"I don't know ..."

"Look, why don't you meet me at the police station and we'll go over things and decide whether to give the detective the tape or not."

"At the station ... ?"

"Which one?" Malay asked, certain it was Judd Kemp's and that was the name she'd left unfinished.

"The central station on Imperial."

"Be there in ten minutes," Malay said. "How will I recognize you?"

"I'm driving a white Mazda 6."

"I'll find you."

Malay raced from the country club parking lot and tore toward downtown San Diego. From Chula Vista to Imperial Avenue should only take him a few minutes in midday traffic.

*   *   *

The mansion looked dilapidated and unoccupied, but Rico Guzman didn't trust such an unconfirmed assessment without proof. He drew the machete from its scabbard and mounted the porch steps, stopping on each tread to listen for any suspicious sound.

At the front door he peeked inside through the broken window lights that framed the entrance. He saw nothing but an open, dirt-swept space. Inside, he crept through the hall and checked each room as they passed his view. The inspection of the house gave him a few clues regarding human occupancy. An unopened bottle of French wine sat on the mantelpiece, ashes in the fireplace looked new, and the fresh evergreen boughs on the floor were matted in places, as if recently slept on. That recent occupant had to be the man he sought. The question now was should he wait in the house to ambush him on his return, or venture outside and hunt him down?

The house smelled of bad air. Guzman stepped outside and made a careful survey of the grounds. Gnarring sounds rose from the earth in the back yard. He took wary steps to where they emanated and ended at what appeared to be a deep hole in the overgrown weeds. Blood trails streamed from the hole, two sets of them. Looking down, he could see the remains of many dead chickens below, but nothing to which to attribute the sounds, so he bent lower and tried to see into the covered passage on the right. Nothing but darkness. As he cocked his head to the left, a huge set of vicious jaws leapt upward at his face and snapped, falling short of their mark by inches. Guzman reeled and stumbled onto the prickly ground. The Komodo dragon jumped to the upper edge of the ditch, his head and front legs chinning and clawing to escape and get at the fallen Cuban. Rico sprang to his feet and retreated several feet and held his machete high. The dragon soon tired and resigned itself to sliding back into its earthen jail.

*　　*　　*

Frank heard the commotion in the yard and spied out from the ajar door of the cabana. It was Rico Guzman, all right. He had to give him credit for making it all the way across the island and homing in on the likely spot where he'd find his nemesis. Frank watched Guzman as he brandished his machete and glared at the ditch. The dragons had missed him. It was time to come out and go on the attack.

Frank loaded one of his hickory shaft arrows he'd sharpened to an icepick point. Its three peacock fletchings shone bright in color near the wire bowstring. He stepped out from the cabana and fully drew back the wire. The oak bed slat creaked as the arrow's point lay on the knuckle of his left index finger. Guzman turned toward the tiny sound as the arrow flew from the bow and punctured his right side below the ribs, its point protruding from his back.

"God *damn* you," Guzman hollered as he staggered from the hit.

Frank abandoned the bow, withdrew his machete, and charged toward the wounded man, who ripped out the arrow and raised his machete. The two men left

347

ten feet between them, their weapons in hand and at the ready.

"Worse things than arrows have hit me, Dugan," Guzman said. "Let's dance."

"Pulling out that arrow may make you bleed out, Rico."

"That little hole will heal as we fight."

Guzman lunged at Frank, slashing with his weapon. Frank side-stepped the attack, but Guzman managed to strike Frank's machete a prodigious blow, sending it whirling into the pool.

"Now what ya got, flatfoot?" Guzman said and prepared another assault.

Frank dove into the pool and disappeared beneath the surface. He descended to the open concrete pipe and swam into it. Thirty feet later, he came out of the pipe and broke into the afternoon sun atop the surf. He was in the ocean near the beach and in a handful of strokes later, was on the sand. He stood and took his knife from his belt and opened the main cutting blade. The dilapidated pier was a few yards to his left. There was an item there that he desperately needed.

*   *   *

Guzman watched the sloshing water in the pool for several moments.

Did the crazy bastard drown?

He searched the water as it cleared enough to make out an object on the bottom, an object like a body, but there was none. He considered going into the pool himself to see how his enemy escaped. Not such a good idea, he judged, and the wound in his side wouldn't benefit from bacteria in the water nor strenuous swimming. *Dugan could be down there with a breathing device, maybe a hose to the outside air, just waiting to attack me and get the upper hand.*

No, Rico Guzman was no fish. He would wait out Mr. Amphibious Dugan until he came back onto the land, and kill him like a man.

*　　*　　*

Errol Malay screeched into the Central Division of the SDPD and swept the public parking area with his eyes searching for the white Mazda. In less than thirty seconds, he found the vehicle and parked next to it. He saw the pretty brunette behind the wheel, left the Mercedes, and approached her driver's door. The woman stared at him through the glass.

"I'm Robert," Malay said. "Are you Daley?"

The woman rolled down her window.

"Yes," she said. "Where should we talk?"

"Here would be fine."

"Out there or in my car?"

"In the car would be better. More private. I mean, this *is* a police station."

Malay circled the Mazda and opened the passenger door. Daley had to move her purse and a manila envelope so he could sit. Malay got in and closed the door.

"Is the tape in the envelope?" Malay asked.

"Yes."

Daley let Malay feel what was inside the envelope, then held it on her lap..

"Seems like the one I got from Mitch."

"Where is yours?"

"In my car."

"I'd like to see yours," Daley said.

"Is this a 'you show me yours, I show you mine' kinda thing?" Malay said and chuckled.

"It really needs to be that way. You know, mutual trust and all."

Malay was prepared to snatch the manila envelope from Daley's lap, if he had to. Once he controlled all the tapes, anything else would be academic or, at worst, a matter of "he said, she said."

"The important thing is, Daley, we don't want to set the cops off on a witch hunt that could seriously harm Mitch. Even get him arrested."

Daley stared straight ahead out the windshield. The slight shake of her head unnerved Malay. It was the trait all court witnesses went through when they wanted to recant their testimony. Daley wasn't going to cooperate willingly. He'd have to do whatever it took to protect himself.

Malay struck like a rattlesnake and grabbed the manila envelope from Daley and moved to exit the Mazda, but stopped. Her car was surrounded by police officers. In the forefront was Detective Judd Kemp.

Kemp opened the Mazda's passenger door.

"Well, good afternoon, counselor," Kemp said. "Working your clients in parking lots these days?"

"Ambulances are so hard to catch," Malay said. "We were having a private meeting concerning one of my clients."

"Ms. Foster here says you're Robert Platt. I seem to remember you as Errol Malay."

"I didn't want to influence her by presenting myself as an attorney."

"I'm presenting myself as Detective Judd Kemp. Step out of the car," Kemp said.

Malay slowly got out and faced the detective.

"When you called Ms. Foster, she was already here. We listened in on the conversation and knew something wrong was about to take place. We asked her to play along so we could see this mysterious Mr. Platt. It was a real surprise to discover it was the most famous defense attorney in California."

"So now what?" Malay said. "I've done nothing criminal."

"You just stole that envelope from Ms. Foster," Kemp said. "We call that theft."

"I fully intended to return it to her after I saw what was in it."

"We did see what was in it. The real tape is in the station, locked in our evidence room."

"What's in this envelope?" Malay asked.

"A small pack of sticky notes," Kemp said and took the envelope from Malay. "You're under arrest for the murder of Ernest Gaither."

Kemp nodded at one of the several officers surrounding the Mazda. The officer handcuffed Malay and guided him toward the station.

"You have the right to remain silent," the officer said. "Anything you say can and will be used against you in a court of law ..."

Malay and the contingent of policemen marched into the station as the rest of his Miranda Rights were given.

*　　*　　*

Judd Kemp stuck his head in the door of Daley Foster's car.

"You did great, young lady," Kemp said. "We're all proud of you. Now I have to try to save a man who's been wrongfully sent to a penal island with men who want to kill him."

"You believe you can save him?" Daley asked.

"That is a most excellent question."

Chapter 45

Frank found the length of hemp rope he'd tossed under the pier. He hadn't figured on needing it since he'd used it to wrangle the two Komodo dragons into the ditch. He'd been confident that he could take out Guzman with the bow and arrow. At least that was the battle plan. But, as he well knew, the first thing to go when the fight begins is the battle plan. Now he scrambled to set his new offense into action.

He hoped he had enough time.

*   *   *

Dan Crawford finished sending the last cart of supplies to the warehouse and sat out on the wood pier as the overcast day was finally going home. He was concerned about Frank. Wondered how he was faring. Hoped and prayed he wasn't dead. He had always despised cops, but Frank was different. Reverent, respectful, and honest to a fault. He never made a claim or a promise that was a come-on to achieve an advantage or get a leg up on anyone. Crawford liked that and felt that there was something purely good about the man the day he met him at Pelican Bay.

Three of the community, besides Guzman and Frank, were missing. He found out who they were and wasn't surprised since they epitomized the worst of hardened criminals. All three were murderers several times over with nothing to lose by trying to escape. But escape to what? The sharks? The naval guns? There was never going to be any escape from the Resort. So where were these men and what were they up to?

Crawford was determined to find out.

* * *

Rico Guzman treated his seeping wounds with wine he'd found in the mansion's cellar. It was still drinkable and a bottle or two made his pain abate dramatically. He shredded part of his tee shirt and strapped it around his body to compress the open holes and stem the bleeding. So far, he was doing okay. Now he needed rest. Tomorrow he'd go look for Dugan or, better yet, his dead body. He had to have drowned. There was a kind of culvert, a narrow tunnel at one end of the swimming pool. If Frank swam into that and got stuck, game over. If it took him out to the ocean, the sharks would dine on his black liver, also game over. But he needed to confirm the death to be able to return to the community. Going back without knowing for sure, and then have Dugan show up alive and well? That would be a shameful embarrassment Rico Guzman's pride wasn't willing to chance.

Tomorrow he'd find that bastard's body or finish him and bring back his bloody head. Either way, he'd claim the kill and the victory.

Rico Guzman would again be king of the hill.

*   *   *

Morning. The waves at the beach rolled in gently in three to five inch laps upon the shore. Frank concealed himself under the pier by arranging a few of the loose walkway boards around him, and waited. Rico would have to at least search for him back at the beach. If Guzman followed the pool flow pipe he'd know it led to the ocean.

He'll be here, Frank thought. *He's not leaving until I'm dead.*

Three hours passed. Frank took brief cat naps and was getting cramps from bunching himself into his hiding place. If he didn't show soon, Frank was going to go looking for him and perhaps lose the advantage he had at the beach. Frank cursed the wait. Patience wasn't his long suit.

The moment Frank prepared to cast off the boards hiding him, something stirred on the paved walk coming from the mansion. It was Guzman, machete in hand, and bandaged about the torso. Frank waited until the Cuban stepped onto the soft sand of the beach and moved to within six feet of the water. Then he stepped out from under the pier, gently, so as not to scare his enemy from where he stood.

"So, you are not dead … yet," Guzman said.

Frank eased into the water, thigh deep, and stared at Guzman.

"What? Do we mud wrestle in the surf now?" Guzman said and laughed.

Frank bent low and scooped up water and washed his arms. Guzman watched Frank's ocean bathing with amusement. Frank prayed Guzman wouldn't move from where he was.

"Maybe I can get you a nice bar of soap," Guzman said. "Clean soap for a filthy fucking cop."

Frank squatted in the three feet of water until he was almost submerged and grabbed the rope hidden in the sand. He burst upward and yanked hard toward the deeper ocean. A large loop of the hemp surrounding Guzman's feet gathered around his ankles and tightened as Frank turned, set the rope over his shoulder, and pulled seaward. Guzman was thrown backward and Frank continued to drag him into the water. Guzman tried to loosen the heavy hemp ligature binding his legs, but the pressure from Frank's tugging defied his every effort. In seconds, Guzman was forced into deeper water and now fought just to keep from going under where he'd be fighting for air.

Frank reached water over his head and had to resort to swimming to tow his captive into greater depths.

Guzman flipped himself onto his stomach and tried to Australian crawl his way to freedom, but Frank's consistent tension on the rope made escape impossible.

It was then that Frank saw the fins of the gathering sharks arriving at their favorite dining time in the moderate shallows. But today, they would find more than grouper and jack crevalle on the menu.

The sharks moved in and brushed Frank with their fine sandpaper skin. They showed no interest in him, but the man in tow was apparently putting out a scent to them that was like pork barbeque to a country boy. The sharks tore into Rico Guzman, so fast he barely got out two screams before he went silent. The water around Guzman was white with froth as razor-toothed heads shot out of the water and dove below the surface again and again. Water and blood sprayed into the air as each shark ripped off a trophy arm or a hunk of calf meat until all went calm except for an occasional last snap at a remaining shred of tattered flesh.

The sharks departed as fast as they arrived and moved on to other feeding pools. Frank swam back to shore, still towing the rope. When he tugged the rope fully back onto the beach, the only parts left of Rico Guzman were his shins and ankles and half of a bloody foot.

Frank squatted on the sand and stared out to sea. It was over. He had won. The monster was dead, but he didn't feel any sense of celebratory victory. There would be no oo-rahs, no drunken dancing in the streets. Killing Guzman would never bring back Amy or Debbie or Billy. Frank almost wished the sharks had found him as appetizing as the Cuban.

Frank had to find one last thing before he gave it all up.

He needed to find a reason to go on living.

*   *   *

Judd Kemp had the video tape copied and converted to the more stable digital media that a DVD would provide. He called a meeting and showed everyone at the station the torture and murder of Ernie Gaither, which also showed the innocence of Frank Dugan, who was trapped in a deep pit during Gaither's bizarre demise.

Next, he would be showing the video to the court and perhaps the jurors who convicted Frank. Once Frank's sentence was overturned, Judd would take the lead in the rescue of his friend and partner from Prescott Island. There was no precedent for this rescue. Folks who were sent to the Resort weren't ever supposed to come back to civilization. By the time the navy got through the government red tape and obtained official approval for his release, Frank could be killed by any of the many inmates who hated him. No. Judd would go in with documents in hand, backed by lawmen, and get the job done.

Judd Kemp prepared for a series of legal battles. The first degree murder conviction of Errol Malay would help ... immensely.

*   *   *

Retracing one's steps through the growing jungle wasn't easy, but Frank made it back to the village in under six hours. He was exhausted and scratched or cut in more places on his body than he could see or touch. Dan Crawford came to visit him in their makeshift infirmary.

"You look like you lost a fight with a bobcat," Crawford said.

"Lotta scratchy shit out there in the jungle," Frank said.

"I trust you got Guzman."

"He is now a man of extinction."

"Still want that police chief's job? You just earned yourself a load of respect points among the inmates."

"What do you know about the weather?"

"The weather? We get satellite cable forecasts, why?"

"Anything big brewing?"

"Like what? A blizzard?"

"The sky the past few days has been threatening. A big storm, maybe. Maybe something bigger."

"What are you getting at?" Crawford asked.

"You know that old seaman's adage: 'Red sky at night, sailor's delight; red sky at dawn, sailor be warned?'"

"Yeah, I've heard it."

"Well, I'm looking for a red sky at dawn."

"To do what? Ironman surfing?"

"Forget it for now," Frank said. "Can you pass me that orange juice?"

"Sure. You want the screwdriver version?"

"You're shitting me. Where'd you get vodka?"

"The pharmacy."

"Jeez, what kind of cruel, horrible, tortuous prison is this place?"

*   *   *

The evidence of the video got Errol Malay convicted of the capital crime of first degree murder, among other offenses. His sentence was, of course, Resort Isle, forever. Trouble was, all this legal haranguing had taken weeks and Judd Kemp was unable to rescue Frank until the real murderer had been caught and tried.

Judd immediately requisitioned a Class A helicopter and a team of LEOs and legal specialists to retrieve Frank Dugan from the Resort. The group wouldn't set out for three days, the time needed to assemble the team and acquire transportation.

Judd Kemp was hopeful, but dread kept creeping into his wishful thoughts. If Frank was dead, he might kill Malay himself, especially if he could borrow the use of those two overhead cranes at the Seaside Marina.

*　　*　　*

Judd Kemp contacted Marty Dimino and Charly Stone to relay the good news about Frank's overturned conviction. They, of course, were beyond elated and well into near-terminal ecstasy. He cut their conversation short because his rotary wing ride was warming on the Central Division's heliport on Broadway. In less than an hour he'd be landing on a cruiser at Prescott Island and enlisting the help of the U.S. Navy guardians there to find Frank Dugan. They would open the locks on the security pier and pass him through to the waiting 'copter.

Judd's heart pounded with anticipation as he boarded the Sikorsky SH-60 Seahawk, capable of over 160 MPH. The crewmen strapped Judd in, gave him a headset, and lifted off.

Words Frank had said to him echoed in Judd's head:

"I'll be okay. God didn't spend all His time nurturing me to see me die like a mad dog on a prison island."

Judd hoped that was the gospel truth.

The pre-dawn surf was light with small waves leap-frogging over each other making barely-audible splashes. Frank sat in the sand and watched the eastern horizon. The top of the sun revealed only a bright sliver as it rose above the far-away line where ocean met sky.

"Sunrise is a beautiful time," Dan Crawford said as he padded up behind Frank. "It symbolizes a beginning; a new day to serve the Lord and accomplish good things."

"I agree," Frank said. "It's particularly beautiful this morning."

"Why is that?"

"Look at the sky out there."

"I see it. So what's special about it?"

"It's red."

"You want bad weather?"

"I do," Frank said and rose. "Today, I'm going on my journey."

"What does that mean?" Dan asked and moved in front of Frank to face him.

"It means I'm leaving this island."

"How?"

"I'm going to swim away."

"Frank, you know you can't do that. Those sharks will kill you before you make twenty strokes."

"I know things that you don't about sharks."

"You sound like a crazy man. That battle with Guzman has affected your mind. Listen to me—"

"You listen to me. I'm not crazy. Sharks don't bother with me. I know that sounds nuts, but it's true, and I've encountered them more than once without a scratch."

Dan looked at the sand and shook his head.

"How do you think I killed Guzman by dragging him into the sharks without them killing me as well?"

"Luck," Dan said with a shrug.

"Luck, my Aunt Fanny. It's the strangest thing anyone's ever heard of."

"So let's say you can avoid being dinner for the sharks, then what? You figure you can make it to Monterey?

"I don't need to swim it to the mainland, only to a place five miles from here."

"Then what?"

"You ask too many questions. Trust that I have a plan."

Frank's plan depended on the navy's heavy reliance on the efficacy of the shark deterrent more than the use of sweeping patrol boats with armed crews. He believed he could handle the sharks. Military men laying down automatic gunfire, not so much.

"Swimming five miles is a crazy plan to begin with. After that, I can't imagine …"

"But I *do* imagine, Dan."

"I never dreamed I could like a cop, but after you walked into Pelican Bay and we talked, I saw a man who wasn't the adversary I'd made him to be. You've given us a place we can endure. Pelican Bay was not endurable. For that, I'll always be thankful to you."

"And now I'm going to try to escape the inescapable place I practically invented."

"You won't escape. And I'll miss my friend who talks of friendly sharks and marathon swims."

"I'm not saying I couldn't use a few prayers, pastor. If I make it, I'll send you a message in something they don't check in your weekly supplies."

"What are you talking about? They check everything that comes here."

"Not this, they won't."

Crawford waved off Frank's comments as the ravings of a crazy man.

"When are you planning to leave?"

Frank removed his tee shirt and gave Dan a bear hug.

"Now," Frank said and quietly slipped into the surf.

The sky was now vivid red mixed with deep gray ominous clouds. Lightning bolts slashed the sky, too far away to make their thunder heard.

Frank felt the storm of the century was brewing.

It was coming to meet a lone man who could swim with sharks.

Chapter 46

The big Sikorsky dropped onto the deck of the USS Cortez, an Austin Class joint command ship refitted for the purpose of oversight at Prescott Island. The helicopter rolled and yawed in the powerful wind churning up spray from the white-capped sea. Judd Kemp bolted from the aircraft as soon as the wheels hit the deck and hurried for the bridge with an escort of two shore patrol sailors. The helicopter had radioed ahead and stated the purpose for the visit, but Judd wanted to head up the reception group who would be stationed at the ocean side of the security pier. He wanted to be the first face Frank would see as he stepped from captivity to freedom.

Judd and the sailors entered the bridge.

"Where are we in finding Frank Dugan?" Judd asked the exec officer of the Cortez.

"We are nowhere," the commander said. "No one can find him."

"The village isn't that big, commander. Don't they have a PA system?"

"They do. We're trying to locate one of the leaders on the island."

The radio sputtered and a scratchy voice said, "We've got a man here named Crawford. He has information on the lost inmate."

The commander keyed his mike.

"Bring him onto the pier and escort him to our side," the commander said and looked at Judd. "We need to go below to the pier gate."

By the time Judd and the commander arrived at the gate, Dan Crawford was on the other side of the locked entrance, cuffed hands and ankles. Two armed SPs stood nearby.

"Let the inmate through," the commander said and the electronic gate opened to allow Crawford passage.

"Are you Mr. Crawford?" the commander asked.

"I am Reverend Crawford," Dan said.

"What can you tell us about Frank Dugan?" Judd asked.

"Not much, I'm afraid, sirs. He went into the jungle to settle an issue with another inmate. Man named Rico Guzman. Neither man has come out. Been fifteen days now."

"Any chance of getting a search party together to find him?" the commander said.

"No chance, sir," Crawford said. "The men sent here have no obligation to do any dangerous outside work. I can barely get them to do the things we need to do to keep the place livable. And they're not fond of going into that thick, bug-infested jungle, especially in weather like this."

"What do you want to do, detective?" the commander asked.

"Can I stay here until we get some answers?" Judd said.

"Aye, sir. We'll set you up in my quarters. You don't want to go anywhere in this weather."

Judd hung his head and trudged back toward the Cortez while Crawford was shuffled back onto the pier and locked out from the seaside gate. He watched as Crawford short-stepped his way down the long pier, his body blown from side to side in the wind. He watched until they unshackled the reverend and released him onto the beach. The only contact he had to Frank was gone and had offered little about Frank's whereabouts. Judd's plans to rescue his friend lay dashed. Maybe they could find Frank. Maybe he'd stroll back into the village, alive and the victor of his "issue" with Guzman.

Maybe …

*   *   *

Dan Crawford had no idea why these visitors from California wanted to find Frank Dugan, but he wasn't about to rat him out so they could fish him out of the ocean and return him where he didn't want to be. He was terrified of what Frank was undertaking, but he respected his wishes to make a run for it. At least he would die a free man. Now he had to ask God to forgive him for lying to those men who wanted Frank for some unknown reason.

367

He looked to the north where Frank had set his course. Where he had watched his strong low strokes ever-pulling the man away from the land. He had watched until he could no longer see his friend in the surging chop, but continued to gaze, imagining his progress. Dan watched until the storm gusted so hard that sand tore at his body and stung his narrowed eyelids.

Crawford prayed for the cop he had come to care about. He hoped one day Frank would shed his pent up anger and find a true home for his chaotic life and be at peace.

Red sky at dawn ... sailor be warned ...

Crawford figured that would go triple for a lone swimmer betting against all the odds.

*   *   *

Frank felt the brush-bys of the sharks as he stroked his way toward the volcanic island. He felt they came instinctively out of curiosity, or for their endless search for food, but maybe to just say hello to a creature they had a strange kinship with. Whatever their reasons, they came and went, seemingly unaware or unconcerned about the heavy chop that now comprised the building white-capped waves.

As Frank reached what he judged to be the halfway point, his limbs burned from the heavy exertion. He turned onto his back and performed the "elementary backstroke" he'd learned in the Boy Scouts. It was restful and recuperative for his weary muscles. The kinder summer water soothed the aching like a warm shower, and was certainly a dramatic contrast to the cold Pacific he'd often experienced in his Marine training in the October waters off San Diego.

The storm was threatening to rage and the atmosphere wielded an eerie pressure that Frank felt in his ears. He had to get back to swimming, and swimming as fast and as steady as he could bear.

Another mile slipped under him and he thought he was either hallucinating or he could actually see the volcanic ridges of his destination.

Half a mile more. The rain was pelting him like water bullets, then worsened by gusting winds to a blinding spray. Exhaustion crept in. Had he come this far to now surrender to the depths? Each stroke was painful. He hadn't judged how difficult the swim would be in such adverse weather conditions. The storm he desperately needed was going to kill him before he could put it to good use.

His thoughts ebbed in and out, then something struck him from behind. Fear rippled through his exhausted body. Maybe the sharks had found a feature appetizing about him after all. Maybe he'd been wrong the whole time about his immunity from their killer instincts. Again, a ramming came from beneath his back that nearly lifted him out of the water. He rolled over to see the attacker that would be taking his life.

It was a dolphin.

*   *   *

God had paid him a visit, Frank thought, in the form of a pod of dolphins that pushed and nudged his spent body into the shallows of the lagoon where the *Esperanza* lay grounded. A few crickety chatters later and they were gone.

Frank slogged onto the land and gazed at the heeled over hull of his beautiful sailboat. The storm now raised the curtain on its Act II surprise: steady torrential rain. Lots of it, pouring from the heavens like the world's largest waterfall. The *Esperanza* rose from her heeled-over position and soon rolled from side to side, and for moments appeared to be fighting to float upright. She was pulling free from the bottom and Frank had to get to her now. Timing was everything.

The lagoon swim to the boat was a cakewalk compared to what he'd experienced in the open ocean, but he was nearly spent. He was so close to the finish line and he now needed a sprinter's "kick" to make it to the imaginary tape that was the swim deck of the drifting sailboat. He summoned the last drop of his strength to stroke the final few yards and pulled himself onto the narrow deck on the stern. He dragged his numb body over the transom onto the aft deck. He managed to stand, but his legs shook with weakness. The erratic motion of the wind-blown sloop twice dropped him to his knees as his uncertain balance was compromised with each roll of the boat.

After a fierce struggle, Frank managed to unfurl and set the jib and felt it surge and fill, its sheets tugging at the mast and his hands as the *Esperanza* pitched and yawed her way into the deeper water. He dared not unfurl the mainsail for fear it would be ripped from the mast in the typhoon wind, but the jib was giving the boat ample headway. The *Esperanza*, after months of lying embedded in the mud of the lagoon, and Frank, after captivity on a prison island, were both sailing free again.

Frank brought her about and sailed her into the ocean. He turned her into the wind and dropped the jib and furled it. He set the bow anchor and went below to wait out the storm, which soon abated and turned northwest.

Later that night, weather permitting, he would set a course for Marina del Rey. Tonight he'd raid the galley, eat a can of beef stew, and drink a couple of St. Pauli Girls.

Tomorrow he would see Captain James Fiske and ask for asylum while he hunted down Mr. Errol Malay. Tomorrow he would head the *Esperanza* toward freedom and a new chance to find vindication.

He was a detective. He needed to solve his own predicament.

Frank smiled as he thought of the name of his boat, *Esperanza*.

It was the Spanish word for hope.

Chapter 47

The *Esperanza* sailed into the marina late at night and tied up at the visitors' dock. Frank waited until daybreak to walk down the quay and approach the door of the harbormaster's office. He peered inside, but saw no one.

"What can we do for you, young feller?" a familiar voice said from Frank's back.

Frank turned to the voice.

"Well, great Caesar's ghost," Fiske said. "Frank Dugan."

"Can we talk inside?" Frank asked.

"Sure, sure. Get yourself in there."

They entered the office and Fiske locked the door and hung the "Out to Lunch" sign.

"I need to buy a little time to get to a man named Errol Malay," Frank said.

"Errol Malay's in jail."

"What do you mean? He got arrested? For what?"

"For murder. The one everyone was certain you did. Everyone but me, that is."

Frank collapsed into Fiske's desk chair.

"Let me get this straight," Frank said and placed his palms flat on the desk. "Malay finally got found out about Ernie Gaither's murder and how he framed me for the crime."

"That'd be the *Reader's Digest* version, yeah."

"When was someone going to tell me about this?"

"Already have…I thought. Feller named Kemp was supposed to fly out and get you back to civilization. Saw it on the news yesterday."

"Oh, shit. Now he's looking all over Prescott Island for me and I'm sitting here."

"Well, why didn't he run into you on the island?"

"Captain, that's such a long story I don't believe either of us will live long enough to fully tell it. Here's the short version. I swam to the island where the *Esperanza* was aground and the storm last night got her up so I could sail here."

"Christ knows, that's short enough, but I get the gist."

"I need to contact the police in San Diego. I'm a little short on cash. May I use your phone?"

"Of course. Pay me when you can," Fiske said and laughed.

"It gets worse. I also need a car."

*   *   *

Judd Kemp's helicopter touched down at the SDPD heliport on Broadway. A waiting police cruiser sped Judd to the Delaney's Restaurant in Dana Point where Frank had suggested they meet, about halfway between Marina del Rey and San Diego.

374

Frank was at the bar when Judd charged in and yanked him off his bar stool and hugged him long and hard enough to make Frank blush.

"I love you too, man," Frank said.

Judd released his grip on Frank.

"Now that we've convinced everyone here that we're gay ... " Judd said.

"Who cares? You know these people?"

"Good point," Judd said. "God damn, it's awfully good to see you, partner."

"Back at ya. Never thought I'd ever see Delaney's again."

"You had to come back for the clam chowder."

They had a laugh and sat at the bar. They ordered drinks and waited until the bartender moved out of earshot.

"So my CIs tell me Malay's in the can and has a reservation for the Resort," Frank said.

"You have the correct intel."

Judd proceeded to relate to Frank the details of acquiring the video tape from Mitch Davis via his ex-girlfriend Daley, and all that went with it.

"So, what's the plan now?" Judd asked.

"I haven't had time to give that much thought. Never figured I'd need to, but I might drift back to my old detective job in Baltimore."

"And leave sunny California?"

"Too many bad memories here, Judd. I need to go somewhere the scenery doesn't haunt me. I look out there at Dana Point and remember Amy and me swimming with the kids. Every place I go there's something to remind me of them. It'll be easier if I don't keep seeing her dancing on the beach and riding Pirates of the Caribbean at Disney with Deb and Billy."

"Those are not bad memories, Frank. Those scenes make up the movie of your life. You will always see those happy scenes. Embrace them. Folks like me never had great ones like that."

"I guess I'm the only one who sees them, so it's my personal—"

"You're not the only one," Judd said.

"Well, I hate having to leave, but I may operate better in Baltimore."

"I get that. I'll miss you, buddy. We'll all miss you."

"Me too."

"Now I want to hear about the fight with Rico Guzman," Judd said. "I got a feeling this is going to be better than ringside at Thrilla in Manila."

"Better get yourself a couple more drinks."

*　　*　　*

Frank returned the borrowed car to Captain Fiske at Marina del Rey and told him to sell the *Esperanza* and keep a twenty percent commission. That would more than cover the long distance phone bill.

There was one more thing left to do. He had to see Marty and Charly Dimino and say goodbye.

They were living at Marty's beach house when he wasn't in Washington and Marty was home for the summer.

Frank parked the rental on the beach road and rang the doorbell. Charly answered.

"We heard the good news," Charly said and clutched Frank like he was her long lost child, tears in her eyes. "God, it's good to see you."

Marty's voice boomed from the bedroom.

"Who's at the door?"

"It's Frank," Charly said.

"Don't let him in or he'll want to stay and suck up our liquor," Marty said, appearing in the hall. "We'll never get rid of him."

Frank came in and embraced Marty.

"Welcome home, kid," Marty said. "I thought we'd lost you."

They sat in the den and had drinks and told stories. After an hour, Frank stood and stared at his favorite couple.

"I see my Bronco's still here," Frank said. "I would've bet it'd be on the police auction block by now."

"Judd Kemp wouldn't allow anyone to touch it," Marty said.

"I'm going back to Baltimore," Frank said.

"You told us why," Charly said. "I understand."

"Write if you get work," Marty said.

Frank stood. The Diminos started to get up, but Frank stopped them with his extended palm.

"Let me remember you two just the way you are," Frank said and went out the door, squared his shoulders, and drove away.

*   *   *

Frank steered the Bronco east onto the Santa Monica freeway and wended his way through the late morning traffic. He reviewed his decision to leave California and decided it was a good one. He would apply to get his old detective job back at the Baltimore City Police Department where his father was a veteran beat cop.

Frank and his father were not close. Years of drinking, gambling debts, and childhood abuse by the father had destroyed any affection between the two men, but Frank would be civil with his dad in the workplace, and on the rare occasions when he felt obligated to visit and offer help to the aging patriarch in tasks he could no longer do.

As a policeman, Frank would continue to pursue and collar the bad guys. If those bad guys were cruel to animals, the helpless, or children, Frank Dugan would bring the whirlwind, the whirlwind from hell.

*   *   *

A local fisherman eased his john boat near the tiny islands dotting the coastline of Long Beach, California. Fishing in this area had often been productive in the past so he drifted among the small land masses hoping to spot a good place to cast his line. Most of these islets contained oil pumps cycling their mechanized arms up and down, ceaselessly. As he passed one without a pump, he was amazed to see a small animal. At first he thought it was a hamster, but upon a closer look he realized it was a field mouse, a brown and white one.

The fisherman floated on by, but wondered what that little creature had done to end up on such an isolated dot of land surrounded by an ocean.

*　　*　　*

Dan Crawford sorted through the items in the supply carton addressed to his non-denominational Christian church, The Lamb of God. In the box were hymnals, sheet music, and a single, leather-bound Bible. A news clipping protruding from the top of the pages in the Bible drew Crawford's attention and he opened the book to the page it marked.

The clipping had a recent date and its headline proclaimed:

FRANK DUGAN INNOCENT
SDPD detective cleared of all charges

There was a portion of scripture from Matthew 16:3 hi-lighted on the right-facing page of the Bible. It read:

"When it is evening, you say, 'It will be fair weather, for the sky is red.' And in the morning, 'There will be a storm today, for the sky is red and threatening.'"

Dan Crawford knew his friend Frank Dugan had, at last, made it home.

*   *   *

Traffic slowed to a crawl as Frank approached the 405 near Culver City. A huge billboard in the distance caught his attention as the Bronco eased closer at ten miles an hour. The message at the top of the advertisement read:

**The Law Enforcement Officers of California
ASK YOU TO HELP THEM STOP
CRIMES AGAINST INNOCENTS**

The bottom of the sign displayed a hotline number and the name of the sponsor for the ad: *Detective Judd Kemp of the San Diego Police Department,*

Chairman, LEOC. But it was the background graphic of the sign, the sign's enormous color photo that had Frank's heart racing.

The photo was of a smiling Amy Dugan with her two grinning children leaning against her shoulders.

About the Author

Paul Sekulich was a Hollywood television writer and script doctor for several years and has now trained his sights on novel writing. He teaches television and movie scriptwriting on the college level, and holds degrees with majors in Theatre and Communications.

Detective Frank Dugan will be his lead character in the series of books he has out currently, including *The Omega Formula* , and several planned for the future. His new novel, *Murder Comes to Paradise*, another Frank Dugan crime thriller, will be making its debut this spring.

Another novel by the author is already out and titled, *A Killer Season*, a thriller about dangerous gambling in Las Vegas, and gunplay that carries into the international arena.

Paul and his wife Joyce live in Maryland.

If you'd care to email or share your thoughts about this book with Paul, or see upcoming works from the author, visit his website at:

http://mdnovelist.com

I can't adequately express, in these few lines, how important reviews are to authors. Please take a moment to leave me a review at Amazon.com.

It keeps writers writing. And it's appreciated beyond measure.
- *PBS*

Made in the USA
Middletown, DE
26 September 2017